TE KORERO AHI KA

to speak of the home fires burning

SpecFicNZ:
Speculative Fiction New Zealand

edited by
Grace Bridges
Lee Murray
and Aaron Compton

with a foreword by
Juliet Marillier

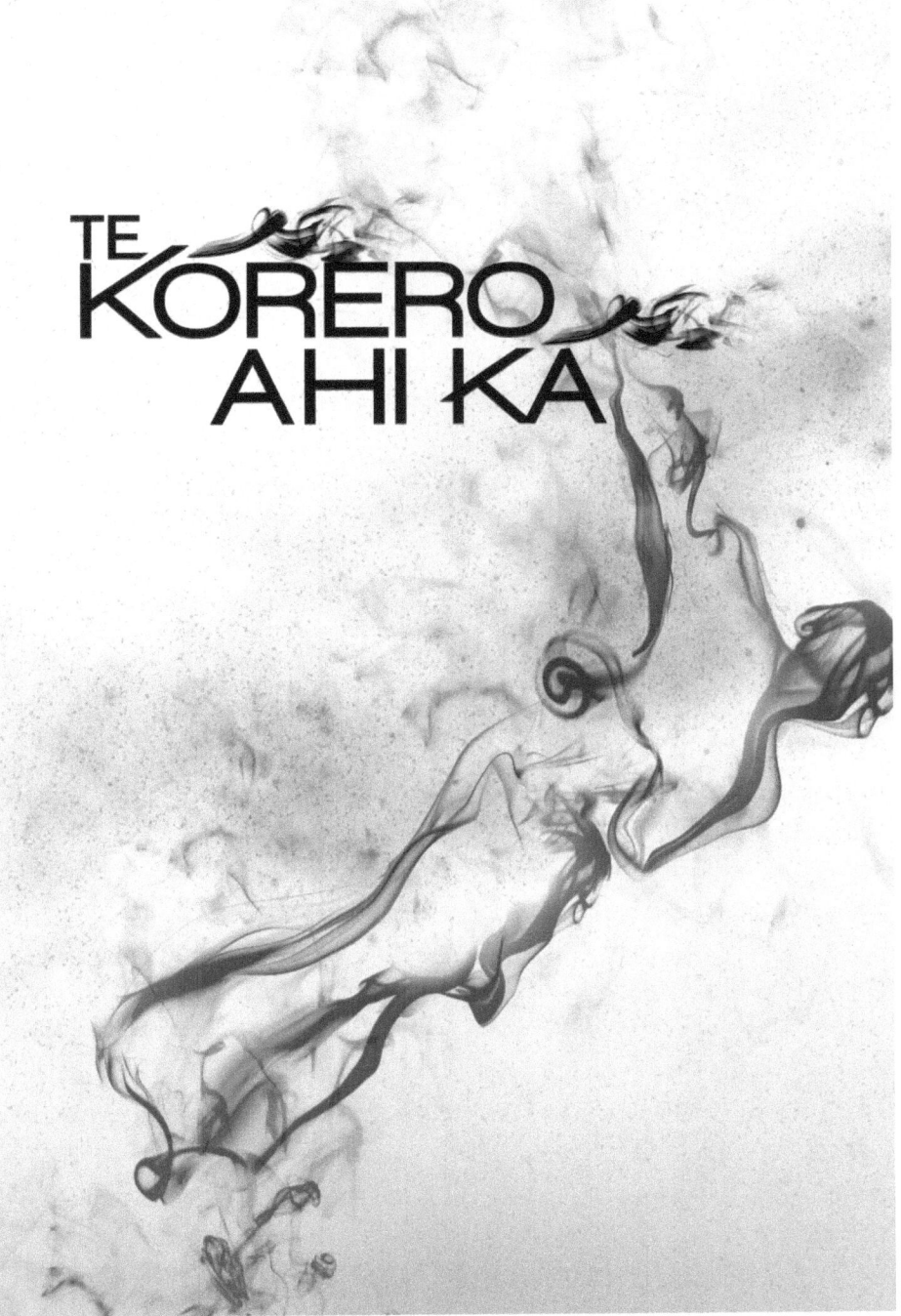

TE
KORERO
AHI KA

Te Korero Ahi Kā: to speak of the home fires burning
Edited by Grace Bridges, Lee Murray, and Aaron Compton

This edition published in February 2018.
ISBN 978-0-473-42834-1 (print)
ISBN 978-0-473-42835-8 (epub)
ISBN 978-0-473-42836-5 (mobi)

Cover Design by Evelyn Doyle
Interior Typesetting by Grace Bridges

Works contributed by the 2017/18 SpecFicNZ Core and the Ahi Kā Editorial Team are donated and unpaid, including: Aaron Compton, Grant Stone, Dan Rabarts, Grace Bridges, Piper Mejia, Paul Mannering, Lee Murray, and Darian Smith. All other submissions were chosen through a blind judging process and their contributors paid. SpecFicNZ believes in fair compensation for work.

Reprints Information

Ahi Kā by Eileen Mueller and Alicia Ponder, winning entry (first equal) in NZSA NorthWrite Collaboration Contest, 2013

Friend, by Grant Stone, first published in *Everything is Fine*, Racket House, 2016

Gatekeeper, What Toll? By Mike Reeves-McMillan, first published in *Cosmic Roots and Eldritch Shores*, 2016

Mother's Milk, by Dan Rabarts, first published in *Regeneration: New Zealand Speculative Fiction 2*, Random Static Press, New Zealand, July 2013

The Eye of the Beholder, by Kevin G. Maclean, first published in *Misspelled*, DAW Books, April 2008

Earthcore: Initiation, by Grace Bridges, first published by Splashdown Books, New Zealand, 2017

To the Centre of the Earth, by Robinne Weiss, winner of the Au Contraire III Short Fiction Prize, 2016

Why I Hate Cake, by Paul Mannering, first published in audio on *Pseudopod*, 2007

The Mysterious Mr. Montague, by Jane Percival, first published in *Bloodlines*, Ticonderoga Publications, Australia, 2015

Selfie, by Lee Murray, first published in *SQ Mag*, Vol 26, *Symbiosis Edition*, May 2016

Wearing the Star Cloak, by Darian Smith, first published in *Wily Writers*, 2012, and *Shimmering Worlds*, 2015

The Iron Wahine, by Matt Cowens, first published in *Flash Frontier*, 2015

TABLE OF CONTENTS

FOREWORD
Juliet Marillier

K ia ora, readers! I'm delighted to introduce *Te Kōrero Ahi Kā* (To Speak of the Home Fires Burning), the inaugural anthology by members of SpecFicNZ. Since it was formed in 2009, this organisation has continued to grow and flourish, with many of its members achieving significant creative success. Providing support and encouragement for speculative fiction creators and editors, both established and developing, is at the heart of SpecFicNZ's work. It was perhaps with that in mind that experienced editors Grace Bridges and Lee Murray were joined by mentee editor Aaron Compton in working on the organisation's first anthology.

In the same spirit, submissions for *Te Kōrero Ahi Kā* were open to all members of SpecFicNZ, from developing to well-established, multi-published writers. The resulting selection reflects the broad range of talent, the diversity and the vitality of contemporary speculative fiction writing in New Zealand. I was honoured to be invited to contribute this Foreword. Although now an expatriate, I never forget that Aotearoa New Zealand is the place of my birth and upbringing. It will always be my artistic and spiritual home.

While I waited for a proof copy of *Te Kōrero Ahi Kā* to arrive, I considered what gives New Zealand and New Zealanders their unique quality, and how these special elements might weave themselves into the stories. There's the irrepressible, downbeat Kiwi humour. There are the unique idioms of everyday language. Then there's the pastoral landscape—sprawling, prosperous dairy farms; high country sheep stations; struggling smallholdings. There's a magnificent, hard-won tolerance of difference and a vibrant multi-culturalism. The strong threads of Maori and Pacific Island tradition, culture and language are vital to the whole fabric of New Zealand society. Underpinning everything is the wild, with its dark forests, lonely lakes, and icy rivers, its crags and cliffs and crevasses. It is a place of extremes, where a person can be tested in body, mind and spirit. If you go out there, if you embrace that wildness, you're likely to come back changed forever. There are ancient stories in that landscape, stories of wanderers and warriors, of tricksters and storytellers and wise elders. There's history and there's what lies far deeper than history: the bones and blood of the land; the heart and spirit of story.

Reading *Te Kōrero Ahi Kā*, I felt a strong sense of Kiwi identity. The anthology has a nice balance of fantasy, science fiction and horror, with some stories blending genres. The writers demonstrate a diversity of approaches, from the tried and trusted to the more boldly experimental. There's time travel. There's future science. There are dragons and taniwha. There are mud eruptions. There are ghosts, molluscs, and sausages. Climate change is a recurring theme, incorporated in different ways by different authors. The theme of family recurs in strikingly contrasting forms. And there are some wonderful stories about the importance of ritual, the handing down of tradition and learning, and how ancient wisdom may re-invent itself in a dramatically changing world.

I hope these stories will delight, surprise, amuse and intrigue you. And I hope the anthology reassures you that speculative fiction writing in New Zealand is not only alive and well, but full of creative energy. The umbrella genre *speculative fiction* is very broad. Each sub-genre—fantasy, science fiction and horror—itself contains many and varied approaches to storytelling. *Te Kōrero Ahi Kā* celebrates that broad range. As well, it highlights the wonderful job SpecFicNZ does in nurturing and encouraging our writers at every stage of their journey. A community of writers is a safe place, somewhere we can thrive and learn and create in the company of like-minded souls. It doesn't matter whether that place is physical or virtual. It is both safe haven and creative crucible. Oddly enough, considering what a diverse bunch of individuals we are, it feels like home.

Bravo, contributors, editors, and all who worked to bring *Te Kōrero Ahi Kā* to fruition! This book has the true Kiwi heart I was looking for. Readers, may you enjoy this publication as much as I did. I hope it's only the first in a series of such anthologies from SpecFicNZ.

Juliet Marillier
Guildford, Western Australia

January 2018

AHI KĀ

Eileen Mueller
and A.J. Ponder

(Prose and interwoven sonnet, *Truth Lies in Fire and Dies in Flame*)

Howls pierced the fog of my dreams. I clutched Ahi, shaking her awake. "Are they real?" Yowling wound through my ear canals, ricocheting inside my head. "The dogs, Ahi, can you hear them?"

She woke, startled. "Hurry, Manaaki. They're coming."

We scrambled out of our bush-clad hideout, dashing up the hillside, sliding in the damp earth, ponga fronds whipping our faces.

Frenzied yelps closed in on us. The creatures' vicious snarling drowned our laboured breathing.

Blue eyes pursued us, hot gas flames in the dark.

Were they real?

I yanked my meds from my pocket. Pills scattered in the dirt. I scrabbled for them. One stuck in my throat before sliding down.

Cry havoc and let us unloose the dogs
the dogs, let slip those hellish brutes of war
for tonight Manaaki will have to choose
to run—

"Hellhounds," Ahi yelled, bounding up the mud and crumbling rock.

Menacing growls raced through the underbrush. Ahi yanked a nail from her fingertip. It flared to light, illuminating the black-hackled beast leaping towards us.

"Ahi?" In all our time together, her fingernails had never exploded into fireballs. I stared at her and swallowed another pill, tasting dirt.

The hound, with pain-stricken yelps, was devoured by flame. Wild baying echoed in the valley below. More hellhounds.

Ahi stood, fingertip bleeding. Her hand, with only four nails, reached out. Warm blood sticky in my palm, she yanked me uphill.

Had my medication stopped working?

To be sure, I gulped another down.

Laugh in the shade of the slavering beast
let fire light his eyes and make death tame
the boy is mad—

The hellhounds thundered behind us. Racing through the darkness, we tripped, smashing our knees on jutting rocks.

I gagged on the stench of the hounds' hot breath. They snapped at our heels—and bit deep. I screamed.

Ahi ripped off another nail, flinging it over her shoulder. The beast yelped and fled, trailing flames.

Fingers spraying glistening blood in the flame-light, Ahi aimed nail after nail at the perilous beasts, until only two nails remained.

The boy is mad to thwart this hunter's feast
the dirt he tastes will never bear his name
and yet he stops and turns—

Ahi flung her penultimate nail through snarling fangs.

The beast combusted. Singed fur and burning flesh. A pale demon loomed behind the hellhound's flaming carcass. Worse than hellhounds. Worse than my lover-turned-stranger beside me, oozing blood from her torn fingertips. Worse than hallucinations.

I screamed.

Ahi smiled through her blood and tears. She tore the final fingernail from her hand and pressed it into mine. "Swallow this," she whispered.

Truth Lies in Fire and Dies in Flame

Cry havoc and let us unloose the dogs
the dogs, let slip those hellish brutes of war
for tonight Manaaki will have to choose
to run through fire and flame or face the maw

Laugh in the shade of the slavering beast
Let fire light his eyes and make death tame
The boy is mad to thwart this hunter's feast
The dirt he tastes will never bear his name

And yet he stops and turns, his wild fear tame
Ahi Kā, Manaaki keep the home fires burning
In blood and fire—with life he stakes his claim
Ahi Kā, let us stand where he is standing

Not hew him as a carcass fit for hounds;
But burn those who chase Manaaki out of bounds.

ON THE RUN
Kevin Berry

t's cray, bro. The zombies invaded the big smoke yesterday. Since then, I've been on the run. I never did no running or sports at school, and I eat heaps of burgers, so I'm slow as. Now I have to be hardout cunning.

For weeks they'd been stuck on the west coast of the South Island. No one cared much about that. There's not much there, eh. Like, no one's going to bust a gut over a few coasters. Some dudes on TV even reckoned it was an improvement. LOL. It could be another tourist attraction, an undead safari park.

The army blocked the mountain passes so the zombies couldn't cross the alps to the main centres. Then some vigilante groups went on weekend hunting trips because, YOLO, and they thought shooting zombies would be sick. Sometimes they didn't come back.

They must have got to Picton somehow. The zombies, I mean. And then some of them must have sneaked onto the Interislander. The ferry ploughed smack into the waterfront with a horrendous crunching of metal, wood and asphalt until it came to a stop, blocking Featherston Street. Hardcore. The whole place was munted.

I was in Macca's, bunking school and having a feed. I left to gawk at what was going on. A shamble of them came out of the ferry. Some grotty and rotting and all aggro, like in the flicks. Some like normal dudes, but with torn clothes and fresh bloody marks on their arms or faces where they'd been infected on the boat.

They snapped everyone who got too close, like those bros who went to see if they could help survivors. What were they thinking? The dudes on the ferry were zombies already. Not human any more. That's legit, bro.

FML. It was a total 'mare.

I gapped it. They pursued me. They pursued everyone.

I crashed in the botanical gardens for the night. Now it was morning. I wanted to take a squizz at what had gone down, suss out what to do next. I reckoned if I stayed in the shadows, I could get down the hill to Lambton Quay, the dead centre of town—or should that be the undead centre?

My arm hurt from when I'd fallen yesterday, and I hadn't had no kai since that half a burger, so I was hungry as.

Heaps of shops had been ransacked. Mean as zombies wandered alone or in small packs we call a shamble. The army had built roadblocks to stop them moving up the Hutt Valley in search of fresh meat. Soldiers circled the Beehive and Houses of Parliament, though I reckon they should have just left the doors open. Dunno if anyone would notice if the zombies got in there. Or care.

I avoided all of them. I'd got wind of the army out and about, shooting to kill anything that moved in case it was a zombie. I dunno if that was true, but I didn't want to take no chances, eh.

I pondered what to do. I thought about my parents and little sister in the Hutt Valley. I would've been there too, if I hadn't been bunking yesterday. I couldn't call them, bro. The cell phone network had been dodgy for hours, and then my stinking battery died. I didn't know if they were alive, dead or zombiefied. And they wouldn't know about me, either.

I wanted to get home. I had to get to my whanau before the zombie shamble did. The zombies could walk there, eh, if they could get past the army roadblocks.

The road would be too dangerous. The trains weren't running. That only left the sea. I sussed out a plan. All good.

I made my way watchfully to the grounded Interislander ferry. It loomed shadowy and quiet in the early morning light, abandoned. Sweet as. I climbed onto it at its lowest point, near the bow, and struggled along the rail against the slope of the tilted ship.

Some of the ship's lifeboats were gone. Maybe some quick-thinking bros escaped the doomed ferry on its way across Cook Strait. I tried to release one of the remaining ones, but I couldn't loosen the ropes. It was way too hard, especially with my crook arm.

I soon gave up on that. I looked around and saw a lifebuoy. Shot. I unhooked it and biffed it over the side onto the road below. Then I climbed down the way I had come, picked up the lifebuoy and slowly made my way to the waterfront, always on the lookout for movement, for danger.

All was quiet there. No army, no zombies. Maybe they'd taken the fight somewhere else. Maybe the army had forced them down Lambton Quay, or driven them inside the Beehive. Yeah. That'd be sweet.

I waded into the cold water. When I could no longer touch the bottom, I grabbed onto the lifebuoy and kicked towards the Petone foreshore like a boss.

It was hard yakka. It took me until late morning to cross the harbour. I staggered from the sea bedraggled, cold, wet and hungry. I kept to the back streets. There wasn't no one anywhere. Maybe a state of emergency was in force or something. Choice. My family would be at home. I was keen to find them.

Knackered, I stumbled home. I grinned when I saw the familiar little white fence, my dad's flash wheels in the driveway, my little sister's trike. My keys, remarkably, were still in my pocket, and I unlocked the door.

Yeah nah, bro, I was stoked to be home.

I surprised them all in the living room. They gasped when they saw me. Maybe it was because of the seaweed in my hair, or the way my arm hung by my side at an unnatural angle. But I reckon it was because half my face had come off when the zombies caught me yesterday.

It was awesome to have found my family.

They were tasty as.

MOA LOVE
Aaron Compton

I stretched out my arm, wafting pungent basil, and the moa swung its long neck around, sniffing and huffing, its breath steaming into the night air.

Ruru hoot-hooted from the forest while I coaxed the big idiot away from the broad beans in the veggie garden. Brown eyes flicked from me to the leaves in my hand. A whole stalk of beans disappeared into its beak. Then it strode towards me across the stepping stones in the soil, light-footed on those great claws. I stepped back. The furry-feathered hump of its back curved as high as my shoulders.

Great-great-Grandfather whispered through my earpiece, "There's someone I want you to meet."

"Now?" I turned to the tekoteko carving of my long-dead man who stood guard above the gabled roof of the main house.

"When you're done there," he said.

The moa boomed an almost-subsonic bass I felt in my chest. I locked the great bird away behind the nearest gate. He'd be lonely for the night, calling for the females waiting in another paddock.

"You and me both, e hoa," I said, although the damned moa would get some action before I ever did. I'd just about had enough of farm life. I was over the gruff orders fired at me by Great-Great-Grandfather, done with these oversized chickens escaping from their paddocks. I could manage this place better without the constant interference of that old kēhua—ghost.

In my heart, the boom of the city called me from over the hill. I headed back to the house to see who was so bloody important I had to meet them at this time of night.

I flopped into a recliner in front of the office cypher-space rig.

"Who is it?" I said, feeling every bit the petulant grandchild of his grandchild.

Triple G, aka Great Great Grandfather, had been a rangatira, a chief. When he died, our people kept him close. He was lucky his accident happened after we were given resurrection germs—before then, all that would've become of him was a grave and the tekoteko on the roof. His wairua—spirit—would have swum across the Pacific to Hawaiki. We would've talked to the carving, and some of us would've heard him answer. After death though, he transformed into an enhanced model of his own brain, every neuron, every dendrite replicated by a colony of microorganisms in a tank.

His village wanted him to run the new community centre, but resurrection changed people. He'd done his time as the big boss, preferred a quiet afterlife. Even his wairua, no longer defined by human flesh, had been transformed.

Fifty bloody years later, he'd run a couple of generations of us into the ground, or away to the big city, and now he was doing the same to me.

The faint whiff of fermentation came from the tanks of the bio-machines in the next room, where Triple G's brain floated in a tank of probiotic solution. It smelled like kimchi. My stomach rumbled. Dinner had been hours ago.

Yawning, I took off the earpiece, replaced it with a rubber Lucidity cap that gripped my skull like a too-tight wig, with filaments of wire for hair, each one connected to a tiny magnet in the rubber. Bundled into a cable at the back of my head, the electric ponytail connected me to the old man.

Lean back. Deep breath. Close eyes.

14

My vision fills with a swirling mandala; a hand reaches out, I take it in mine; the mandala swallows me.

Lush burgundy and gold carpet under me, tasteful landscape paintings on the walls around me. A huge chandelier sparkles. Rich cooking smells, spicy and savoury. A string quartet plays in one corner. The murmur of other diners talking. The clink of cutlery on crockery. Triple G sits by the big window, wearing his good suit, about a hundred years out of style, but dapper anyway. Medals hang on his chest. A fit fifty-year-old, his short hair shows only a hint of grey. We're on a cliff, the ocean below us.

The woman across the table from him stands when she sees me approaching. She's blonde, white, and slightly more fashionable, in a flapper dress about thirty years out of style—short, strappy, sequined, with a matching headband. "Esme, this is Boy," Triple G says.

"Boy, hello. I've heard so much about you." Her accent is American, Southern, and her smile reaches into her blue eyes. I smile back and kiss her cheek.

Triple G grins like the dog who got the cheese, crinkling the green-black lines etched in his brown face.

What must a Southern girl think of these tattoos?

They didn't use a needle gun for tā moko in Triple G's day; they carved the swirls and spirals from living flesh with a tiny adze, then pressed ink into the wounds, leaving a shallow, pigmented scar. He's a good-looking man, and the design of the tattoo accentuates his cheekbones, his broad forehead, the cheeky twinkle in the old man's eye. If he sits still and expressionless, he could be mistaken for the carved wooden tekoteko above the house. Sometimes, I reckon that would be better.

I look from Esme to Triple G and back again. An odd match, this white girl and an old Maori chief.

"Where did you two meet?" I say. "In a database somewhere?"

Esme's brow furrows for a moment, as if confused, then she grins. "Oh, no, it's not like that. I was at an online grain auction with Daddy. Ata was there as well. I just couldn't take my eyes off him."

15

I look at Triple G. I'd assumed she was a bio-machine like him. Her style of dress made me think she was from the nineteen twenties, but if she's living, she's most likely as young as she looks—while he's from another era.

"Now, Boy, before you say anything—" he starts.

"You mean, you're alive?" I say. Liaisons between the dead and the living are not forbidden, just awkward.

"Never mind that," the old man says. "Here's our kai."

A waiter puts a plate in front of each of us. I shouldn't be surprised that it's hāngi—moa, potato and vegetables buried on top of hot rocks and cooked slowly in an earth oven, absorbing the flavour of the earth.

Triple G mutters a karakia under his breath. After all this time, after life with no death, the missionaries still have his soul colonised. His fork trembles in his hand as he waits for one of us to smell it. Esme looks into Triple G's eyes and takes a deep sniff. This is what he was waiting for—his face melts in delight, his fork hovering above the succulent meat.

The dead have no noses, taste buds, or skin. Except for sight and sound, from cameras and microphones, they're sensorially deprived, and it can drive them mad. They need the living. In the dreams they induce in us, like this figment, they bleed our senses, smelling, tasting, feeling the world.

Esme provides the sensual detail Triple G craves. She lifts the flesh to her teeth.

Triple G nods and follows suit. He moans, ecstatic, as he chews a mouthful of meat and kumara. Esme returns his hungry gaze.

I don't eat.

After dinner, Esme snuggles up to Triple G on a couch, the two of them sipping coffee liqueur. I lean forward over the low table and say:

"Esme, what does your family think of this?"

Triple G glares at me.

"Oh, they don't know," she says. "They think I'm playing Chewy Crush. My Dad isn't the most tolerant of men." She looks out the window, her gaze on the horizon. "I'd do just about anything to get away from him." She looked back at me and, realising I was listening, shook her head, put on a grin, and turned to Triple G. "And boy oh boy, was my daddy pissed when your grain got a higher price than his! Hooo! He might not understand this at all."

"Grandfather, I'm not trying to ruin this for you both–"

"Then don't!"

"...but even if Esme isn't playing out her Daddy issues, trying to rebel, how can you possibly make this work? You're a century older than her and you don't have a body!"

"Boy," Esme says, "that's a very unkind thing to say! I'm here because Ata is the most fascinating, kind, and thoughtful man I've ever met."

Triple G leans forward—*oh god, they're going to do it*—and kisses her.

"Our first kiss," she says, her lips still against his.

Her hand goes to his face, strokes the artful scars there. He's purring, I swear, although he can't really feel her.

"I love these tattoos, and this face."

"I may be just a brain in a bottle," he says, "but I'll find a way to return your love."

That's it. I'm out. It's not enough the old prick does a job a young man like me can do, now he's taking a living woman. Jealousy is ugly, but the dead should make way for the living. I stand, fiddle with my pocket watch, and exit cypher-space for flesh-space.

In the office recliner, the rumbling of my stomach accompanies the distant booming of the bull moa, calling for a companion.

The big feathery bastard was still booming the next day. After I'd fixed the garden fence, I opened the gate to lead him to another field, this one lined with rows of fodder trees and undergrowth. The females, even bigger than he was, were already pushing at the fence. They reached over the wire towards the bull, their necks like huge feathered serpents.

He ran through the first gate, pushing so hard against the second one that it flew out of my hands. I left him there for the giant hens to fight over.

"Good luck, buddy." I locked the gate.

If only life was so simple for humans. If only there was some village girl straining at the fence for me.

I walked to the farm buildings, the heels of my gumboots clop-clopping on the hard dirt track. Daffodils bloomed alongside the track. They were early this year.

"Boy, I need your help," Triple G said in my earpiece. I'd been waiting for this.

"I know what you are going to say," I said. "Don't bother. It's too weird."

"You'd deny your rangatira?"

I laughed. "You gave up being a chief a long time ago. No, I won't do it."

"There's nothing here for you, Boy. You want more. I'm making plans for you. Help me with this and I can help you."

"What can you bribe me with? A promotion? Doubt it. No. Nah. Not happening. It's wrong and just…gross." I kicked a stone along the track. "Final answer. No."

I expected anger, but all I got was silence.

Another farmhand was in the big shed.

"Kia ora, Boy," said Nancy, looking up from the seed spreader she was working on.

"Kia ora, Nancy," I said. Her husband was an old mate so I made the effort to not look at the way her overalls stretched as she worked. "Hear the booming?"

"Yeah, spring is coming, huh?" she said.

"Yeah eh, they're gonna need some more feed, I reckon."

I climbed up behind the wheel of the tractor, pulled a chain from my pocket and plugged my ignition bead into the slot, and pushed the button.

Nothing.

I tried a few more times, then swore.

"Won't start?" Nancy opened the hood and peered at the engine. "Try again."

I pushed the button and she shook her head.

"Not even sparking."

I climbed down and looked in.

"Can you hit the ignition for me?" I said.

She climbed into the driver's seat, put her own bead in the slot and pushed the button. Sparks clicked and small flames jetted underneath the angled rows of sealed cylinders. In a few seconds, the pistons inside began clicking, faster and faster until the clicks became a quiet whirr and the flywheel spun.

"That's odd," Nancy said.

"Damn him!"

He'd revoked my access.

I went into town and found I hadn't been paid. I borrowed the bank's phone.

"You can't just deny me my wages, we have a contract!" I said, trying not to let the teller overhear.

"Your contract gives you a responsibility for my welfare, which includes sensory stimulation, so as to avoid mental distress. Technically, this could include—"

"You old shit!"

I couldn't argue the contract. He had me by the short and curlies.

Esme wears a silver, low-cut dress that clings to her curves. Her hair is down this time, long blonde waves hanging over her shoulders. Part of me aches just looking at her.

I'm in the khaki dress uniform of the Te Ngau Mounted Rifles, a regiment that was disbanded in the eighteen hundreds. I feel ridiculous. Triple G insists it's the height of masculinity. He wears the same, except his insignia is a higher rank.

We stand in a large gazebo, wooden posts supporting an open framework of beams and lattice that drips with bunches of purple wisteria and fragrant white jasmine. There's no entrance—thick vines enclose us. I push aside some leaves to look out, but there's no out, just blackness. A private figment.

From the darkness, I hear a booming call. I glance at Triple G, who doesn't look away quickly enough for me to miss his grin. Cheeky old devil. He controls every aspect of this place; that boom is his little joke.

Triple G takes a long-stemmed rose from the huge four poster bed in the centre, then turns to Esme and I, both of us hesitating at one side of the gazebo. He hands her the glistening red bud. She accepts it with a smile and concentrates for a moment. The bud grows fuller until the petals spread open into a mature bloom, dripping with nectar. She holds it out to me.

She doesn't let go when I take the stem, not until I look into her blue eyes. I inhale the sweet perfume, then pass it to Triple G. He breathes deeply, then sighs in satisfaction.

She pulls me towards her. I hesitate, but Triple G's hand is on my back. I'm in her arms, her mouth on mine, her tongue between my lips.

She peels off my uniform. I almost rip the silk dress off her. I rub against her, her skin on mine. I smell her, taste her. I take my time, feeding my senses, so Triple G might experience her. We both moan when I move between her legs.

All too soon I stand back. Triple G's uniform has vanished. Esme holds her arms out to him. His buttocks and legs swirl with carved tattoos.

Esme lies him down. I'm only here so he can bleed my sense of touch, but before she lowers her head to kiss him, her eyes meet mine, and it's my chest that aches.

My heart.

Days later, my bead glowed in the ignition, the particle of Luciferous Aether pulsing with light to let me know the boss wanted to talk.

I was still thinking about Esme.

I pulled over, jumped out, the quiet whirring of the old truck engine slowing to a fast click as I walked to the phone booth.

The screen inside the booth was intact so I plugged in my bead, expecting orders to pick up something from the hardware store.

It was her. Esme. My heart leapt. Her smile pushed her cheeks up, making her eyes smile too.

Those eyes…

I was being foolish—did I really have a crush on my Great-Great-Grandfather's girlfriend?

"How did you get through?" I said.

"Ata patched me through. He wants me to talk to you. He thinks you are having problems with…what we did?"

I hoped the camera wouldn't pick up my blush.

"It's not my problem, Esme. It's yours. How are you going to deal with this when your family hears about it?"

"Yes, I hear you. Pa has told me that as long as I live under his roof, I ain't to have any boyfriends."

"How would he feel about you having a tattooed boyfriend who died decades before you were born?"

She laughed but the smile was gone from her eyes. "Oh, he would flay me alive, I'm sure."

"So…?

"Do you like me, Boy?" she said. "Because I sure like you."

My throat closed up tight. I choked on my words.

Two weeks later I was digging moa manure into a garden bed when Triple G whispered in my earpiece:

"Look up."

A giant cargo ship floated above the forest, heading towards town. The blimp was V-shaped as if two giant rugby balls had been stretched and joined at the nose. The triangular space between them was the cargo bay.

"Are you feeling strong? There's a package for you to pick up," he said.

When I got to the airport the huge ship was being tethered to concrete anchors. Chains rattled, a ramp thudding onto the dry grass. A forklift drove down, crates high on the forks. It towed three trailers behind it, the wheels bumping over the lip of the ramp.

Men unloaded boxes and cases. I asked an official with a clipboard if there was a package for Mamae Ātaahua. He ran his pencil down the list, found Triple G's name, then took me to the last trailer and pointed me at a leather trunk. I grabbed the handle and hefted it up.

Bloody heavy!

"What the hell is in here?" I said, under my breath.

Behind me, she said: "That would be all my worldly possessions, so please treat them well."

I spun.

Esme.

She was here, in flesh-space.

In my ear Triple G, more beautiful than any carving, said: "I told you, I had plans for you."

I put the trunk down and she was in my arms.

In the forest a moa boomed.

AN EXTRACT FROM THE DIARY
OF PETER MACKENZIE
Daniel Stride

T*he following is reproduced with the permission of the Hocken Library, Dunedin, New Zealand.*

Monday, 7th September, 1896.

A week out from Kurow, but it's a Monday so at least Wilson is bearable again. Fellow spent yesterday lecturing me about the wrath of God, until I fled the tent for some peace and a swig from the hip-flask he doesn't know about. Between that beard and those brows, my partner makes a passable Elijah, all the more so at 63, and I do not doubt he could summon the fires of Heaven with the best of them.

Not that he needs to: looking at the horizon, Our Lord has plans enough.

Tuesday, 8th September, 1896.

No chance of further work or travel today; it was all we could do to keep the rain off the brand-new theodolite. We would look right fools, returning to Oamaru with £50 worth of surveying equipment wiped out, and the Department on the warpath. Wilson may be winding down—he says he's voting Liberal for King Dick's Old Age Pensions Bill—but I am 25, and a product of the Otago School of Mines. I have a future to think about.

Sir John has been skittish for days, even before the thunder. My Uncle William once told me horses are wiser than men.

Wednesday, 9th September, 1896.

The weather has cleared, but the Waitaki River fair rages. One hears it from the tent, never roaring but always present, always gnawing at the mind.

Spent the day trooping up and down the tussock slopes with my Abney Level, calling out the angle measurements, while Wilson scribbled results into the book. From dawn to dusk, I heard nary a word from him, not even about religion or the incompetence of the Department.

Thursday, 10th September, 1896.

Wilson's silence is getting to me. I have decided to confront him about it.

Friday, 11th September, 1896.

"Memories," Wilson grunted, over dinner.

"Which memories?" I asked.

"I'll tell ye soon enough, laddie, but yon plates and pots wilnae wash themselves."

Later, as we sat outside with food in our stomachs and good tobacco in our pipes, Wilson told me of another expedition.

Years ago, soon after he arrived from Scotland, the then Wellington Provincial Government had tasked him with surveying the Wanganui up north. Since the riverbanks were infested with thick bush—ne'er touched by man since the Creation, in Wilson's words—the journey was a canoe trip with a Māori guide.

"We passed a muckle cave-mooth," he said. "Black as the gates o' Hell. Worse, singin' came frae the depths, as if the Sirens had leagued with Satan himsel'. The wee Māori wouldnae talk aboot it, but I pushed him tae tell me. 'Twas the taniwha."

"A taniwha?" I exclaimed. "A mythical water-serpent?"

"Aye," said Wilson. "The guardian o' the river. Lang ago, wise men would gang into the cave, but nae mair. Naebody kent the richt prayer. So the bush aboot grew thicker, an' the cave-mooth darker, an' the tui-birds nae langer sang in the trees. E'en the puir eels swam awa'. Meanwhile, the taniwha waits."

24

"Waits for what?" I asked.

Wilson did not answer.

Saturday, 12th September, 1896.

More surveying further along the Waitaki. Wilson is no more talkative, and I have given up prodding him.

Sunday, 13th September, 1896.

No work today. Sir John seems hell-bent on confirming the old proverb; I lead him down to the river for a drink, and he kicks up such a fuss I must bring him a bucket instead.

Kurow assured us Sir John was the sturdiest pack-horse they had, but I have never seen a beast so flighty. The hire-company shall have explaining to do when we return.

4 p.m.: Wilson still sits cross-legged in the tent, poring over the Psalms with a face like an Easter Island statue. His loss: I am sunning myself on the riverbank.

Strange to think that in the years to come there will be road and rail through here. Perhaps even a dam, as though man hasn't despoiled enough Edens over the years. Makes one rather melancholy, even if we are the men responsible.

Monday, 14th September, 1896.

Raised yesterday's thoughts with Wilson. My partner is less romantic.

"Genesis 1:28," he muttered, as we loaded the theodolite back onto the cart. "An' God blessed them, an' God said unto them, Be fruitful, an' multiply, an' replenish the earth, an' subdue it: an' have dominion o'er the fish o' the sea, an' o'er the fowl o' the air, an' o'er e'ery livin' thing that moveth upon the earth. 'Tis progress. The Lord wills it."

"But what if there's a Waitaki taniwha?" I asked. "Do we have dominion over it too?"

"Nae mair talk o' the taniwha," Wilson snapped. He dabbed his forehead with a handkerchief.

Tuesday, 15ᵗʰ September, 1896.

Dreamt of the taniwha last night. I was sitting alone in a boat, and it swam over to me: a twelve-foot-long serpent with great shining eyes and scales of jade, its forked tongue quivering. It said something too, but for the life of me, I cannot remember what.

Wednesday, 16ᵗʰ September, 1896.

Rained solidly all day. Put my coat on, and went for a walk down to the river. There was nothing to see.

Thursday, 17ᵗʰ September, 1896.

Weather cleared in the afternoon, so we took more measurements. Afterwards, I sat with pencil and paper, sketching the landscape from the river up to St Mary's Range. If we must destroy this place for progress, at least I shall record what was lost.

Wilson nods approval at my skill. In truth, I could have been an artist, but my father pushed me into the School of Mines—a veteran of the Victorian gold-rush, he loved money too much, and beauty too little. I will not be the man he was.

The more I think, the more I fear we make a terrible mistake. Some creatures ought to remain outside the ken of mankind, some paths left untrodden. Blasphemy or not, what if Genesis errs?

Friday, 18ᵗʰ September, 1896.

Yesterday's sketch now shows a long, serpentine tail rising from the river, and I would swear on my mother's grave I did not draw it.

I have hidden the sketch from Wilson. I need a stiff drink.

Saturday, 19ᵗʰ September, 1896.

The serpentine tail is still there, though now it has moved. Only an inch, closer to those rocks in the foreground, but it has shifted or I'm a Dutchman. Wilson is looking at me strangely again. Let him; it is my turn for taciturnity.

I go about my evening chores, the old Shakespeare quote ringing in my ears:

There are more things in heaven and earth, Horatio,
Than are dreamt of in your philosophy.

It is clouding over in the south too, though we may evade the worst of the rain.

Sunday, 20th September, 1896.

A day of calamity.

While Wilson hovered over his Bible, I slipped out into the misty rain to study Thursday's sketch. The serpent had crawled from the river, and now looked right at me with its mesmerising eyes.

Next I knew, I was sitting amid the tussock, pouring strong liquor down my throat like some crazed Irishman.

Worse, Wilson was shaking me.

"Ye blaspheme the Sabbath, ye daft fool!" he shouted. "May the Guid Lord strike ye down!"

He seized the hip-flask, and flung it into the Waitaki. Numbly, I watched it float away.

Wilson would be no match for me at fisticuffs, though that afternoon he was angry enough to try. If only he had tried. If only it had ended there…but Our Lord had other ideas.

Thunder rolled away to the south, and Sir John reared up in a right panic. Before either of us could move, the pack-horse fled away over the slopes.

I ran after him, calling his name. Wilson grabbed the rifle from the cart.

Sir John swerved, and suddenly stumbled, collapsing into a screaming heap. To my horror, I saw his rear left leg had shattered.

Wilson put a bullet through the poor beast's head.

"If I had the sense the Guid Lord gave an ant," the old man panted. "I'd do the same to ye. But I'll nae breach the Fourth an' Sixth Commandments."

I shuddered, but not from the threat.

We were stranded.

Monday, 21st September, 1896.

We have abandoned our expedition, and all our valuable equipment, in order to return to Kurow on foot. Our packs are stuffed with what remains of our food supplies. At least the weather has cleared again.

Wilson trails me, clutching the rifle and cursing my name. I ignore him; the gentle rumble of the river is a more welcome companion, and all through the walking, my mind drifts into daydreams of dark pools and icy springs.

Tuesday, 22nd September, 1896.

According to Wilson, Sir John's demise was divine punishment for my dalliance with the demon drink. Demon drink, my foot. I hurry on ahead, and only the river stops me from leaving him behind altogether.

Wednesday, 23rd September, 1896.

The taniwha returned to my dreams last night. This time I forgot nothing, neither its scales glistening beneath the water, nor its terrible eyes, nor the soothing hiss of its voice. It told me what I had always known.

Wilson has angered the taniwha. He and his ilk would chain the river, enslave it to man and his little gods. He must pay for his crime, or the taniwha will never let us go.

When I awake, I am holding the rifle.

Thursday, 24th September, 1896.

Wilson has vanished. I sat on the riverbank, letting him catch up, but though I waited until the sun was high in the sky, I saw neither hide nor hair of him.

I have doubled-back to look for the old fool.

Friday, 25th September, 1896.

Wilson is dead. I found his body some three hours away, face-down in the tussock. There was a single bullet wound in the back of his head.

It can't have been me—how can it, when I was so far ahead? No, there has been some terrible mistake.

The taniwha did this…it told me to punish him. To save the river. I have done that, but I didn't kill Wilson. I can't have killed Wilson. The taniwha, I swear on my mother's grave, the taniwha…

Editor's Note: The manuscript trails off into incoherent rambling after this point. Mackenzie arrived back in Kurow on 27th October, a hairy half-starved madman in the words of one witness, and once his rantings and ravings had been deciphered, he was placed in police custody. Peter Mackenzie never stood trial for the murder of James Wilson; judged criminally insane, he was confined to Seacliff Lunatic Asylum outside of Dunedin. He died there on 25th May, 1913, of tuberculosis.

As for Mackenzie and Wilson's surveying efforts, the proposed extension of the Kurow Branch never eventuated, and the terminus of the rail line remained at Hakataramea.

FRIEND

Grant Stone

The rap on the window startled him. Andy jumped and cold coffee splashed across the paper, turning the weekend weather forecast a muddy brown.

Andy slid open the door and the sound of cicadas rushed in like an off-tune radio. Nigel stood a few paces back, looking down at his boots and the muddy footsteps he'd left up the stairs.

"Kettle's boiled, if you want one," Andy said, but the look on Nigel's face told him that wasn't going to happen.

"I was just up the hole," Nigel said. "I think you need to see something." Nigel's voice was a little higher than normal and ragged around the edges. Had the silly old bugger run down the hill?

Andy sat on the steps and pulled on his boots. Not even nine a.m. and already the smell of heat in the air. Today would be a scorcher. Nigel stood silently, looking away towards the sea. Bruce Tinsdale's boat was already heading out, full of Auckland tourists, their preloaded fishing rods sitting in their harnesses, the lures sparkling like fresh rain.

Andy fumbled with his laces, gritting his teeth against the glass in his fingers. Most of the time when he saw him like this, Nigel would ask why he didn't just get a pair of gumboots and save himself the trouble. But Nigel didn't say anything today. He started up the track while Andy was still climbing to his feet.

Nigel had been Marie's friend first. They had worked together in accounts and had been the supporting pillars of the social club for years. Andy would see him several times a year: Christmas parties, on winery tours or when the social club had booked an entire cinema for the latest blockbuster. There should never have been any more to their relationship than that. It should definitely have ended that January when Andy was woken by Marie's crying and she told him she wanted a divorce. Or a year later when she moved into Nigel's Newmarket flat. Perhaps it should have ended with shouting and a few awkward punches on the street. Instead, somehow, they ended up firm friends. Squash on Tuesday nights, beer on Thursday. A ritual that went on for years.

They had stood side by side when Marie had left them both, the two of them shouldering a coffin that felt far too light to contain someone as full of life as her.

It was funny, sometimes, how long you could live with someone in your life before you realised they were a friend.

Andy had retired up north, lucky enough to find a house with million dollar views across the water during a downturn in the property market. A developer had bought the lot behind a few years later and got as far as ripping out all the native bush before his line of credit ran out. Andy had watched as gorse invaded the newly-emptied space.

Andy had been ready to order a couple of industrial-sized barrels of weed killer when Nigel called to say he'd finally decided to retire and sell the flat in Newmarket.

Nigel bought the section and parked a caravan in Andy's driveway to live in while he built a house. No trouble getting the labour—there hadn't been a lot of building going on up north the past couple of years and Nigel was paying cash. He should have been able to move out of the caravan and into the new house in a couple of months, four at the outside.

A contractor came in to dig a hole for the water tank. He'd barely got the digger back down to the road when the sky turned grey. No drainage yet. Ten days of rain, the worst the locals had seen in a lifetime, left the hole three-quarters full of brown water. Nigel had shrugged, unconcerned. It wouldn't take too long to drain away or evaporate. If it wasn't gone within a week or so he'd get a pump in to drain it. No big deal and didn't it show how great a spot it was for the tank?

That had been nine months ago.

Nigel's boots crunched on the seashell path and Andy wondered again how he could have missed hearing him approach earlier. Had he fallen asleep at the kitchen table with a coffee in his hand? He'd fallen asleep in front of the TV enough times in the last year or two. Maybe it happened more than he knew. It was just easier to spot when you were watching James Bond one moment and an infomercial the next.

Andy laid a hand on the fencepost that marked the boundary between his section and Nigel's. It wasn't much of a slope, but it seemed to take a bit out of both of them, especially in February, when the sun roasted everything except the cicadas. He made it up the hill, past the pump that lay discarded at the side of the track, its thick black pipe extending over the path and optimistically down into the hole.

Nigel stood at the lip of the hole, his arms wrapped around his gut. Andy joined him and leaned over while his heart slowed back down to something approaching normal.

"So what. Did you. Want to show me?"

Nigel continued to stare into the hole and said nothing.

Andy couldn't see anything different. The hole was still three-quarters full of muddy brown water, same as always. He crouched, wondering what Nigel was so worked up about. Perhaps a possum had died and fallen in, or—

The water changed colour from brown to a deep black. It was as if all the silt and sand had been sucked towards the bottom. Andy frowned. "Is this some kind of oil?" Nigel opened his mouth to speak, closed it again. Shook his head. Their reflections, dark and indistinct, stared up at them.

The reflections moved.

Andy was still crouched, hands on his knees, but now his reflection straightened. The rippling of the black water made his arms seem longer and thicker. Andy gasped and toppled backwards onto his arse.

Reflection Andy reached out and grabbed Reflection Nigel around the throat. Andy looked up at Nigel who had not moved; he continued to stand, frozen, staring into the water.

In the hole, Nigel's reflection raised a flailing arm. Andy's reflection bared its teeth, both arms around Nigel's throat now. Ripples in the water distorted the reflections; their form changed, from oversized wrestler to matchstick thin and back again.

Nigel's reflection fell to his knees. The real Nigel gasped, but still did not move. Reflection Nigel fell to the ground and Reflection Andy kicked. Reflection Nigel rolled, then fell away from view as if—as if he had been kicked into a hole.

The reflections faded. The water changed again, from black to its usual muddy brown. It was only when the chirrups of the cicadas started up again that Andy realised they had been silent before. The sky was still blue, but Andy saw black in it too, as if a storm had just passed. As if he had been pressing the heels of his hands hard against his eyes until his vision passed through red and into black.

Nigel sniffed and when he spoke his voice cracked as if he were a teenager again. "It did the same thing before, when I was up here by myself."

Andy tried to stand, but his legs were shaking. "What is it?"

Nigel wrapped his arms around himself again. "The truth. It hasn't happened yet, but I think it's the truth."

Nigel turned and walked back down the hill before Andy could reply. Andy looked back into the hole. His reflection stared back at him, baleful, both fists clenched, for a few seconds more. Then it turned and walked away.

The sun had gone beneath the horizon by the time Andy walked back down the path. Nigel's caravan was sitting in the driveway, same as always. Andy knocked on the door and got no answer. Tried the handle and found it locked. No light shone through the closed curtains. He was sure Nigel was in there. He should speak, he knew, see if Nigel wanted that coffee now, try and apologise for…apologise for what? For something he hadn't done, would never do?

Andy returned to the house and when he blinked he found himself sitting at the kitchen table, a half-eaten plate of dinner he couldn't remember making in front of him. The kitchen bench was littered with pots and plastic bags. He stared at the mess, trying to figure out how long he'd been out. How long it took to boil water, throw in pasta, brown mince—he remembered walking back up the drive from Nigel's caravan. That was it. He dumped the rest of the pasta in the compost.

He turned off the TV and fell into bed, but sleep did not come. Every time he closed his eyes he saw Nigel's caravan. He should check, he knew. Just in case. But he didn't move.

The moon was full and its reflection on the sea was bright enough to throw light onto his bedroom ceiling. Light that rippled slightly, as if he were staring up from the bottom of a deep pool.

It was funny, sometimes, how long you could live with someone in your life before you realised they were a friend.

BACKCHAT
Mark English

Eugenie Hildegarde (Genie to her friends) closed her front door firmly and leaned against it, her mind reeling over the conversation she'd had with her new neighbour. He'd said the most odd…no, the most *correct* responses to her polite door-step enquiries, but they had all been slightly at odds with the conversation. She couldn't quite put her finger on what *specifically* was wrong. She *hmmed* for a moment, then paced to the kitchen where she frowned her way through brewing a pot of tea.

Once settled into her overstuffed armchair—a cup of tea steaming on the side-table (gingernut biscuit perched on the saucer)—she rested her sharp elbows on the antimacassars and put her equally sharp mind to work on solving this mystery.

Genie had always taken a deep, near-spiritual joy in meeting new people. The arrival of a new neighbour (an elderly bachelor according to the real estate agent) had been a source of great planning, hat arrangement, and face powdering in preparation for her first foray to the freshly painted red door adjacent to her lilac one.

The man had answered Genie's knock before her knuckles could rap a second time on the wood. He hadn't stepped out, but had peeked through the narrow opening as though a timid sort, showing her three-quarters of his face bisected by a security chain.

"I'm very well thank you—delighted to meet you. I'm Pars Vicisson. Sorry, I can't invite you in—unpacking to do, you know?" He offered a hand through the gap.

"Hello there, I'm Eugenie, Eugenie Hildegarde, but you can call me Genie—everyone does! I live next door—how do you do?" She shook his hand. His skin, she noted, was feather-soft to her touch.

"No, no, I'm fine thank you, quite fine, and fully provisioned." His head bobbed behind the chain.

Genie paused at the unusual response, then charged onwards with her planned introductions. "I fully understand, quite a busy day I expect. Is there anything you need right now: milk, sugar perhaps?" She ducked her head, and stood on tiptoes to see past him.

Pars ducked and stretched in time with Genie as though they were swans mating. "No, not now thank you—perhaps tomorrow? Yes, tomorrow would be good—say around 10?"

Pleased at the positive response, and the invite—she would be the first in the close-knit community to report on his décor and chattels—she backed off the door-step. "Righto. I'll go home now and make myself a cuppa. Are you sure you don't want one?" Pars bobbed his head once, smiled then closed his door with a peremptory snick.

Genie blinked and stared at her faint reflection in the bright red paint. Though she'd made inroads to getting to know her neighbour, there was an oddness to his responses that bothered her, but she couldn't put her finger on it. She blinked again, and turned, her mind chewing away at what it was that was out of kilter.

It took Genie two cups of tea from her kitten-cosied pot before a tetrapod of an idea surfaced from her sea of thought to lie gasping for breath on the beach of her consciousness. Genie picked up and dunked her gingernut in her tea while she reviewed this new idea. From instinct, she lifted the sogged biscuit to her mouth before the ginger mash could flop into her beverage. The consequence of that thought excited her...but there were several options: Mr Vicisson could be an imbecile, a charlatan, an alien or just plain vexing!

Before the appointed tea-time, Genie prepared her handbag with props to test her various hypotheses. At the last moment before leaving the house, she reneged on the alien hypothesis and removed the tin-foil lining from her hat. It had been getting a little hot in any case, and she could return to this test if the others did not deliver.

The shiny red door snapped open after her knuckles tapped but once, but this time it opened full wide to reveal Mr Vicisson in neat tweeds and an ironed shirt. To Genie's eye, he cut quite an appealing profile and she looked forward to learning more about him.

"Mrs Hild...Genie, please come in. Perfectly on time I notice—something I have a great deal of respect for. And please call me Pars." He swept out of the way, and gestured for her to enter the parlour, where a cosied pot awaited their attention on the side table.

"Hello again, Mr Vicisson. I do hope you weren't expecting me to be fashionably late!" She bustled in, switching her bag from hand to hand as he took her coat and hat. Genie thanked her lucky stars she had taken the tin-foil out. How on earth would she have explained that away?

Pars continued talking whilst he draped her belongings over a stand tucked behind the door. "I've travelled extensively in Africa—there are places, you know, where you never have to converse with another soul for months on end."

"What wonderful decorations and ornaments, Mr V!" Genie gazed at woven wall hangings, pottery and carvings presented in a tasteful, yet uncluttered way throughout the room and into the hallway beyond. "You have certainly been overseas in your time, haven't you? It must have been very exciting." Her agenda in exploring the mind of Mr Vicisson was momentarily clouded by the image of the wide eyes of her tea club as she regaled them with snippets about this exotic explorer.

She surfaced from the brief reverie to find Mr V, facing away from her, evidently pouring tea. He turned his head to her and nodded.

"Oh, thank you. No sugar, but yes to milk," she said.

"I have a range of biscuits. Please take your pick." He brought her tea in a fine bone china cup and saucer, and in his other hand he offered a tin of biscuits. He smiled as though amused.

"Do you have any gingernuts?" she asked. "I find them very good for the brain, especially at our age!"

"Please Genie, call me Pars." He sat back in his chair and picked up his tea. "I stumbled on this place in the back of a travel magazine—it was about to be used to light a fire—the magazine, that is. I was craving something new to read, and snatched the magazine so quickly I near took the poor fellow's hand off! I'd been away from people for several years, and the article plucked a heart-string for the old country. So I decided to give it a go." He sipped his tea and closed his eyes momentarily as he savoured the rich taste.

Though Genie had partially worked out how to approach this meeting, she experienced a sudden wave of light-headedness, and an urge to move onto the next question. "Tell me—has your life of travelling led you here, or is this a short sojourn before you voyage forth again, Mr V?"

"By the look of this place, one could certainly settle down with pets and treat them in the manner to which they might wish to become accustomed." Pars placed his cup into the saucer, a slightly pained expression twitched across his face.

The same light-headedness assailed Genie again, stronger though. "Do you like cats?"

"Purple." Pars gently moved his cup and saucer to the side-table, then ran his hands through his hair.

The urge to ask her next question became unbearable, as she fished in her mind for what it was she intended to ask. "What colour is my hat?"

"Red."

Her next question snapped out, almost beyond her control. "What colour is your door?" She stood, slopping tea into the saucer. "Say nothing, Mr Vicisson. Your manner of speech vexes me, and fogs my mind. Say nothing!" She placed her saucer next to Mr Vicisson's. She breathed deeply then sat once more, hands placed calmly in her lap.

Genie took a deep breath, and looked directly at Pars. "You seem a decent enough man, of some experience and standing, but I detect you have an affliction or you are perhaps deceptive, No—say nothing!" She raised a hand, palm out and shook her head as he went to open his mouth.

She reached for her handbag. "I have some questions written out here—ten of them, and I will pull out three, one at a time, so I do not know which they are. I have noted you craft your words carefully to not stand out, but I ask—because I like you, Mr V, and we would make great neighbours—do not obfuscate." She deflated him with a hard stare, and waited until his wilt had settled into a more comfortable posture.

Pars looked at her, his mouth a thin grey line drawn on a paler face. "Ceylon." As the word left his mouth he looked as though he was going to sicken before her very eyes.

Genie plucked the first question from her bag. "Which do you prefer, Ceylon or China black? I guess we know that one."

"Quiet music, perhaps a radio show and reading a good book in an overstuffed armchair. Genteel company." Pars steepled his fingers.

Genie's hand darted into the bag once more. "What relaxes you of an evening?"

Pars blushed, returning some colour to his cheeks. "This may sound rum, but...three men in a tub."

"Oh!" said Genie, blushing herself. "I think I know what's next then." Her hand streaked into the opening of the bag like a weasel into a warren. "Complete the following rhyme: Rub-a-dub-dub."

Pars leaned forward and locked his gaze to Genie's. "I have ever been this way. I seem to lose my way in a conversation; I hear what will be said, so answer—though I know it will be heard in the context of what went before. So I hedge my terms. Right now, as of this point in the conversation, I'm in anguish. I know how disjointed and odd I must seem!"

Genie smiled tightly at Pars. "I think I have diagnosed you, Mr V. I had wondered if you were reading my mind, and were playing a rather horrid word game with me. But I now believe you are afflicted." She felt once more the light mental nudge that had been missing from the written questions. "Tell me, what's happening to you?"

"Oh, Genie! Thank you so much for not baulking at the first hurdle and dismissing me for a mad fool!" He clasped his hands over his mouth, moisture rising in his eyes.

"Yes, as I suspected—you are living very slightly in the future, or we are in your past—I do not know which. Neither do I know truly if it is your answers that guide some of my questions, or that to meet your answers, my questions must be asked."

Pars reached a shaking hand towards his cup and saucer. "Let us sit and enjoy this fine tea for a while, in companionable silence. I'd like to settle my nerves by contemplating your very fine and most incisive mind, Mrs H— Genie."

"Hardly, Mr V. It's been a fabulous exercise for the little grey cells, as they say."

A full hour passed with only the sound of passing footsteps in the street and the kitchen clock pacing them towards noon. Both enjoyed another cup of tea—Genie's served before she asked; though she asked in any case.

As the clock ticked on to mid-day and the morning tea had extended beyond the usual polite interlude, Pars stood. "I'm sorry you have to leave, but tea tomorrow would be marvellous—at the same time?"

Genie rose, smiled at Pars and placed her empty cup on the side-table. "I have to go, I'm afraid—household chores. Would you care for morning tea tomorrow?"

He smiled back. "Hardly likely, not now we've got to know one another."

"Yes, 10 a.m. sharp. Don't be late!"

He ducked to peck her farewell on the cheek. Genie pulled back, her smile growing into a grin, and wagged her finger at him—although she did not utter a single word, Pars understood her meaning. And he understood it at exactly the same time.

"Now, now, Mr Vicisson! You really are getting ahead of yourself!"

THE LOST
Gregory Dally

Stay gentle on yourself, good sir. That girl means for you
such things you'd only dream.

You could even assay Nirvana
via the dimensions of her indeterminate smile.

In the dazzle of a vision designed for the sightless,
someone might trick himself that she cares.

Scholar, you research comets and other
signs of a heart and a mind that aren't yours yet.

The cosmos rolls these around, all in their time, omens
trailing clever phrases you haven't said.

Together, silent, you'll take the path that snakes a hillside,
then entangle yourselves in rest beneath the tōtara

at its summit, the giggles you'll effect
just ever so slightly dishevelled in her momentum.

Right now, acting casual on the stroll along a harbour,
your stride is matching hers, easy and true. She's lazing,

as sirens are apt, visiting at leisure
to lead a careful life's undoing.

It seems right to shake up the sand. You might as well strut.
As you thresh, you dislodge myriads of atoms

to a vortex in the storm tide of her saunter. A year
you've missed her. You haven't exhaled for a minute.

GATEKEEPER, WHAT TOLL?

Mike Reeves-McMillan

The dust transformed the boy into a bronze statue, freshly cast and yet to gain a patina. He trudged, limping every so often as his bare feet struck the pebbles which persistent sun had flaked from the rocks of the desert.

I took stock of my own appearance as he approached. Middle-aged, plump, unathletic. A uniform, neither new nor crisp, stained under the armpits. Symbols on the pocket, which the boy would read as "Bill". At my side, a truncheon, chipped and worn, with only remnants of polish remaining. I sat in an open-fronted booth with my feet up, smelling the alkaline dust and my own sweat.

The Gate took the form of a cave mouth in a cliff. A turnpike, made from an imperfectly-peeled tree branch nailed to a leaning post, stood in front of it, a merely symbolic barrier.

"So," I said to myself, "an easy one this time."

As the boy came closer, I made out a crown of curly hair, dark eyes full of determination, and the lean frame of a lad who'd been given more labour than food. With decent rations and the right exercise, his shoulders might yet fulfil their promise of broadness.

When he came near enough to make himself heard through the dust in his throat, he coughed some of it out and greeted me politely. "Good morning, sir. Is this the way to the Gate of Worlds?"

I let my feet thud to the ground and hauled myself upright, bending over my paunch. Indicating the Gate, I said, "There it is."

"That?" he said. "That's the Gate?"

"At the moment," I replied.

"I've heard it looks different to each traveller," he said. "That the way it looks says something about you." He regarded the rickety turnpike with a dubious expression.

"I've heard that, too," I said, wondering what jongleur, cloaked wanderer, or winged messenger had told him of the Gate, and what touch of strange blood or fate enabled him to find it.

He looked at me, up and down, and I treated him to a blank look in return. He seemed to remember something, and cleared his throat again.

"Gatekeeper," he said, "what toll?"

He'd been properly instructed, then. "The knowledge of your name," I said. "Your destination."

"Alexander," he said, and, "somewhere I can train."

"Train for what?"

"For war."

"There's war where you come from?"

"Not yet," he said, narrowing his eyes.

I saw him next emerging from lush forest. He rode at the head of a group of companions, fit and well-favoured, and he was the youngest. He had filled out, as I had predicted, but remained lean and wiry. Yet the biggest man watched him as a dog watches his master.

The smallest man, red-haired, with a sharp, cunning face, I immediately thought of as the Fox. He looked everywhere but at his leader, because danger could come from any other direction, but not, he thought, from Alexander.

The last of the party was a woman, disguised—convincingly—as a man, but she moved like a wolf. She didn't look at Alexander either, but in a way that told me she feared to fall in love with him, and that it was already too late.

I've seen many stories come through the Gate, and, looking at Alexander among his companions, I feared that I knew this one.

I was a sergeant this day, younger than when I'd seen him first, and I had troops, to either side of the Gate. The Gate itself looked like a heavy iron grille set in a thick wall of grey-black stone. Beyond it lay another forest, and different, alien trees towered above the wall.

"Gatekeeper," said Alexander, "what toll?"

"Let me speak with each of your companions alone," I replied. He considered, and nodded.

I told each of them the same thing. The Dog glared and set his jaw, clenched his fist. He would tell his master as soon as they were through the Gate. The Fox cocked his head, sceptical. The Wolf looked aside, not meeting my eye. She already knew.

"Where's old Bill?" Alexander asked, as they mounted up again.

"Not needed any more," I said. "No more than the desert, or the caves."

"I found this in those caves," said Alexander, touching a sword that swung at his side as if part of him. The hilt, bronze wrapped in leather, had no jewels or decoration. It was a sword for basic fighting, not for looking at, and the scuffed scabbard spoke of hard use.

"It's served me well," he said.

"Or you've served it," I said. "Have a safe journey."

He grinned in my face and led his companions through the Gate as my troops swung it wide.

Time passed, and travellers. I saw the jewelled lizards of Am-Skek pass by in palanquins, borne by muscular animated statues of silver and gold. I saw merchants out of Vesin on their six-legged mounts, and pilgrims from Tel in their vessels with the leaf-green sails. An old witch trudged by, and, as she passed the gate, I saw her change, become a princess attended by birds. To each of them I showed what face was appropriate to their need and their attitude at the time.

When I found myself a stern young captain commanding fifty musketeers, I anticipated Alexander.

He led a troop of lancers on tall steeds, and the youth had gone out of his face, though, by his time, I knew it had not been many years. His eyes assessed me and my troops, and he nodded to me with respect.

"I see your Fox and your Wolf," I said to him, indicating his close companions, "but where is your Dog?"

It puzzled him only for a moment, then he gave a laugh, and, as quickly, turned serious again, his bronzed face closing.

"Dead," he said, quietly, and, even quieter, with a catch in his throat, "my fault."

Of course it had been his fault. Nothing happened within two days' ride of a man like Alexander that did not have to do with him.

"Gatekeeper, what toll?" he asked, and I answered him, "Your banner." It floated above the Fox's head, a golden, many-rayed sun in a deep blue field.

He did not hesitate, but signalled that the Fox should strike the banner and give it to me—which told me that he knew the troops followed him, and not it. I swung open the tall, iron-bound oak doors of the Gate for him myself.

"Where away?" I asked him, as we watched his lancers pass through onto the plain beyond.

"There's war in Es Terin," he said. "They're paying well for troops."

"Which side?"

"It doesn't matter," he said, and mounted his beast. He bore the bronze sword still, but a flintlock pistol balanced it on his thick leather belt. The beast's nostrils flared as he guided its shaggy shoulders through the Gate.

The Wolf approached the Gate alone, except for her mount and a spare. The mud and rotting foliage of the swamp clung to her and to the beasts. She stopped before my booth.

"I have passed the Gate twice under the authority of another," she said. "May I pass a third time on my own account?"

"How did you find the Gate?" I said.

"A tugging in my gut." She touched her belly gently, and I knew how she came to be there.

I regarded her. "You may pass, if you pay the toll."

She stared at me a long time before she asked, "Gatekeeper, what toll?"

"Your story," I replied.

She shrugged. "He passed through my village. I knew I must follow him, so I disguised myself and fought beside him, as his companion."

"And this?" I said, indicating her midriff. I saw that she knew I knew.

"Drunk after a victory, he called for a woman," she said. "I said I would arrange it, then put on women's clothing, veiled myself and went to him." Her mouth twisted.

"It was not as you had hoped," I said.

She shook her head. "You were right in what you told me when we first met. He is a dangerous man to follow, you said, and he will fail you."

I nodded and waved for her to pass through the Gate, bearing Alexander's child and the fate of kingdoms.

When I next saw Alexander, he rode in a motorised conveyance the colour of old blood, uniformed as a general, and followed by a thousand riflemen. They marched across rolling hills covered with purple grass, and stopped before the Gate.

His Fox sat beside him, watching him closely. He had finally worked out that Alexander was the most dangerous factor in any situation.

I hailed him from the outer breastworks of the fortifications. They offered no entrance to anyone who did not have the means to cast them down, unless I willed it.

"General Alexander," I said. "I do not see your Wolf."

"He left," he said in a clipped tone. "I don't know why."

Because she loved you, and you didn't even pay her enough attention to see through her disguise, I thought. Because she was never more than a tool to you in either guise. Because she had just enough fate of her own to break free from your story. Because her leaving moved your story forward anyway.

Because she is a wolf, and not a dog.

"Where away?" I said.

"Gatekeeper," he said, "what toll?"

"That depends on your destination." Beside me on the ramparts stood troops, cannon, mortars, all I would need to stand him off. I would not have them if I did not need them.

"I go to where I came from, Colonel," he said. "Back when you were old Bill and I was a barefoot boy."

I smoothed my hand over my close-cut silver hair.

"Then the toll," I said, "is your army."

He glanced behind him, back to me. "I understood your function was to keep the Gate and let people through."

"My function," I said, "is to keep the Gate, as I see fit, and charge such tolls as I assess."

"I see." He considered, then ordered his driver to turn around, his troops to withdraw out of cannon-shot.

He camped, and began to dig trenches.

I went myself to parley with him.

"I thought you a better general," I said. "It is pointless to besiege troops who have the Gate of Worlds at their back for resupply." Even if they ate, and mine do not, though I chose not to mention that.

"This is not a siege," he said. "It's a blockade."

I looked at him, puzzled.

"It's almost the time of the Migration of the Clans of Evenholt, from what I understand," he said. "They will not be pleased to see the Gate blocked."

I nodded to him without changing my expression, returned to the walls, and sent a messenger through the Gate.

After an interval, a king joined me on the walls.

"How can I assist?" asked Kenthin, Lord of Iron.

"I require a blockade broken, and I thought of you."

"I see," he said. "I believe we can do business."

"Three free passages of the Gate," I said. "For you and your descendants."

"Acceptable."

He descended on the inner side and consulted with his engineers.

Two nights later—it was a place with nights, but no moons—I opened up portals in the walls, and by morning, iron shields stood close enough to Alexander's troops that the artillery drawn up behind the shields could be brought to bear, without itself being vulnerable to rifle fire.

I did not order a bombardment, but waited for his response.

Alexander himself rode up to the walls beneath a sign of truce, and looked up to where I stood.

"Well played," he said, his dark eyes blazing with rage kept barely in check.

"You can pay your toll," I said, "with the lives of your men, or you can leave them here alive and go on without them."

"Allow me twenty rifles," he said. His voice and his eyes did not plead. They demanded.

"Ten."

He nodded to me, as to an equal one acknowledges, but who is not one's friend.

"I shall not forget this," he said.

"Do not," I replied, opening the wall.

The Lord of Iron watched as Alexander, his Fox, and the ten riflemen passed through.

"Why did you wish to confiscate his army?" he inquired.

"With a thousand rifles, he could conquer without effort, and would rule without legitimacy. With ten, he will have to conquer by cunning, alliance, and the unpopularity of the existing ruler. Or, he will fail."

"I did not know you had such discretion. Or cared."

"I, too, must pay my toll," I said.

Years passed, and cavalcades. The Evenholt clans migrated, and migrated back. Envoys from the Court of Yance, seeking an alliance, their long crimson plumes bobbing above their heads, followed twittering tourists from the Upper Glades, and preceded explorer-scientists of Taft, who sought the legendary Islands of the Stars.

The wind howled and whistled as a boy, clad in furs, topped the snowy rise. He hesitated, seeing the Gate, and descended, his footprints erased almost as fast as he made them by the blowing snow.

"Gatekeeper," he cried above the roaring of the gale, "what toll?"

"The knowledge of your name and destination," I replied.

"Alex," he said, casting back his hood, and I noted his bronze features and his wolfish movements. "I go to seek my father, now that my mother is dead."

I nodded, and hauled open the rough wooden barricade for him.

"Thank you, Bill," he said.

The Gate lay on the edge of a desert, and, far off in the twilight, I saw an elderly man.

He trudged, favouring one leg from time to time, and his back bent with weariness, but he retained the bearing and manner of a king—a king on his way into exile. White hair and a white beard, a plain cloak flashing velvet beneath, tall leather boots, a signet ring gleaming in the last light. A sword.

"Hello, Alexander," I said.

"Hello, Bill." For once again I was the middle-aged turnpike guard.

"Gatekeeper, what toll?" he said, and I answered him, "Your sword."

His hand leaped to the hilt, paused, and withdrew, his face becoming a bronze mask. "No. Not the sword."

"You gave me your banner, once."

"I was much younger then. Besides, the sword has always meant more to me than the banner."

We shared a long look. At last, I saluted him, and he returned it.

His back straightened. He turned away into the desert and the night, and marched to meet his fate.

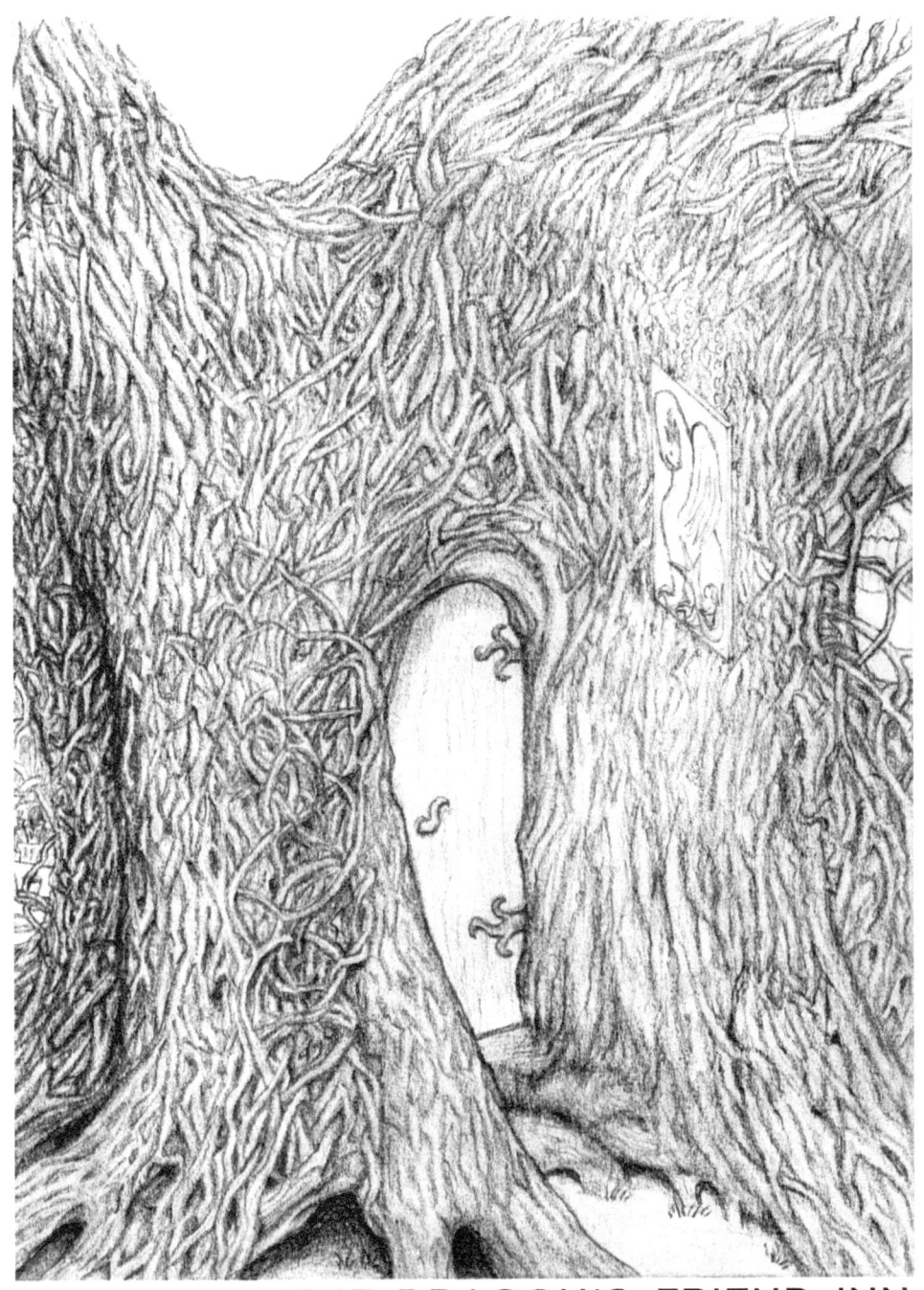

THE DRAGON'S FRIEND INN
by Serena Dawson

THE BIG BAD WOLF
Kevin G. Maclean

The Big Bad Wolf strolled up to the door of the House of Straw.

"Little pigs, little pigs, open the door and let me come in!"

"Not by the hair on my chinny-chin-chin!" cried the First Little Pig, and emptied his AK-47 through the door.

The Big Bad Wolf watched the bullets fly past from where he stood *beside* the doorstep, then retreated behind a nearby tree. "Then I'll huff, and I'll puff, and I'll blow your house down," he called. And with that, he called for air support, rolled himself a small spliff, and sat down to wait.

But when the helicopter arrived, and blew all the straw away, there was nothing for the Apache to train its Vulcan on, because the Three Little Pigs had gone out through the back wall.

Some weeks later, the Big Bad Wolf strolled up to the door of the House of Sticks.

"Little pigs, little pigs, open the door and let me come in!"

"Not by the hair on my chinny-chin-chin!" cried the Second Little Pig, and rolled a grenade under the door.

The Big Bad Wolf pulled his head down into the ditch where he'd taken cover, and crawled away to a large rock where he'd set up previously. He dialled the house on his cellphone.

They answered quickly. "Little Pig Residence. How do you want to be porked?"

"I'll huff, and I'll puff, and I'll blow your house down," said the Big Bad Wolf, and hung up without waiting for any more cheek from the Pigs.

And he called for artillery support, rolled himself a medium-sized spliff, and sat down to wait.

But after the shells arrived and reduced the house to matchsticks, all the Wolf found was an escape tunnel.

A few months later, the phone rang in the House of Bricks. It was the Wolf.

"Little pigs, little pigs, open the door and let me come in!"

"Not by the hair on my chinny-chin-chin!" cried the Third Little Pig, and pressed the button that blew all the claymorettes along the garden path and fifty metres up the road.

The Big Bad Wolf grinned and opened up from four hundred metres with Mabel, his old reliable Browning M2HB machine gun, turning the interior of the brick house into a hell-storm of supersonic shards of glass and brick from which there was no escape.

He leaned back and chuckled with satisfaction. "If you want a job done right, you gotta do it yourself." He extracted a full-ounce spliff from a case on his webbing harness. "Time for a little huff and puff." He lit the joint on Mabel's barrel, and took a long slow toke. "I am Bad!" he declared to the universe at large, and blew a smoke ring. He decided he liked the taste of those words in his mouth.

"I am Bad! I am B, A, D, Baaaaad!"

He stood, checked his flashbangs and his carbine, and staggered off to get his kill confirmations. He hoped there'd be enough left for it to double as a munchies run. "Hoo-ee," he giggled to himself. "Ain't I the biggest, baddest wolf in the whole wide world?"

AUTHOR'S NOTE: It may be that there's a moral to this tale, but somehow I doubt it.

BREACH
Robinne Weiss

"Come on, girl. Don't you have a little more for me?" Mary worked the cow's teats for another minute, but gained only a few drops of milk for her effort. She sighed and stood, stretching the kinks from her back. Opening the head bail, she patted the cow on the rump. "Off you go, Bess."

The cow made her leisurely way from the milking shed, rejoining her companions in the dusty brown paddock. Mary poured Bess' milk into the large stainless-steel jug, and then heaved the jug into the chiller. She wiped the sweat from her face with her shirt.

A drink. That's what she needed. A glass of water, and then she'd go to the south paddock and weed the millet. She stepped into the glaring sun and walked to the house. Dust rose up at each step, and the breeze sent it eddying around the yard. She touched the water tank as she passed it. This ritual reassured her, but didn't alleviate her fears they would run out. In a month, they'd be drawing nothing but silt from the well, and the rainwater they'd stored during winter would have to get them through the hottest days of summer. It was always a struggle—this year would be worse. Winter rain had been light, and the tank wasn't full.

When she reached the kitchen, she found Les already there. His face was streaked with dirt and sweat. She smiled and swiped at his face. "You look like a zebra."

"How was the milk this morning?" Les asked, pouring himself a glass of water from the pitcher they kept cool in the chiller.

Mary held out her glass for him to fill. "Not as much as yesterday." She sighed. "I think those N'Damas were a mistake. They're just not giving as much as the Sahiwals." She pulled out a chair from the battered kitchen table and sat down. It creaked under her weight, and she wondered how long it would be before she had to fix it again.

Les sat down across from her, leaning his elbows on the table. "Remember, those N'Damas are also giving us beef. Bess and Lily's calves sold for more than any of the others."

Mary sighed. "I suppose. Still, their milk production is lousy. I think I'll cut some extra acacia for them today. Maybe I can boost their production with a little more feed." She frowned. Extra feed now meant extra need for water later.

Les leaned across the table and kissed Mary on the nose. "It'll be okay. We'll make it through this year." He shrugged. "A dry year is good for prices." He downed the last of his water and stood. "Speaking of prices, I should be going if I'm going to get to Port Geraldine and back today."

"It seems ridiculous we should have to take the milk all the way down there, and pay the agent, just to sell our milk on Banks Island."

"Yep, but since those rich bastards out on the Island raised the West Melton ferry fees, it's cheaper this way."

Mary grunted. "You know they only raised that ferry fee so they don't have to put up with us poor Mainlanders on their pristine streets." She stood, picking up both their glasses and carefully wiping them with a towel before replacing them in the cupboard.

Les put an arm around her shoulders and kissed her sweaty forehead. "We're doing okay, Mary," he reassured her. "We're still getting good money for the milk." He pulled away and brushed a wisp of hair from her face. "Need anything from town while I'm there?"

"Here's a list." Mary picked up a scrap of paper from the benchtop and handed it to Les. She kissed him on the cheek. "I'd kill for some more of those Stewart Island cherries, too, if they're not too expensive this week."

"I'll see what I can do, though I'm not sure I'm willing to resort to murder." He winked and returned her kiss.

After Les was gone, Mary grabbed a hoe and headed to the south paddock. On her way, she stopped to scratch the cows' ears. She loved her 'girls', as she called them. Her herd of fifteen was one of the larger in the region. Few farmers bothered with dairy cattle on the Canterbury Plains; the climate was simply too hot and dry for it to be profitable. For that matter, few farmers bothered with the Canterbury Plains at all—only those who couldn't afford more forgiving land elsewhere. But Mary's family had been farming dairy in Canterbury for hundreds of years. Her father had always told her she had milk running through her veins. As a child, she was surprised to see beads of dark red blood whenever she cut herself.

Her herd was composed mostly of Sahiwals, well-adapted to the heat and drought. Bonnie, whose reddish-brown hump Mary now scratched, was the boss of them all. She insisted on first milking, first scratch, first feed. She was a good milker, too, and four of Mary's other cows were Bonnie's offspring. The pair of N'Damas had been a gamble. One Mary didn't think she'd repeat. Not only did they not produce as much milk, but they looked strange, with their grey pelts and flat backs. She gave a parting scratch to one of Bonnie's daughters, promising to return with food for them later.

Les still hadn't returned from Port Geraldine when Mary began the evening milking. She was dreaming of ripe cherries as she sat coaxing milk from one cow after another. The girls knew the routine; all Mary had to do was open the gate, and they'd file in one by one. The rhythm was relaxing, and Mary greeted each cow by name as she entered the milking shed. She finished with Bess, disappointed again with her production, and bent down to press the lid onto the milk bucket.

When she straightened, she let out an involuntary cry. Her eyes went wide as a huge animal stepped up to the bail and poked its head into the feed trough. Black and white patterns over its hide gave it a bizarre look, and its sheer bulk was intimidating. It was a cow, no doubt about that, but it was like nothing Mary had ever seen before. Her eyes skimmed along its broad flat back and down to an udder bulging with milk.

She gave a nervous laugh. Where had this animal come from? Had Les brought it home? But, no, she hadn't heard the truck return. And where would he have gotten *that* thing from? She looked at the animal's udder again and began to calculate how much milk must be in there. It would well make up for the shortfall from Bess and Lily. And wherever the cow was from, she needed to be milked—that udder was taut. Warily, she closed the bail to keep the cow in place. She emptied Bess' milk into the jug, then sat down beside the giant cow.

Timid at first, not knowing how the beast might react, she began to milk. The cow munched placidly, ignoring Mary, and she relaxed into the rhythm of the job.

An hour later, when Les came home, Mary was leaning on the fence, watching the new cow grazing with the others. He came up beside her and slipped his arm around her waist. Then she felt him stiffen.

"What the hell is that?"

"A cow." Mary giggled.

"That's not a cow, that's a house. Damn, she's big!"

"And she gave twice as much milk as the others. Twice. It just kept coming."

"You milked her?"

Mary nodded.

"Where the hell did she come from?"

"I have no idea. She just showed up in the milking shed. Followed the others right in, came up all quiet-like to the bail and stood there to be milked."

"Do you think it's from the Parnhams' place? Have they gotten a new animal? Shit. I've never seen anything like that!"

"I don't know."

"They're going to be pissed off you milked her."

"She was bursting, Les. What could I do?"

"Well, we'll have to ring them and see if they're missing an animal." He turned to go into the house. He took a look back at the cow. "Damn."

The cow didn't belong to the Parnhams. It didn't belong to the McCormicks either. Or the Browns. It seemed to have materialised out of thin air in Les and Mary's paddock.

"Well, shit. It has to have come from *somewhere*." Les was watching Mary milk the cow the following morning.

"Here, pour this into the jug." Mary handed Les her bucket. "There's still more coming," she added as she took the empty bucket back from him.

"What are we going to do with her?" Les asked.

"I say we keep her. We've asked the neighbours, and she doesn't belong to any of them. If someone's lost this animal, they'll surely come looking for her. Until then…" Mary shrugged. "It's a hell of a lot of milk."

Les frowned. "She'll need a hell of a lot of feed, too." But he didn't contradict her. The cows were Mary's responsibility. It was her decision. And she was probably right. Someone would come looking for the cow, and until then, well, who could blame them for taking advantage of the situation? Better than letting that milk go to waste and risk the cow getting mastitis.

Two weeks passed, and no one came for the cow. Mary vacillated between wishing someone would show up for her, and hoping no one did. The cow ate so much food. Mary was cutting twice the amount of acacia from the alley cropping as usual, and she began to worry about having enough feed for the year. If they had to buy in feed, it would cancel out any benefit of having the extra milk.

And the extra milk seemed to be drying up, too. By the end of two weeks, the giant cow was only giving a little more than the others, and she seemed lethargic. Was she still not getting enough feed? Mary simply couldn't give her more and hope to have any left by the time the autumn rains started. The cow wasn't grazing much, either. She stood in the shade of the hedgerow most of the day, not venturing into the sun at all. The healthy fat layer she had on arrival had wasted away. Mary began to think that whoever had bought this cow had gotten a bad deal. She hoped it wasn't sick. She didn't need a new disease to infect her herd.

And then, sixteen days after the cow arrived, it vanished again. No one came for it, no one rang. It just disappeared as mysteriously as it had arrived.

Mary wouldn't have minded much, except that Bonnie disappeared with it. When she asked around, none of the neighbours had seen either animal.

"She's my best milker. My breeding stock! What am I going to do? We can't afford to replace her right now."

Les sighed. "I don't know, Mary. Maybe wait a couple days. She might turn up again."

But she didn't. And two days later, Bess and Lily vanished.

"Someone's stealing them," Mary suggested at dinner that evening. She pushed her beans around her plate, too upset to eat much.

"But why take Bess and Lily? They're the worst animals in the herd."

"The thief doesn't know that. Not until they milk them."

"Have you contacted the police?"

Mary scoffed. "Like they'd do anything." She sighed. "But, yes, I filed a report, for all the good it will do." She set down her fork. "I'm going to spend the night in the paddock tonight."

Les nodded. "We can trade off nights." Les stood, his empty plate in his hand. "Take the gun with you." He kissed Mary on top of the head. "And eat. It won't do any good to starve yourself."

When Mary sat down in the paddock at dusk, the cows drifted over to her, curious and eager for scratches. After satisfying their curiosity and itches, they settled down next to her. Mary smiled, surrounded by the sound of chewing cud and the sweet fermented smell of bovine breath. She leaned back against a fencepost, closing her eyes for a moment to savour the cool night air.

She woke with a start some time later. The cows were no longer arrayed around her. She squinted into the darkness and saw them grazing about fifty metres away. She counted. Twelve. She hadn't lost any more. But something had woken her, she was sure of it. She stilled herself, opening her senses to everything around her.

The smell. Something was different about the smell. Had it rained? No. That was ridiculous. It wouldn't rain until May. The sky was clear, and Mary was dry. Why, then, did the air smell so...so *green*? A cool breeze wafted over her and she shivered. And why was it so cold? She stood and wrapped her thin jersey more closely around herself.

Three of the cows raised their heads, sniffing the air. So they smelled it, too. Mary walked into the breeze. Two more cows raised their heads. She stepped cautiously, wishing she'd thought to pick up her torch. The smell seemed to grow the further she went. She closed her eyes for a moment and breathed deeply. It was the smell of moist soil and green grass. Entirely out of place, and so seductive she couldn't help but follow it.

Maybe she blinked, but she didn't think so. One moment she was walking on the hard, dry ground of home, and in the very next step, her foot came down on thick, springy grass. She cried out in surprise and peered down. It was hard to see in the dark. She bent and ran her hand across a carpet of plants. She grabbed a handful and pulled, bringing it to her nose. She inhaled deeply. Grass. Lush and tall, and utterly impossible. She turned, looking back where she'd come from. She sucked in a sharp breath and dropped her handful of grass.

Her cows were gone.

Her paddock was gone.

Stretching away from her was a vast expanse of grass, dotted with enormous black and white cows like the one that had mysteriously appeared, then vanished. There were hundreds of them, their white patches glowing faintly in the starlight like wisps of fog.

Turning in a slow circle, Mary could see nothing but lush grass and enormous cows. Was she dreaming? Surely, she must be. She walked a few more steps into her dream. The smell of moist soil was intoxicating. One of the giant cows noticed her and lumbered toward her. A few others followed. Mary staggered back, intimidated. Then she spun at a noise behind her. More giant cows walked toward her. Feeling terribly small, she was beginning to think this dream was about to become a nightmare. Well, if she was dreaming, she could wake up.

"Okay Mary, wake up," she said aloud. The cows stopped for a moment at the sound of her voice, and then continued to pace toward her. "Now."

But she couldn't wake. Maybe if she retraced her steps, she could find her way back to the beginning of her dream and out of this place. But the shifting livestock and her own spinning had confused her sense of direction. She had no idea which way she'd come from. And the cows were all around her now.

"Go away!" She waved her arms at the beasts and they scattered like flies. Mary laughed nervously. "Well, that was easy. Too bad I can't wake up as easily." She would just have to wait it out. This strange dream couldn't last forever. She hoped it wouldn't keep her from waking, should someone arrive to steal her cows.

She sat cross-legged on the ground. The damp slowly seeped through the seat of her pants, and she wondered at her own ability to imagine sitting on wet ground when it was something she'd never felt before. She listened to the cows around her, their steady munching relaxing her.

But even the sound of grazing cows couldn't keep the panic from rising as the hours passed and Mary didn't wake. When the sky began to lighten, she had to acknowledge that she wasn't dreaming. Whatever this was, it was real.

The rising light revealed an alien landscape, greener than anything she'd ever seen. The grass seemed to stretch forever. It was a cow's paradise.

And now the cows were slowly making their way toward a low shed in the distance. The milking shed. It must be. And at the milking shed would be a person—she looked at the hundreds of animals around her—lots of people who could tell her where she was and perhaps explain what was going on.

She dusted off her trousers and followed the cows.

Her eyes grew wide as she neared the shed. It was more like an airplane hangar in size, and as noisy as the planes that flew overhead at home. In spite of the noise, the cows walked calmly into a narrow chute and up a slight ramp into the shed. Mary hung back. She wasn't going to go into that chute, to be crushed by giant cows. There must be another way into the shed. She clambered over a metal gate and skirted around the building.

One side was entirely open, and as she rounded the corner, Mary's jaw dropped. Dozens of cows stood shoulder to shoulder, head inward on a giant, raised, slowly rotating platform. Pulsing tubes were connected to their teats and milk flowed through the translucent tubing. At first she saw not a single person. Then, as she scanned the vast space, she saw one man managing the cows as they entered and exited the shed. He let them into each stall on the platform as it turned, and opened the gate for the ones who had gone all the way around so they could step off the platform.

Movement at ground level caught her eye and she watched a woman deftly pull the tubes off a cow who had gone around the circle. One after another she removed the tubes, and they retracted out of the way. She was in constant motion, only barely keeping up with the carousel of cows. Mary reasoned there must be another person putting the tubes on the cows on the other side, where they entered. Three people to milk maybe four hundred cows! Mary stood dumbfounded.

"Um... Can I help you?" The voice came from behind, and Mary jumped in surprise. She turned to see a burly man in coveralls. He was clean-shaven, and his short-cropped hair was mostly silver.

"I...um...well..." What could she say? She waved a hand toward the milking shed. "What is all this?"

The man frowned. "What do you mean? It's a milking parlour. This is a dairy farm. What did you expect to see?" He looked her up and down. "And who are you?"

Mary shook herself and held out a hand. "Mary McPherson. I live—" she waved a hand vaguely in the direction of the paddock "—nearby."

"Mary McPherson, huh?" The man didn't take her proffered hand.

"And you are?" Mary dropped her hand, feeling decidedly uncomfortable as the man scrutinised her.

"Ian. Ian McPherson." He let the name sink in for a moment. "I'm surprised that a Mary McPherson I've never seen or heard of lives nearby and has to ask what a milking parlour is. So, what do you do, Mary McPherson?"

"I...well...I'm a farmer. My husband and I have twenty hectares in dairy and millet."

"Millet? Who the hell grows millet in Canterbury?"

Mary frowned. "Well, what else *can* you grow?" She looked around at the green expanses of grass. "Obviously you've got some source of water here. And the money to pay for it."

"Look, I don't know who you are or where you're from, but I'm going to have to ask you to leave."

"But I'm not sure how to get home from here. I've…I've never seen this place before. I never knew this sort of place *existed*."

Ian's manner changed. He looked at Mary for a moment, and then spoke slowly, as if explaining something to a child. "How about I take you inside? Do you have someone you can ring to come and get you? Someone who takes care of you?" He took Mary by the elbow and turned her around, steering her toward a large house nearby.

"Someone who takes care of me?" She pulled her elbow out of Ian's grasp. "I take care of myself, thank you very much. And I'll thank you to treat me as an adult." Then a gasp escaped her. "Bonnie!" She broke away from Ian and rushed to a small pen where Bonnie stood chewing her cud. Bonnie greeted her by stretching her neck over the fence for a scratch. "Oh! And there's Bess and Lily."

Mary greeted all three of her cows, and then turned back to Ian. "These are *my* cows. They were stolen over the past couple of days. Where did you get them?"

"Whoa!" Ian held up his hands. "I haven't stolen anything. Your cows appeared in my paddock. I think before you accuse anyone of theft, you should check your fences." Then he made a face. "Why you'd care about such lousy stock, though, I don't know."

"Lousy? Bonnie is my best milker—fourteen litres a day." Mary paused. "The two N'Damas…well, they are pretty lousy. But for a dual-purpose breed, they're not bad." She glanced back at the milking shed, with the hundreds of giant cows, and barked a laugh. "I suppose, with that herd, my animals do look pathetic."

Ian nodded. "I get thirty-two litres a day from each of my cows."

"Yeah, that one that showed up at my place gave twice the milk Bonnie gives."

"The one that showed up at your place?"

Mary laughed. "Yeah. Maybe you need to check your fences, too."

Ian rubbed his chin and frowned. "I did have one go missing for a while…Came back yesterday looking like hell—like she hadn't eaten for a week. Thought I might have to put her down."

Mary grimaced. "Sorry. I tried. I fed her as much acacia as I could cut, but she was so huge. She just ate whatever I could give her and wanted more. I don't know how you get this much grass to grow." She waved her hands around. "And no shade for the cows? How do they manage the heat?"

Ian's brow was furrowed. "I really don't understand anything you're saying. If these are your animals, you're welcome to take them. I penned them up, worried they'd pass some disease to my herd. Figured someone might come looking for them. You got a truck to take them home in?"

"No. I...I walked here. Through the paddock." Mary frowned. "It was the strangest thing...like...like walking into a different world."

Ian's eyebrows rose, and Mary knew he thought she was a nutter. She was beginning to think the same, herself.

"Look, I was on my way out to Christchurch. Can I drop you somewhere along the way? You can pick up your truck and bring it back for your animals."

"Christchurch? Where's that?"

Ian's eyes widened. "What rock do you live under, lady? Surely you know where Christchurch is."

"Um...no. I've never heard of it. Is it on Banks Island?"

"Banks *Island*?" Ian took a deep breath. "Okay. How about we just go inside and ring the police. We'll get you to wherever it is you need to go."

Mary let herself be led into the house. It was large and clean, with carpeted floors and strange-looking appliances. "This is amazing!"

Ian scoffed. "Just a house. How about a cuppa while I ring the police?"

"Um...sure. Thanks." Mary looked around the immaculate kitchen. She vaguely recognised items—a kettle, a chiller, a cooktop and oven—but they all looked oddly angular and blocky. Then her eyes landed on a calendar pinned on the wall. She froze.

Her voice came out in a whisper. "Two thousand and seventeen?"

"Huh?" Ian looked up from the kettle he was about to lift.

"Two thousand and seventeen." Mary pointed. "Is that the correct year?"

"Yeeees. What year did you think it was?" Ian filled the kettle from the tap.

Mary swallowed. "Where I came from, it's two thousand four hundred and ten." She turned to Ian. He was staring at her with his mouth open, the kettle forgotten in his hand.

"That's impossible. It's insane."

Mary nodded. "But I'm not. Me, my cows...we live in the year twenty-four ten. I walked from my paddock into yours last night, without crossing a single fence. One step I was at home, the next step I was here."

"You're saying you stepped through time." Ian's eyebrows rose. "Look, I don't know whether you've been smoking something funny, or whether you're a little bit cracked, but you can't just step from one time to another."

Mary sighed. "I know that. I haven't been doing drugs, and I swear I'm not insane." She frowned. "At least, I feel like my usual sane self. Except for this." She waved her hands around at the kitchen.

"How could you possibly come from another time? Time travel's not possible."

Mary shook her head. "I know, but…Look, you're a McPherson. I'm a McPherson. My family has been farming the Canterbury Plains—this piece of land—since the 1800s. You and I have never met because we're not neighbours, we're…we're living on the same land. In different times. I don't know how it happened, but I stepped through time from my paddock into yours."

Ian stood frozen for a moment. "This is fucked." Then he laughed. "You could be my great-great-great-whatever granddaughter." He set the kettle down with a thud.

Eventually, they both recovered enough to make a cup of tea and sit down at the kitchen table to talk. Mary explained what had happened with the cows over the past two and a half weeks. She described her farm and her crops.

"Why don't you run Holsteins like we do?"

Mary laughed. "I've never seen Holsteins before. If the performance of the one that visited me is any indication, they can't survive in my time. I guess it's too hot and dry."

"And you milk by hand?"

Mary shrugged. "It's the only way I know how. There isn't a lot of dairy on the Canterbury Plains. Small holdings like mine are about it. We supply milk to the towns on Banks Island."

"You mean Banks Peninsula?"

"No. Banks Island."

Ian stood and rummaged in a kitchen drawer, producing a map which he spread out on the table. "We're here." He tapped a spot on the map.

Mary sucked in a breath. "And this is West Melton? So far inland?"

"Yeah, and here's the Banks Peninsula."

Mary looked up from the map and met Ian's eyes. "In my time, West Melton is coastal. The Banks Peninsula is an island. All this—" She looked down and swiped a hand across Christchurch, Lincoln, Prebbleton, and half a dozen other towns. "Is the sea."

"Well, shit."

Running her finger across the map, Mary traced the coastline as it was in her time. "The water at West Melton is shallow. Great beaches, but no port there. We take our milk and grain either down here, to Port Geraldine—"

"Geraldine! That's practically in the mountains," Ian interrupted.

"Or up here, to Port Omihi."

"And it all goes to Banks Pen—Banks *Island*? None of it is exported?"

Mary laughed. "We can barely support New Zealand. There's nothing left over to send elsewhere."

"Fuck."

"You really produce enough to export?" Mary's interest was piqued. "Can I...can I have a look around?"

Ian smiled. "Sure. Come on." They went out to the milking shed, where the cows were still rotating through the milking. He showed her the machinery and the giant milk storage tank. They hopped into his ute, and he drove her around the farm. He showed her the enormous centre-pivot irrigation system, the towering stack of baleage. To Mary's increasing amazement, Ian described his farming system, and how his milk was sent as milk solids all around the world. How New Zealand was a major exporter of dairy products, wool, beef and lamb, fruits and vegetables. She watched, with her jaw in her lap, as the double-trailer milk tanker arrived to carry off the milk to a processing plant in Darfield.

Returning to the house for a late lunch, Mary was astounded at the plentiful food—slivered ham, cheese, beautiful lettuce, soft white bread, crisp apples, and strawberries. She wanted simultaneously to inhale it all in case it vanished, and savour it slowly so it would never end. Ian put the kettle on for more tea.

While they ate, she and Ian continued to compare notes about their respective times.

"So the economy is largely based on agriculture?" It was hard for Mary to believe that the big AI and space aeronautics companies that dominated New Zealand in her time didn't even exist in Ian's time.

Ian nodded. "Agriculture's the biggest, but tourism is big too. People come to see the natural beauty—mountains, hot pools, glaciers."

Mary cocked her head. "What's a glacier?"

Ian's eyebrows rose. "Snow and ice that never melts. The mountains are covered in them. Franz Josef Glacier, Fox Glacier, Tasman Glacier? You've never heard of them?"

Mary shrugged and shook her head. "I've never seen snow."

They drank their tea in silence for a minute. "Sounds like global climate change turned out worse than predicted." In response to Mary's questioning look, he added, "Climate change? Don't they talk about that in your time?"

Mary shook her head. "No. The climate is just what it is. Oh, we learned in school that it was different hundreds of years ago, but we don't talk about it much."

"Well, I suppose the state of New Zealand in your time is the fault of us in this time." He frowned. "I wonder what we'd do differently if everyone knew what was coming." He rose and refilled the kettle. "There's a lot of talk about reducing our use of fossil fuels, reducing our carbon dioxide emissions. Talk is cheap." He shrugged. "So we talk, and that's about it." He looked at Mary and his expression changed. "I'm sorry."

Mary looked around at the signs of wealth. The big house, soft carpet, gleaming appliances, plush furniture…This was her family's wealth. Where had it all gone? Her own unending slog to scratch a meagre living out of the hot dust of the Canterbury Plains recalled none of this opulence.

"Yeah. I'm sorry, too."

Mary put down her cup, feeling hopelessly out of place. "I should go." She stood. "Thanks for the tour, lunch, tea…"

"Where will you go?"

That was the question, wasn't it? How was she supposed to get home?

"If you don't mind, I'll take my cows and…I guess I'll go back out to your paddock. To the place where I arrived. Maybe I can get back from there?"

Ian nodded. "I guess...It's probably your best chance." He rose suddenly. "But wait a minute. Let me send some things with you."

"Really, you don't need to—"

"Nonsense. You're my great-great-great-whatever granddaughter. I should spoil you like I do my grandkids." He scrutinised Mary. "Now, let's see...what is it you need?"

Mary laughed. "Water. But you can't exactly give me that."

Ian's shoulders slumped. "So, what is it you want?"

Mary thought for a moment. She thought about her life. There were a lot of things she didn't have. A lot of things she'd never be able to afford. Her house threatened to blow away in the fierce nor'west winds. When it did rain, the roof leaked. The floor was rough and softened only by a few battered throw rugs. But she had Les and her cows. She thought about Ian's herd of hundreds. He didn't know each of his cows by name. He didn't talk to them every morning and evening while he milked them. His milking shed of noise and frantic activity wasn't the place of peace and reflection that hers was. She smiled and shrugged.

"There's really nothing I want, except to go home."

In the end, Ian pressed some things on her. She left with a bag full of fruits and vegetables exotic to her—apples, broccoli, silverbeet, blackcurrants. She also carried a nearly-full bottle of drench, because Ian's cow had returned from her place infested with intestinal worms, and Mary admitted she couldn't afford drench.

"Wait," Ian said as they were about to head out the door. "One more thing." He ducked into what looked like an office and emerged a minute later with a handful of coins.

"But these are no good in my—" Mary began.

Ian held up a finger. "They're no good as currency, and if they were, they'd be worth bugger all. But in your time, these are four-hundred-year-old coins."

Mary smiled as she understood. "Thank you." She held out her hand, and Ian dropped the coins into it.

"Hold out for a good price. Get all you can for them."

Ian helped Mary tie baling twine leads on her cows. They didn't necessarily need them—her cows followed her without leads—but she didn't want to leave any behind when...if...she crossed back to her own time.

Ian accompanied her to the paddock, where his own cows were once again grazing. The sun was already dropping toward the horizon. She'd spent the entire day here, four hundred years in the past.

"So…now what?" Ian asked. "How did you come across before?"

Mary shrugged. "I just walked into your paddock. I…I smelled it. The grass, the moisture."

"Did you see anything?" Ian peered around the paddock, as if looking for a magical doorway.

"Well, it was dark, but no, I don't think there was anything to see. It was just the smell."

"So…do you smell anything?" There was doubt in his eyes.

Mary closed her eyes and breathed in, not entirely sure what home smelled like. She'd never really thought about it. She opened her eyes again.

"Nothing."

"Hm."

Mary began to pace slowly across the paddock, sniffing. Ian and her cows trailed after her. As the minutes ticked by, her thoughts became more and more panicked. What if she couldn't find the way home? What if she was stuck in 2017 forever? What would Les do? What would happen to her cows? Her farm? She struggled to keep her breathing even and to focus on her sense of smell.

"Mary?" Her frightened thoughts were interrupted by Ian's voice. She turned to look at him and he nodded toward Bonnie.

Bonnie's head was up, her nostrils twitching. She began to lumber away from Mary, tugging on the lead. Mary, Bess, and Lily followed. Ian didn't move. After a few steps, Mary looked back at him. "You sure you don't want to come with me? Just to visit?"

"Nah." Ian's face was pale and he swallowed. "I'll just stay here."

Mary smiled, then hurried up to walk abreast of Bonnie. Five, ten, fifteen steps, and the pair vanished. The only indication they still existed were the two leads trailing from Mary's hand to Bess and Lily. The two cows ambled forward until they, too, disappeared.

Ian stood blinking at the spot for a long minute.

Then he turned to survey his farm. Four hundred years. He tried to imagine his lush paddocks a dry, hot wasteland. Christchurch gone, nearby West Melton a beach community. He sighed and shook his head. Four hundred years was a long way away.

Hands in his pockets, he slowly made his way back to the house.

MOTHER'S MILK
Dan Rabarts

Angelica was pleased, and a little relieved, and only a tiny bit sad, the day the milk went sour.

The sky was grey. Rain fell cold and quiet in straight lines down the windows. The sound of boots crunching over wet gravel receded as she pushed her teacup away and looked up at her reflection in the mirror behind the sideboard. With a wrinkled finger she pushed a stray grey lock behind her ear. It wouldn't be long now, she knew; it never was when the milk turned sour. Just as well, too, for he had started to talk about covering up the windows. They all reached that point, in the end.

Man spends all day out there in them hills, paddocks, looking up at them trees. Don't need to be seeing them of an evening as well, looking back at me when my day's done and time's come to put my feet up. You make sure those drapes are drawn before I get in, or I'll take to them windows with a few good sheets of iron.

Or words to that effect.

Yes, the time was almost right. They had had a pretty good run, and he wasn't getting any better a lover as the years wore him down. Pushing back her chair, Angelica carried her teacup to the sink, tipped out what remained to twist in milky white ribbons down the plughole, and then made for the back door. Hiking her skirts up off her ankles, she stepped into her boots and donned her raincoat.

The police would probably come again, like they had the last time, and the time before that, with their notebooks and their questions and their shovels, but Angelica didn't mind. They were always so *handsome*. Besides, Angelica did nothing wrong, had *never* done anything wrong. The milk had turned sour. That was all that mattered. With a small, dignified grunt, she hefted the mattock over her shoulder, gripped the shovel in her other hand, and set off up the ridge.

The rain was falling right steady by the time Charles got the cows down into the bottom paddock, but Charles didn't mind the rain so much. Reminded a man he was just a small thing in the world, and it wouldn't do no good to shiver and hide—not from the rain, nor from the world. The cows clattered their noisy hooves over the old patch of broken stone near the track, the sound like the rattle of gunfire in the trenches. Rain and mud and shellfire. Long time ago it was, but it was still awful clear back there in the shadows behind Charles Reardon's eyes.

As the rain drizzled off his oilskins and the cows wandered down the paddock towards the creek, Charles leaned against the mossy old brickwork that had once been a fireplace and imagined himself warmed by its heat, long since fled. Tugging his hood further over his face, he reached into his pocket and pulled out the sandwich she'd made him, wrapped in a linen napkin. Light on the butter and ham and heavy on the mustard and pepper. Chrissakes, even after all this time, she still couldn't fix him a sandwich the way he liked it. No wonder her husband had upped and disappeared, all that time ago, and she had trouble keeping help on at the farm. Mind you, for an old bird she still liked to keep the sheets warm, and Charles didn't mind one bit being the help, with benefits. He grinned a little at that, even though he knew the last few times he'd tried to make things happen, things hadn't... happened. Never mind. It was the trees that he blamed, *them* trees, always looking over his shoulder as he went about the place, always whispering past him in their harsh crooked voices off beyond the windows in the dark.

As if hearing his thoughts, the blighted old bastard up on the ridge caught the wind, sucked it in, and sent it whistling away in a maudlin dirge that drove a cold shiver right down Charles' spine. Like the whine of falling artillery shells, the Stuka's howl. Too many nightmares in those sounds.

Charles craned his neck to look up at Old Man Pine. The creaking bastard clung to the ridgeline, one side all black and blasted from some ancient thunderbolt, its other flank grown wild and bent and ragged, somehow desperate, misshapen, tenacious. Through the haze of rain and by the motion of the wind, it seemed to rock back and forth, back and forth, measuring him in eyeless contemplation.

"Damned hazard," Charles muttered aloud to his sandwich, as the dogs barked and corralled the herd down the paddock, toward the creek. "Time to take to it with a saw. Make a good stack of firewood, it will. Better'n having it sitting up there on the side of the cliff waiting to come down in the next big rain." He chose not to consider the fact that Old Man Pine had stood through more downpours and windstorms than he had had hot dinners. Not for the first time, Charles wondered about the bones of the building he leaned on, thought about the tree overhead, its blasted side. He wondered if there was any connection between the burnt tree and the ruins. Angelica could probably tell him. Lightning, maybe, a burning branch falling, setting the house aflame. It wasn't entirely unlikely. Damned hazard.

Damned tree.

As he shoved his napkin in his pocket and trudged back into the rain he heard the laughter. Always down here, in this paddock, under the twisted old pine and by the cackle of the creek, damn kids laughing like their parents don't know better'n to let them run amok in the rain, when the creek's running high, high as drowning, dark as mud. Damned dangerous places, farms. Kids ought to be kept working, not left to run and laugh in the mud and the wet. That's how it was in his day.

Damned kids.

"You won't really cut it down, will you?"

Charles paused mid-stride, turning to peer back through the rain at the tumbledown chimney, and saw the waif of a thing crouching beside it, her pale clear eyes staring intently at him. Rain sluiced off her in thick streams, her hair loose and lank in her face.

"The tree. You won't cut it down, not really."

Charles scratched his head. Had he been talking aloud? Maybe. He did that sometimes; good to hear a human voice out on the farm, even if it was his own. He shook a fist at the girl. "Get out of here, get yourself home. This is private property, hear? You're trespassing."

"You won't cut it down." It wasn't a question.

Charles started back towards her, limping only a little from the sliver of shrapnel Jerry had left in him as a parting gift way back when. Then both the dogs began to howl. Spinning about, Charles saw a cow's mad flailing legs, wrapped up in fencing wire and posts as it thrashed in the mud, sliding towards the creek.

"Damn it," he grumbled, and set off at a jog to save the damned stupid beast before it drowned itself. Then he'd have a damned fence to mend. He risked a glance back, saw the girl still standing there, rain in her face, her pale blue eyes watching him go.

Damned kids.

Angelica placed her cup down with a small tinkle, and gave the policeman a ghost of a smile. He had been here before, she remembered, but he had seemed so much younger then. She pushed a dark, thick lock back behind her ear, enjoying the way her skin felt, so soft and smooth beneath her fingertips. She reached for the pot. "More tea, Detective?"

The aging policeman glanced back up at her from his notes, his brow furrowed in concentration. "Urm…" he fumbled.

"The milk is very fresh. I got it in just this morning."

He waved vaguely at his cup, and she obliged by pouring for him. "Just to be clear, Mrs Harrington, you *are* the self-same Angelica Harrington I personally interviewed here with regards to a missing persons case on this very farm, one Mister Albert Dreckmann, some, er, fifteen years ago? Is that correct?" He looked back at her from his stack of notes, years of worry and concentration burrowing across his forehead like ditches, or trenches, or mass graves.

"Indeed." She smiled again, enjoying how full and rich and complete a feeling it was.

"The same Angelica Harrington who married William Harrington in…March of 1896." His gaze this time was piercing, laden with suspicion and—hidden deep, but not so deep that Angelica couldn't see it—fear. It was very important, the fear. The taste of fear was sweet. When the fear ran away, like blood in the rain, that was when things turned sour.

"Well, Detective, we girls used to be married very young, back in the day."

"You've aged very gracefully, then, Mrs Harrington."

"They say Cleopatra used to bathe in mare's milk to maintain her youth. So much nicer than all that blood of virgins stuff. Very messy, I'd think."

The detective might've frowned, but he was doing his best to hide his discomfort from her. "Perhaps."

The old house was empty when Charles got back. He shucked off his soaking oilskins in the porch to dry. Feeling damp to the bone, Charles stumped through the lounge towards the bathroom, looking forward to the feel of warm water on his skin. As he trooped past the high-backed recliner there by the hearth that he'd long since claimed as his place of ease, he noticed that she'd drawn the curtains, mostly. Most, but not all the way.

He stopped. He looked. There was a gap in the curtains. If he had been sitting in his armchair, looking up at the window...

He leaned down, the recliner creaking beneath him, and he saw it.

The old tree swayed raggedly in the wind. It was all he could see, filling what little sky lay beyond the bay window, grey and bleak and scudding as it was. Charles stamped across the room and pulled the curtains shut tight, blocking the view. Blocking it, the tree, maybe, from looking in.

Charles' eyes weren't exactly what they used to be, no sir, and he was suddenly blind in the darkness. Damn fool should've turned a light on first, but the tree, the goddamned *tree*, it sent shivers up him like no hunk of timber and pinecones ever should. It was just a *tree*, damn it all. Just a tree. Tomorrow, first thing, he swore he'd take to it with the saw. Be a good winter's firewood in it, for sure.

Charles turned around and almost walked straight into Angelica. He stumbled back, clutching at a tightness in his chest. "Holy croupiers, woman, you damn near gave me a heart attack. Why are you sneaking up on me like that?"

She smiled her thin smile and offered him a steaming mug. "It's cold out there. I brought you warm milk."

Charles took a breath. Relaxing, he accepted the cup and stepped past her, heading for the bathroom.

With the water running and steam frosting the window and mirror, Charles eased out of his damp clothes. Allowing himself a moment's respite, he swigged a mouthful of milk.

Angelica heard him before she saw him. His howl of outrage echoed down the short hallway from the darker bowels of the house. No-one ever likes sour milk. Her lips crinkled slightly, dry like old paper.

He stumbled out of the bathroom wrapped in a towel, his skin damp and drooping around his sagging frame, rage writ plain across his face as he stormed into the lounge.

"Damn it, woman!" he began, but the words died on his lips as she turned her head slightly to look his way, her body rigid. The sight must have had the desired effect; the curtains were parted behind her, just slightly, her aged frame somehow regal alongside the distant spectre of Old Man Pine.

"Damn it," he said again, the red rage draining away as a light seemed to come on in that perennial dimness behind his eyes. "Damn milk was sour. Didn't you check the milk? Told you this morning it was sour, didn't I?"

Angelica said nothing—she didn't need to. His eyes were already sliding past her to the ridgeline, the ragged silhouette that loomed against the sky, rimmed in a rare beam of sunlight as a momentary cleft appeared between the towering ranks of clouds. The tree quivered and swayed in the wind.

"Damn it," he said again, like they were the only words left to him, and she could hear the shudder in his voice, hidden deep, as men were wont to hide their fears deep. "Shower can wait."

She watched him go, then turned back to the window. In the few minutes it took him to pull his clothes back on, shrug into his coat, and stomp out of the house, his boots crunching on gravel, the rent in the clouds closed over, and it began once more to rain.

The sliver of sunshine that had forced its way through the clouds for those few precious moments could not last. Today was not a day for sunshine. Today was a day for rain, and cold wet earth, and sour milk.

"Now, what can you tell me about Mister Reardon? You know that the government takes the welfare of our veterans, especially those who served in both World Wars, very seriously." The policeman sipped his tea, glancing around at the small dining room's dark furnishings, its bric-à-brac suggesting relics of a bygone era.

"As they very well should. He *did* go out in that awful storm to move the cattle. They were down in the bottom paddock, you see, and it often floods down there. There was an old milking shed down there a long time ago, you know, but I guess it flooded once too often for them, maybe. Tragic, it was."

"How so?"

Angelica shrugged, her grin warm and mischievous. "I've only heard ghost stories, Detective, and you can't trust *those* now, can you? Some say the farmer and his girls got caught down there and drowned, others say the girls begged the storm to spare them death by drowning, so it threw down a bolt of lightning and burned the place to the ground instead." She leaned over the table, dropping her voice to a confidential whisper. The detective's focus was drawn back to her dark hair, her clear pale eyes. "Do you want to know what else I heard? I heard that the man who once lived on this land had two daughters, but he was not a good father. He was a cruel man, not a man suited to the distance and isolation of making a home in the dark wilds of a foreign land."

A cloud must have passed over the sun, for the room seemed suddenly darker, closer, colder. "It was not enough for him to love only his wife, if you take my meaning, Detective. But we're decent folk. We need not elaborate on the details of what an unwell and unhappy man might do to his daughters far from the watching eyes of society. Suffice to say that a mother's love for her children is a powerful thing. They say she hit him over the head with an iron off the stove, then dragged him up the hill to that tree—yes, that one that you see up there now, though it was much younger then, and not yet burnt like it is now. There she took a rope, a good heavy rope, and wrapped it around his neck, and tossed it over a branch, and pulled.

"But the climb had tired her out, and she lacked the strength required to complete the deed. Her efforts roused him, and him being a resourceful man was never without a knife at his belt. That was how the girls found them, at the tree, him with knife in hand and covered in her blood. There was a madness in his eye, Detective, the likes of which one such as you is like to know from those who have stepped over the line that divides the rational from the insane. He left her body there and led the girls down to the creek, where he took one of them into the water. He held her under while she thrashed and kicked and fought, and the other girl watched, and cried. It was all she could do, you understand. The girls, they were only young. So very, very young. It was all those girls ever wanted to be; young, young forever, not old and bitter and sour like their father, or broken and desperate and lost like their mother.

"He made the daughter who was left carry her sister's body to the tree; made her dig a grave. It was raining then, you see, and dark. He made her bury them there, daughter and mother both, then took her back down to the milkshed.

"The girl knew there was no reason to go into the milkshed after dark, in the rain, down there in the paddock where the creek sometimes ran high and flooded. I'm sure I don't know how it happened, but the story goes that there was a fire in the milkshed, and the father's burnt corpse was found there later, but no-one ever saw the girl again. Perhaps she just asked the earth to open up and—" Angelica smiled, splaying her fingers suddenly, causing the detective to flinch back. "Swallow her."

As if on cue, the clouds passed, and the room become warm again, and light.

"But that is just one story, and I'm sure there are others. These hills have their share of ghosts, and sometimes they want their stories told, and sometimes they don't. What do we sacrifice, Detective, to believe such stories? Because after all, nothing is won without sacrifice, am I right?" Her smile was no less charming as she took up her teacup and blew delicately across the surface.

Charles hefted the axe over one shoulder and took the biggest single-handed saw he could find in the cavernous old shed in his other hand. He glanced longingly at the new-fangled two-person petrol chainsaw on its shelf, and shook his head. It'd be an hour or more to get someone in to help him wrangle that noisy beast up the hillside, and it was more time than the old bastard deserved. He'd go this alone. It was just a goddamned tree, after all.

Back into the rain he went, trudging through the mud as he whistled for the dogs, water sluicing off the cold sharp steel he carried. Mud, rain, and steel, just like the old days. The world was full of monsters, he now realised, though some of them wore the faces of men, while others instead buried their evil, burrowing their roots deep into the earth. Charles remembered digging, digging endlessly, amidst the crack of artillery and the rake of machine-gun fire, listening as other men's evil savaged the earth, the earth which greedily lapped up the blood of good men, innocent men, brave men. No amount of digging would ever cleanse all that blood from the soil, nor strip that evil from the dark places where it lay hidden. All a man like Lieutenant Charles Reardon could do was cut the monsters down where he found them. What he wouldn't give right now for a grenade, or a stick of dynamite.

A solitary figure, he stumped up the ridge towards the tortured shape of Old Man Pine. He was halfway there before he realised that the dogs, who were normally always at his heel, weren't beside him. He paused, turned, looked down through the rain at the house where it sat perched on the hillside like the crows he had watched from the trenches—its black windows like the black eyes of those black birds waiting to set upon the leavings of battle with beak and talon. The house seemed to look back at him, old and tired and hungry. Charles repressed a shiver, refused to think the thought that arose unbidden: *Caught between the gaze of two monsters.*

Charles whistled for the dogs, but against the soughing timbre of the ancient branches, his call was a thin, reedy sound, drowned out by the pelt of wind and lashing rain. "Damn dogs," he muttered and turned away, carrying on up the hill, more alone than before and smaller by the step as the tree grew ever larger, more twisted, more impossibly *watching* the closer he got.

Casting a glance over the edge of the ridge, down into the bottom paddock, he saw the ancient stone footprint of the building that had once stood below; what remained to be seen of it, at least. He saw the fireplace he liked to rest his weary bones on. Maybe it had been the first homestead some intrepid colonial had dared to build on this land, back when the hills had been dark with ancient forests and alive with birds, whose calls now existed only in history and memory. He wondered if the homesteader had lived alone, or if he had raised a family on those draughty stones. Wondered how it must have felt to watch it burn to the ground, or be swept away by a flood, or whatever might have happened to so completely strip it from the face of the earth.

Charles had watched things die, seen things burn. But there was a strange sadness in knowing that this fragment of the pioneering spirit had met such a sad, sorry end. Life went on, he knew. He had seen too many horrors and yet carried on, working and eating and sleeping and shitting, one day to the next, to be able to believe anything else. One house is taken away, those who remain build another, to bury their grief and hide from their dead.

Somewhere, Charles heard a cackle of laughter, and he paused, glancing behind him. "Damn kids," he grumbled, yet his shoulders itched. The sound was thin, and cruel, and cold, and rose above the groan of the branches and the shriek of the wind. Not like a child's laughter. A trick of air, was all; echoes and figments and waking ghosts. He forced himself to chuckle, just a little, at his own apprehension. He was too old to be frightened of ghosts.

Wiping the rain from his eyes, he nearly started forward, but caught himself. "What in the...?" Before him, yawning open at the base of the tree, was a hole. It was several feet deep and appeared to have been hacked out of the ground in a desperate hurry. Charles knew the look of a hole dug in haste, and this was just such a hole. He had dug many such holes, places to crouch and shoot and pray that the next shell didn't fall too close.

Charles had seen too many such holes become graves.

As he looked into the hole, at the slashed remains of thick roots in the muddy slurry at the bottom, he thought he saw pale fluid dripping slow and viscous from the wounds in the tree's deep tendrils. The liquid ran down with the rain into the mud below, pooling in sickly shades of brown and yellow. Yet even over the rich smell of freshly dug earth and autumn rain, Charles caught a whiff of something else. Something rank, rotten.

Sour milk.

Charles knew this wasn't right. For all the miles of trenches, all the foxholes that he'd dug in two great wars for freedom, he'd never known earth to stink of rotting milk. He took a step back, the question finally arising from the dark, primitive parts of his mind, the terrified reptilian sub-brain that had been screaming at him for some time now—perhaps minutes, perhaps hours, perhaps for the months grown to years that he had been on this cursed farm: why would someone have dug this hole, here, now?

He heard the laughter, yet no footfalls, and knew he was no longer alone on the ridge.

He turned as a cloud fractured briefly, a lance of sunlight piercing its cloak; turned in time to see the girl, the rain glistening in the sun as it touched her, settled on her, ran *through* her. Saw her pale eyes, pale like milk; saw the rain wash her innocence away like blood and milk and pain and hunger, all melting into the cold wet earth. Turned to see her thin smile crease her white skin, skin soft from too long in the dark and the damp, in places no-one could see, like the bodies that lay too long in the mud and the fear and the shit in the bottoms of the trenches, flecked black from fire and ash, and flies spawning greedily under that soft, rotting flesh. Heard the laughter turn to a grunt as the girl swung the mattock, up and over her head, the dirty blade singing like wind through the tree boughs above.

A solitary figure stood at the base of the old pine, shovelling dirt into a hole. Far away, the dogs howled.

The policeman slid his papers back into his folder, a little too hurriedly, his face a little too pale. "Thank you Mrs Harrington, that will be all. We'll be in touch if there's anything else we need."

"Of course." She smiled.

The detective turned to go, then paused, as if something had occurred to him. He opened his folder, rifled through the papers, seemed to find what he was looking for. "One more thing," he said, turning his gaze to her.

She could tell from the tension in his shoulders that he was struggling with something quite terrible. She suspected she knew what he wanted to say, and the prospect of it warmed her. Rarely had anyone come so close to the truth. Not that he would ever believe it.

"The farmer who originally built on this land had two daughters, as you say. Their names were Mary and Angela. All we have are their birth records; no-one knows what happened to either of them as adults."

Angelica met his gaze. He held it for a moment, and she saw the haunted look there. It was the look that said that the truth was much too terrible to be real. He looked away.

"Good day, Mrs Harrington."

"Good day, Detective."

And it would be. She was rather looking forward to walking the ridge, where those handsome young officers would be digging on the hillside on account of one of the other detectives saying they had found 'disturbed earth'. They'd be up there, shovels in hand, their shirts tossed aside, sweat glistening on their shoulders. They would find nothing, of course. They never did. And perhaps one of them might decide that he would like to stay for a cup of tea and maybe…a little more than tea. That would be quite delightful.

"Oh, and Detective? If you know of anyone looking for work, I have a position available, long term."

"I'll keep that in mind."

"Thank you kindly. I can always use an extra body around the place."

She sipped her tea. She did so like it when the milk was fresh.

THE EYE OF THE BEHOLDER
Kevin G. Maclean

"I want you to understand, gentlemen, the precarious position in which you find yourselves," Prince-Consort Bertrand said.

The three priests wisely stayed silent, though the leader nodded slightly to indicate understanding.

"The Queen is furious."

This time all three nodded.

"Seven years ago, she came to the Temple of the God with Two Faces with a simple request—that her unborn child should be 'as white as the snow and as red as the rose'. *Most* people would have understood this as a request that the child be beautiful…"

"It is a sign of most extreme divine favour, Majesty," said the priest on the left. The other two stared at him in horror.

"What? To be an albino with a strawberry birthmark covering the whole of the right-hand side of her face? Do you have any idea what your typical seven-year-old makes of that? She is my daughter. And she is the heir to the throne. In ten years, gentlemen, she is going to be thinking of marriage…"

"The mark was quite hard to see for the year Princess Dual was black, Majesty," put in the priest on the right.

"*What* did you just call her? It better have been Jewel, not what I thought I just heard, because if you give me any good reason to suspect that you have not been acting entirely faithfully to the commission Her Majesty gave you, or contrary to my daughter's best interests…well, let us just say that so far I have protected you from the Queen's wrath, and that I love my daughter…"

The Prince sat for a moment, his face unreadable, though his left hand gently and automatically checked his sword was loose in its scabbard. Then he sighed, and the priests could breathe again. "No, gentlemen, I want my daughter to look at least halfway normal. And the Queen still wants her to be beautiful. In fact, she paid you a great deal of money once, and more since, to ensure Jewel would be beautiful, and, to put it bluntly, she isn't beautiful, she's scary. And when she isn't scary, she's ugly. Every time you try to fix the problem, she's different, but a new problem appears."

The High Priest began, "We have a new—" but stopped under the Prince's withering gaze.

"Are you prepared to bet your life, and that of every member of your Order, that this new spell will work to the Queen's satisfaction? Because that is precisely what you would be doing."

The High Priest didn't have to think about it long. "Err…No."

"Well, take it from me, the most pleasant part of what she has planned for you if you aggravate her again will be the ravens tugging on your entrails. Stay out of her way."

The priests stood in white-faced silence.

The Prince continued. "She has lost faith in your ability to set things right. To quote her very words, 'Those two-faced priests of that two-faced god are worse than useless. Find someone who can and will do the job.' And so, gentlemen, I shall."

"Not the witches?" gasped the priest on the left.

"No. Her Royal Majesty has no wish to be beholden to the worshippers of the Triple Goddess, even if she thought they could do the job."

"Dealing with Hell always has too high a cost, Majesty," the High Priest cautioned.

"Just how stupid do you think we are?" the Prince snapped. He held up his hand. "Wait! As you value your lives, do not answer that." His aide took the opportunity to slip a document where the hand had rested. "Gentlemen, Her Royal Majesty has been both patient and generous for seven years, and has seen no progress. Consequently, it would be an act of prudence to offer to pay for someone else to do the job. Have I made myself perfectly clear? Ask now, because any misunderstanding could be fatal for you…"

"Yes, Highness. Perfectly clear. But where will you find such a powerful mage?"

"Faery, gentlemen," the Prince said. "I am sending an emissary to Faery." He waved them away. "I have taken the liberty of arranging you a guided tour of the torture chamber. Pay close attention. If you manage things right, you may never see such a thing again. Go on, shoo! The guards will escort you."

Beth was sure she had made a mistake. No, that wasn't right. She'd made lots of them. First, she should have let Josie get her own clothes down out of the trees. Second, she should never have told her mother what she was about. Third, she should have told everyone concerned to keep their mouths shut—no, that would never have worked...

She was startled out of her reverie of self-recrimination by the arrival of yet another interrogator. This one bore himself with the unmistakeable air of a military man, and one of high rank. He was accompanied by a finely-dressed man who poured a glass of wine for him before retiring to a side-table with the rest of the wine and the remaining glasses. Beth noted with amusement that this flunky wasted no time pouring wine for himself and getting comfortable.

The officer cleared his throat. "I am General Robert Longley. You are Beth Hawkins, from the village of Grimley-on-Tyde."

Beth, of course, had heard of him, but since the last half-dozen interrogations had all been conducted by men who held the power of life and death over her, she was no more frightened by this one. She nodded in acknowledgement.

"This will hopefully be the last interview for you. Lying or attempting to mislead us at this stage will be construed as treason. Any changes in your story will not be held against you. We just want the truth."

"I understand, Sir. But to tell the truth, I've been questioned so long and so hard that I'm no longer sure what some parts of the truth *are*." This brought a scowl from the General, and an understanding smile from the flunky.

"How about you just tell us your story, and tell us which bits you're sure of, and which bits you aren't?"

"Well, Sir, me and a bunch of the village girls went down to the swimming hole, and after we undressed, Josie insisted on putting a religious medallion on top of her clothes. I forget which god's it was, but she insisted it would protect her clothes."

"And you argued over this?"

"Yes, Sir, and eventually I told her that if she upset the Fae, whatever they did would be her own damned fault, beggin'-your-pardon-sir, and let her do it."

"What made you think it would upset the Fae?"

"Well, my gran's ma used to say that openly displaying any religious symbol in the woods was a bit like carrying the Pretender's flag into a royal castle. They just could *not* let it pass."

"And this grandmother's mother, she was something of an authority on the Fae?"

"Oh aye, Sir. Friends with some of them, she claimed, as much as mortal can be friend with Fae. Strange, she said they were, and uncanny."

"And she taught you about them?"

"No, Sir. She died just before I was born. But Ma talked about her a lot. And I've worked out a fair bit for myself."

"Why was none of this in the reports?" The General's voice was low and terse, straining not to shout in angry frustration at his absent subordinates.

"No-one asked, Sir," Beth said. "They kept telling me just to answer the questions, but they wouldn't ask the right ones. They seemed much more interested in hearing about the Puck catching us naked in the swimming-hole, and what Josie did when she found her knickers flying like a flag from the top of a pine tree."

The General closed his eyes in despair. "I see. And the milk and whisky?"

"An apology, Sir, and a bribe to get the Puck to bring her clothes back. He may be terrible mischievous, but there's no real harm in him."

"You've had frequent dealings with the Fae, then?"

"Oh, not that frequent, Sir. Maybe twice a year, someone's cow will get lost, and I'll talk to the Fae, and give them a gift, and next day the cow will show up. That sort of thing...It's dangerous to have too much to do with them."

"But you do know how to contact them?"

"Oh, that's easy enough, though they can be tricksy and wild. Just a matter of etiquette. It's not like they're scarce, y'know."

There was an awkward silence.

Finally, the silence got too much for Beth, and she said slowly, "You didn't know?" Then it came to her. "Of course you wouldn't. You've never been out of a town without your weapons and armour and a great host of men scaring away even the boldest of beasties. No wonder they never let you see them."

There was a rustle of silk as the flunky stood. He strolled across and perched himself on the edge of the table and quietly poured her a glass of wine. "I think, General, that we may have found our emissary." He smiled at her.

"I think, Highness, that you may well be right."

To her credit, Beth did not faint.

She could have said no to the General, with his Duty and Honour. She could have said no to the Prince, with his offers of honours and wealth. She could even have said no to the Queen, with her tears and her threats. But she hadn't been able to say no to a sad-eyed little girl, so she cursed herself for a fool.

And there she sat in the woods, under a great, spreading oak, with a small untouched cup of good whisky in front of her, and another set out for an unknown guest who hadn't arrived yet. A small donkey browsed nearby, hitched to a travelling pack and its saddlebags. She had been able to talk the Queen out of sending a full entourage, but not out of equipping her, and providing a donkey laden half with travelling supplies and half with the Prince-Consort's best whisky. She'd tried to explain it was too much—that the Fae weren't drunks—but to no avail.

The crack of a twig announced the arrival of a guest. Politely, she turned her head toward the distraction, then looked back. The cup opposite was untouched, but a quarter of hers was gone.

"Oh, it's you, Puck," she said.

A peeved-looking Puck showed himself and picked up the cup again. He tasted it again carefully, and pulled a face. "Arr, your great-grandmother's was better...And how did you know it was me, anyways?"

"Anyone else would have taken this one," she said, and leaned over to pick up the untouched cup.

"It's the curse of all Pucks," he said, woebegone. "Too much cleverness and the compulsion to show it."

"Well then," she said and raised her cup to him. "To all Pucks everywhere—may their cleverness never fail them."

"I'll drink to that," cried the Puck, leaping to his feet with cup still in hand, and never spilling a drop.

"Of course you will," she said. "You'll drink to any-bloody-thing."

He clutched at his heart melodramatically. "You wound me, mistress. I may be overly fond of strong drink, but I am not such a tosspot as that."

She smiled fondly. "No, you're not, but you have to admit it was funny." She leaned over and topped up his cup.

"Could it be, mistress, that you are trying to out-clever a Puck?" The Puck wasn't sure whether or not he should be offended.

Beth carefully hid her smile. "Nay, never, for that were foolhardy indeed, and doomed to certain failure."

Honour satisfied, the Puck perched himself on a great gnarly root, and attended to the whisky.

After about three cups, Beth broached the real reason for her visit...

"You want to *what!!??*"

"I want," she repeated slowly and patiently, "to talk to a Faery mage powerful enough to sort out what those priests have done to Princess Jewel." She topped up his cup again. "Do they exist?"

"Oh, they exist all right!" The Puck was too disturbed to even think about the whisky. "And tell me, lassie, how long have you been hankering after death or something worse?"

"Worse?"

"They are a strange and uncanny lot, yon mages. And they all have a whimsical sense of humour and no regard for others. There's no telling what they might do to you. I saw one poor mortal turned into a fish." He shuddered.

"And what was so terrible about that?"

"He left him like that for thirty years, *and wouldn't let him die, or get near water...*" He closed his eyes in horror. "The mage was just amusing himself. Nothing personal about it at all." The Puck looked at her slyly. "Still want to talk to one?"

"I don't really have a choice."

"Then on your own head be it!" He made a single pass across her field of view with his right hand. "Sleep now!"

She slept.

She came awake with a start. The Puck was still sitting facing her. "How long was I asleep?"

"Who can say? An instant? A moment? Forever?" He gave an enigmatic smile. "Ask me not when, but where, for you, my lass, are now in Faery."

"It doesn't look any different."

"Can ye no see it? Look closer."

And she *could* see. There was a *difference*, something subtle in the way the light danced perhaps, a life in the wind, an awareness that even the trees might be sentient, or the rocks...*Or maybe it was just her that was different...*

The Puck stood. "Night comes," he said. "We had best be getting you somewhere out of reach of the nightwalkers."

"Nightwalkers?"

"You know what a nightmare is?" He waited for her nod. "Here, they're *real.*"

Suddenly, it seemed like a very good idea to be moving. She packed quickly and followed the Puck.

It was evening when they reached the palace: an alabaster edifice, elegant and rather smaller than Beth had expected.

"Who lives here?"

"The Duke of the Western Marches. He's an elven sorcerer, and your best bet for getting your princess fixed."

"Is he powerful enough to do the job?"

"He's one of the great lords of Faery. The question is not 'Can he help?' but 'Will he?' Catching his interest could be tricky. He has about as much care for the concerns of mortals as you do for the cares of ants."

"Oh," Beth said, chastened. She fastened the donkey's lead rope to a small tree outside of the garden perimeter. "Will he be safe here?"

"For the meantime. I'll see to moving him later."

"Thank you." She strode through a gap in the boundary hedge. "Even the garden is perfect."

"No horseshit in the courtyard neither," said the Puck. "Me, I like things a little more natural."

The guards paid them no attention, but the same could not be said of the courtiers inside, as all eyes followed them as they approached the Duke. They stopped at a respectful distance and waited.

Eventually, the Duke finished his other business and turned his attention to them. "Well Puck, what have you brought me this time?"

"An emissary, Your Grace, from a queen in the mortal realms."

The Duke snorted. "And what do they want this time? A sword to carve them an empire? The Key to All Knowledge? Or mayhap just a charm to smite their enemies with the Itching Pox?" The wide grey eyes fixed on her and she trembled like a rabbit transfixed by a polecat. "Well? Speak up, girl!"

"If it please Your Grace, Her Majesty is in need of a working of magic. One small to one of your obvious puissance, but beyond the reach of her own powers."

"Get on with it, girl."

"Well, Your Grace, a spell was cast upon her then-unborn daughter, and, oh Your Grace, they made such a mess of it. Instead of making the girl beautiful, she has a face straight out of a bad dream. They have tried all they know, but nothing has helped."

"There would be a price…"

"Her Majesty has told me she is prepared to be generous."

"Indeed? I will think on it. Steward, show our guest to suitable quarters and see she is provided for. I will send for her once I have reached a decision."

The room Beth found herself in was small, but immaculately appointed. She sat down on the edge of the bed and removed her boots. She had a moment of fright when she heard the key turn in the lock behind her and realised that there was no other way out of the room, but they did not seem to intend her harm. She lay back and let herself drowse.

Beth came awake suddenly, and would have cried out but for the small hand across her mouth. It was full night, and moonlight streamed through the window slits.

"It's me, the Puck," a voice whispered in her ear. "Be as quiet as you can. Put these elfboots on. We're leaving."

Beth struggled to put the strange boots on. Eventually, the Puck gave up and put them on her.

"Now," he whispered. "Follow my lead. Be quiet. Do *what* I tell you *when* I tell you, and we'll get you out of here."

They stepped out between two sleeping guards. The Puck relocked the door and hung the key back on one guard's belt. Then they slipped into the shadows and away out of the court.

After several miles, she stopped to catch her breath.

"Come on. Come on." The Puck jigged up and down in anxiety. "We must be well away before daybreak."

"I'm not going a step further until you tell me what's going on."

"I heard them talkin'," said the Puck nervously. "They was going to put you to sleep."

"So?"

"They was arguing whether forty years would be better or fifty…"

A sudden chill ran up her spine. "Oh…Thanks are definitely in order, then. And we'd best cover our tracks."

"No need while you're wearing those," he said. "Best elfboots, them. No noise, no tracks, never slip. The scout I stole them from will be livid.

Now come on."

"What about the Duke's hounds?"

"Well, when they wake up, in about a week, the trail will be too cold. Now come on."

And so she did.

"You can speak normally now," said the Puck. "We're safe here."

"Where are we?"

"Oh, this is just a hidey-hole I made for when I need to keep out of sight. Being a Puck means sometimes you have to avoid certain people until they cool down. First, the water rushing past the end of that corridor is a waterfall. We get water, light, and air that way. Second, that way comes up under a rather large, unruly, and extremely thorny blackberry bush. Third, that way comes up between the roots of a tree, though you'd have to cut your way through some spider-webbing."

"Isn't anyone who finds one of those going to investigate it?"

"Not unless they're a Puck, or one of the wee folk. Yon elves would just think it was a mouse hole. They don't have size-mastery."

"Oh. So I'd be what—half an inch tall?" She thought about this a moment, and decided not to think about it more, because it made her dizzy. She sat down.

"There's a bed over there," said the Puck. "It's yours as long as we're here."

"Thank you." She moved in the direction indicated, and located the bed by touch. "Is it always this dark?"

"At night, yes." The Puck was amused. "I'll shut the water-door, and then we can light a candle." He did so.

Beth sat on the bed and began to remove the boots. "I still don't understand why you'd risk the wrath of one of the great lords of Faery over me," she said.

The Puck nibbled on a fingernail. "Well," he offered, "it's not like I'm unfamiliar with the wrath of great lords. But mostly, it's for your namesake, Old Beth, your great-grandmother."

"Gran's ma? But she's long dead."

"Oh, I wouldn't count on that—her being such a fearsome strong woman an' all. Half the Fae looking after her house think she's coming back. You know some people called her a witch?"

"Never to her face, I'll bet."

"No, never that. Not twice, anyway. But I owe her. And it's one of those unpayable debts."

"Why? What'd she do?"

"She faced down a King of Faery for me."

Beth looked at him and raised one eyebrow.

"He's hunting me seriously—hounds and all. They've just about caught me when I see Beth's door standing open, so I duck inside. Beth takes one look at me and grabs her staff and heads out the door I'd just come in. I hear a few yelps, and sneak a look out the window. There's twenty-odd Fae Hounds prowling up and down this white line she's drawn across her garden. Any of them is at least as big as her. Presently, His Majesty comes trotting up on his grey horse and looks at the line. She tells him it's a courtesy line, which is to say a line that he can cross if he really wants to, but which he can't cross without crossing her, as it were. Then he demands me, and she tells him no, that I am under her protection, and that he may not hunt me, or anyone else for that matter, on her land without her permission. And at that time, the Fae reckoned her territory as stretching at least ten leagues in every direction from her house. She lets him bluster and threaten a bit as his retainers come trotting up, and then she looks at them and tells him, yes, his hunting pack is a pretty fair imitation of the Wild Hunt, but if he doesn't get those horses and hounds out of her vegetable patch quick smart, he'll get a much closer look at the real thing than he really wants. His Majesty tries to stare her down, but she just lifts one eyebrow and smiles slightly in that dangerous way she had. He jerks his horse's head around and heads off with all his retainers and other hounds behind him. And you know what? She never even asks me what I've done."

"And what had you done?"

"Well, the King has been romancing this sweet thing for months, and finally she gives in, and the two sneak off to the royal bedroom, only to discover that some evil person has short-sheeted the royal bed."

"Oh. And the King didn't think that was funny?"

"*I* thought it was hilarious."

"*You* would…And, of course, you got blamed."

"As is only right, seein' as I'm the one what done it. A Puck's got his pride."

Beth laughed. "You're mad, I vow. Completely off your rocker."

The Puck leapt to his feet and gave her an extravagant bow. "Why thank you, Mistress. 'Tis the nicest thing anyone's said about me these many years." When Beth's giggles had subsided, he added quietly, "You know, you're not going to be able to go back."

"What?" Beth said, momentarily stunned by the rapid change. "What do you mean?"

"I mean that if you go back to Grimley-on-Tyde, you'll find all your old friends aren't your friends any more. You'll be the strange one, the one who left the village, and talked back to the Queen, and went to Faery. And they'll never quite believe any of it, but they'll make those signs they think ward off evil when you walk past."

Beth's eyes filled with tears. "I know," she whispered.

"And when that happens," the Puck went on, "you'll have two choices. You can run away before they stone you, or…" and he posed dramatically for a moment, "…you can move into your great-grandmother's cottage."

"I don't understand. How would that help?"

"Ah, now listen to the Puck, for he is mad. Completely off his rocker. Fear and respect are but two sides of the same coin. The one will get you stoned; the other gets you a place in the world. Your great-grandmother was a Wise Woman, and a wise woman as well. It is a place in the human world that will let you be strange, nay, even requires it in some measure. Moving into that house would be a declaration that you are to be treated with respect."

"Does it still stand?"

"Oh aye, did I not tell ye there were Fae looking after the house? And half of them expecting *her* back? And you were named for her, because you were born shortly after she died. And half those Fae suspect there is more of Old Beth in you than would be accounted for by bloodline."

"And what do you think?"

"I think that it doesn't matter. Even if you were Old Beth come again in her entirety, you're still yourself, and that's as it should be. And you'll be a great Wise Woman…"

"How can you be so sure?"

"Because I'll make sure. And, of course, because I'm mad. Completely off my rocker. Didn't a Wise Woman just tell me so?"

She heaved a chunk of moss at him and rolled over, knowing she'd've missed. "Good night."

She did not hear him leave, but then, he was, after all, a Puck.

Beth awoke to a strange crunching sound. She carefully rolled over to locate the source. The donkey rolled one eye at her, but left his muzzle in the bucket of oats.

"How did you get here?" she asked.

"I stole him, of course," said the Puck, sauntering into the cavern and perching himself on a rock. "And seeing as there was no pursuit yet, I brought him here. And as to your next question, don't ask, because I ain't tellin'. Just take it from me that following the tracks he left is a waste of time."

"So what now?"

"Now, we wait until the hunt dies down. Should only be a few days. Make yourself comfortable."

"Then what?"

"Then we go looking for a mage again. Only it can't be an elf, because the Duke will have alerted them all."

"Doesn't he have any enemies?"

"Oh, plenty, but they're just as nasty as he is, or worse. And it won't be so easy to escape a second time. They weren't really expecting you to up and go, because it never occurred to them that I might help you. They know better now."

"So who do we try next?"

"Well, it's no use asking a unicorn. They don't like travelling out of Faery. And they can't do magic, only undo it, so if the girl is naturally ugly, that's how she'd end up." He scratched his head thoughtfully. "I think your best bet is a dragon. They're powerful, very magical, and don't care what elves think. Yes, a dragon would be best."

"Ah, don't they *eat* people?"

"Yes, but they're intelligent. No self-respecting dragon would eat a person who could deliver them half-a-dozen oxen, and I imagine your Queen would gladly give every ox in the country for this little job. And they're quite protective of their own offspring, so they can understand a parent's concern, which gives us a slight advantage. And don't forget they're vain. You can use that."

"I see."

"Just don't aggravate the dragon, and you should be able to rely on its greed to see you through. But cheat one, insult it, steal from it, or try to harm it or its offspring in any way, and that dragon won't be happy until you've met a gruesome death."

"Such as being a dragon's breakfast..."

"Exactly!"

A fortnight saw them in the foothills of the mountains, approaching the lair of the dragon Fwooshka.

"I'd better change back to my old boots soon. Wouldn't want him thinking we were sneaking up..."

"Good thinking."

Her steps still sounded disturbingly loud to Beth by the time they crested the final rise, and there, basking in the sunlight near the opening of a cavern, was a large dragon, which Beth correctly took to be Fwooshka.

The Puck pointed towards a rock entirely too close to the dragon. "We'll just sit down there until he wakes up."

The donkey sensibly declined to follow, so they led him back over the ridge before making their way down to their chosen seating.

No sooner had the Puck sat down than an eye snapped open. The dragon sat up and stared at the Puck. "Why are you here? Could it be that you have brought me a sssssnack?" He eyed Beth hungrily.

"Oh no, Great Fwooshka! I have come to you with a rich proposition befitting your magnificent self," Beth said quickly. "There will be many oxen in it for you, and gold..."

"Oxsssen? Gold? Magnifissscent?" Fwooshka polished a claw against one massive shoulder. "I approve of your mannersss, human, and sssssince you do not offend as much as mossst of your unattractive speciesss, you may continue. Go on…"

So she did, and they haggled, and finally agreed that, for a fee of eight oxen, the dragon Fwooshka would fly to the mortal lands on the night of the next full moon, and there he would inspect the princess, and negotiate directly with the Queen for the correction of the spell.

The Queen was mightily pleased with herself. For a few dozen oxen and a mere hundredweight of gold, the dragon had agreed to remove all the existing enchantments from the princess, and then to make her beautiful. The only hard bit would be getting the gold out of those priests, but she could take it from the royal coffers and deal with them later.

The peasant girl had been granted the patch of abandoned land she had requested, and sent on her way laden with gifts.

The oxen had already been set free in the wilds for the dragon to collect at his leisure. All she had to do now was get the gold to the agreed clearing in the forest on the night of the new moon and leave Jewel there alone with the dragon while he worked his magic. And the next morning, her little Jewel would be *beautiful*…She could make *plans*…

The Queen and her ladies-in-waiting approached the clearing. The Ladies just wanted to get back to civilisation, but the Queen was more anxious to see her now-beautiful heir. She needed to know the exact appearance of the Princess, so she could choose which of the neighbouring kings to offer her to. Red hair would be good—that would attract the lust of King Randolph, and his kingdom was large and rich, and adjoined her own.

Anxiously, they entered the clearing. The gold was, of course, gone. They looked around and spotted something.

"Aww…what a cute little dragon…" said one of the Ladies.

"Such exquisite patterning!" enthused a second.

"She's beautiful. Just look at the way the light plays on those iridescent scales..." said a third.

"But where is the princess?" demanded the Queen.

It was some minutes before the awful truth occurred to her.

SOMNIUM
Gregory Dally

Everything is always present tense. You exist in an incessant now, an eternity that's afforded by Dreamland. It's so cool.

Everyone in this alt-realm wears a manic grin—except the Irie. They stand to the side of the dance hall, slumped against the elegance of art deco tributes to Zeus, looking unconcerned. Their coyness doesn't trade on fripperies such as smiles and other adornments of the face. If you're already lovely, you can sidestep trivialities like curvatures of the mouth that give out flimsy qualities à la likeability.

In this milieu you're immune to categories. That's a salve. Given that you can't even answer the essential question—your place of origin—it's as well that you lack a definite entity.

Oh, that could change, because here comes the head sherang. Today she really is solely a head—although you accept that. If you intimated that you didn't, she'd have yours. As it is, your self-expression has been restricted by the guardians of this zone. Anything you say could be taken down and bent into a slogan, one that slanders only you. Travellers who speak inside a trance are apt to err. Sensing this, you relax and stick to gliding, a vitality loose on theories.

Unlike Cheap Trick's *Dream Police,* those chameleons—the symbolists dressed as symbols—live all over, not exclusively in your head. In your alert life they're there, urging you to get back to the somnolence. One might be a helpful shop assistant, he who knows each savoury and many kinds of rice. Another could be your pharmacist, so diplomatic and restrained, so very necessary. Laced in everyday dealings, they're potentially lethal. You can't leave a jot that you experience unexamined. Either in the so-called actual or here, immersed and rolling through the immaterial, the journey makes itself valid through random learning.

Your schooner is smashed on the Cape of Loose Threads and your soul is a nest of emus. You have the head of a gryphon and your given name is Lemuela. This is the sort of crap your mind throws out if you've had too much cheese. In a fit of self-analysis, a montage highlights recent habits—all the late night snacking, unheralded munchies centred on an attachment to septic fromage. On decamping from the dream, you'll get to a clinician.

You've got your anorak, your homburg and several other accoutrements of the unreal. Who the hell wears a gaberdine in the evening, especially if a turquoise sky is raining stoats and easels? You haven't a clue who sent you here or what is happening; yet the guy in the silt coloured vest, yes, he has your number. The fact that the numeral is negative seems irrelevant, for you have scribbled out a secret code and hidden it in ambrosia. Sometime later in the dilation known as this head trip it'll resurface. You've stashed a magician's skill to save you, resourceful one. After the doubters read the prophecies you've collected, they'll take you as their leader and adore you.

Of a sudden, there he is—the dream guy. Rehearsals are over, and you're on. Let's cue him in, your saviour, announced by the lilt of ambient grooves you extol in dance moves. Lord hail the imagination.

The Shelleys would have treasured you, designer of near-humans. The pop-up guy is your ace of invention, a cosmic type layered in shimmers by this reverie. Unrelated to anyone you've met in your supposed real life, he arrives in these absurdities full of aplomb and ready to have you.

That's to come, however. At this instant the crinoline hero simply recasts your dancing. In his thrall, your jumps ape a madrigal, the munters' strut of yore. Only risk-takers shed of rhythm can abide it. Therefore you munt out. Ravers who join you do so in a spirit of emotional retrenchment. They're extremely careful, appearing to be free as they prance and hop, aflutter in their shirt sleeves ruffled, electric hair made up nicely. They'll never show it, but they've taken to you.

The one thing you care about is getting in tune to him, the self-made one. Even though he's swapped his crinoline Versace for a tie-dyed mauve paisley tee, he still looks superfly. The joy is, protagonist, that in the land of the muted sun outdated adjectives have an exalted role. You can say superfly, rad, groovy, bitchin' and sweet till the bovines return to their abode—against all likelihood, you'll remain in vogue. Ain't it the shizzle?

The dance implodes, and everyone staggers to the margins. Amongst the throng of ignorance, the one who matters is cognizant that you have value. The dream dude sashays up to you out of a tangerine moonrise. That's his thing. Someone praised him for his suaveness under half-light once; thereafter he got savvy and employed that angle to enchant those he liked a lot. In his lapel is a portrait of you on your best day, covered in laminate so the sorcery can't be dispelled. It's all on.

That tryst you enjoy with the dreamt one, très loving and self-redeeming, it happens from the template of your ideals. You're the last one who says 'tryst' these days—devoid of others' laughter, too, floating in your airs. You reason that it's your spirit, and as long as you're unconscious everything is authentic. Any trope is contingent on thought, indulging its Maker.

You're like Lazarus or other righteous escapologists—you expire, reconstitute, revive. Oh so many times. Deleted, yet still here. You've got that Jesus talent sussed, you magus suprema. Here in the interior universe, you're remaking the paradigm and its sense at any moment. In itself, the idea of a 'moment' is down to you. Disregard Steven the Mancunian surrealist asking, 'How soon is now?' You're in charge of divining forever, of setting its imminence. In Dreamland you've already outlasted concepts as meagre as 'infinite time.' It's about reliving favourite scenes as you see fit, just for the hey of it.

As sudden as any happenstance, the ceaseless life you inhabit crumples on you and is over. Amethyst hued solar gleams cleave your mind, and you're emerging reformatted into light. As logic is passé, all ideas have turned sacred in the absolution of a self-creator. You depart. It is, of course, ephemeral, this return to the conscious. The exit has mana, though, since the imagined guy has vanished and you've leapt onto the self as a deliverance. As you revisit the alt-state, imperious, his successor may fête you. In that dimension once more, you could have revoked all care for others' liking. The quality of transcendence, it seems, is in the leaving.

DANCE, TINY PARTICLES, DANCE
Sean Monaghan

I n the last five sevenths of a second of her life, Georgia Kerridge realised
she still had some things to do.

There was the birthday card to write for her grandfather. A load of
laundry on the line that needed to come inside. The dryer would take off the
last of the damp.

Katie would need her dance uniform first thing tomorrow. Grading lay
in the near future and everything needed to be right. And there was a chicken
to be defrosted.

Georgia's eyes were open. Her corneas continued to transmit light. Her
retinas continued to receive it. Light can cover plenty of ground in five
sevenths of a second.

Her brain processed the information faster than she was used to. That
was a surprise, though perhaps in the lab she should have expected it.

What she saw were shards of toughened, heat resistant glass spinning in
the air. The splinters reflected light from their faces and edges. Georgia saw
whole scenes within the glints.

An icy landscape, bergs calving from the leading edge of blue-white
glaciers. Foamy white suds of sea bursting up as the skyscraper-sized chunks
plunged through the surface.

A forest. She could even smell the damp, piney, earthy world. Tawny-
coloured owls, wings wide, sifted through the branches hunting for voles and

mice.

Mars. Dry, dusty. Decorated with the spangly remainders of dozens of robot rovers. That small abandoned human base like a stone in an icefield.

Four sevenths of a second left.

Georgia wondered how she knew how long she had with such precision. Four sevenths of a second.

The shards spun. The bioquantum mix hung in droplets. Suspended like air bubbles in ice. Georgia knew she'd absorbed some. Right in the moment before Jacobs had activated the scanner, when the beaker broke.

Clive Jacobs. Thirty-two. He had a wife, Bernie, who owned a corporate jet rental company. He laughed sometimes that it was so lucrative he would work at the lab for free. Every few weeks they would fly to the Bahamas or Fiji or somewhere for the weekend.

Even though they'd been lovers, once, Georgia could barely stand him now. That arrogance. She could barely make her car payments, and she didn't know how she was going to manage next semester's dance fees.

Should she feel guilt for being glad he was already dead?

The arc from the reaction chamber had struck him square in the chest. He still hadn't hit the ground.

Bioquantum should have been fast, but not this fast. There was no possible way that she should be able to perceive what was happening.

No way she could know how long she had to live.

Less than four tenths of a second now.

Time moved fast.

Jacobs kept falling. Extrapolating his angle back, the look in his eyes, and the settings on the gauges she knew what he'd been doing.

Intuition leapt in. Jacobs had been running different lines. Off experiment.

Three sevenths of a second.

Time moving fast.

Some of the droplets had aerosoled. More than hanging in the air, they swirled. She couldn't have inhaled any yet. Not in that space of time.

Georgia checked her passages. She could smell camphor and incense. Her nasal lining showed contact with the aerosol.

Likewise her tongue. The residue tasted like fish. With teriyaki sauce.

This was uncomfortable. How, in this moment, could she be

experiencing all this? The bioquantum might, in theory, push some boundaries.

Always their intention had been to build computing capacity. Quantum states were one thing, but the prospect of physically building them outstripped anything they'd come up with. Until she'd hit on the idea of exploiting some of the new bioprints out of Korea.

Jacobs, of course, claimed he'd thought of it.

Conniving prick. Deserved what was happening to him right now.

She wondered if he was really dead.

Reaching out, she felt through the air. The molecules, oxygen, nitrogen, carbon dioxide, with free argon and neon, vibrated. So much information contained within them.

Jacobs was already dead. Some brain processes functional, but it was all too late. The electrical stab had stopped his heart.

Georgia actually felt sad. They'd been at loggerheads over some of the latest progress but she had respect for his knowledge and insight.

Even this morning they'd spoken about the new trials.

No, she'd said, *you're getting too far ahead.*

But what if it works?

Jacobs had wanted to try pushing up the pressure a hundredfold.

Fabulous if it works, she'd told him, *but there's no experimental trial. You're operating on a hunch.*

So what? Sometimes that's what you need to push things along.

And who will publish it?

Stop it with the publication railroad again, he'd said. *You know what this offers. The money we could get for this.*

We're not in business, Clive. We're funded by the university.

Did you ever think who funds that? You're so naïve.

You're too rash.

That had been the end of it.

She wondered if he had ramped up the pressure anyway. That could have been behind the rupture.

Peering closer through the atoms, she looked right into him.

Dead already. Anything happening in his mind was simply residual. Dopamine slithered around and there had been a brief surge in adrenalin.

She wondered if there was some way to save him.

Time had slowed, that was for sure, but she couldn't turn it back.

Two sevenths.

Georgia looked around the lab. She couldn't move her eyes, but there was enough detail on her retinas, and outside, to build up a picture. The first aid kit, emergency dousing shower, fire blanket and fire extinguisher were meters away on the wall.

In real time, she could get to them in perhaps two seconds. Maybe three.

There was an emergency button too. Red. Capped by a hinged plastic shield to prevent accidental activation.

Real time. That was a distinction.

Could it be that the bioquantum was affecting her? Or was she simply caught in that drowning loop of reliving her life over in the moment of death?

Ice cream cones with her family at Cape Henlopen when she was six. Seeing bison in Theodore Roosevelt National Park a year later. So huge and placid.

Flying a kite over Baja. Getting stoned in college with Thad Derwent. Creep.

Shaking the chancellor's hand as she accepted her first degree, her parents out in the audience with their phones, trying to figure out how to work the camera.

Meeting Alan.

Making Katie. That had been fun.

Watching Katie grow and grow. Listening to her get argumentative, even belligerent. Smiling as she danced with such fervour.

Farewelling Alan at the hospital, not knowing at that moment that she would never get to greet him again.

Holding Katie so close.

Coming back to work. Trying to focus. Trying to stop Jacobs from taking over everything.

A life.

Some smart-alec had pointed out once that people in the situation of reliving their life at its final passage, were essentially immortal. At the moment when the reliving of their life arrived at their death, they relived their life again, and then again and again. On and on in ever-decreasing slivers of time.

Time was all slivers, she saw now. An awful lot could occur in a single seventh of a second.

Lives could be saved.

Probing deeper, deeper through the atoms, into the protons and electrons, into the rough texture of the neutrons, she saw so many connections. Almost as if the world here at this level was linked the way a brain was put together; every neuron connected to dozens of others. Every particle connected to *every* other particle.

On down.

Neutrons hid leptons and quarks and bosons. Charms, ups and downs, muons and Ws. It was like walking through a vast field of fragrant, brilliantly-coloured wild flowers.

Axions. Gluinos. Didn't they sound like the names of gorgeous blooms?

At Theodore Roosevelt, her father had told a long intricate tale about an early English settler called Mr Higgs, who had started a buffalo farm. The man had a sign at the gate reading, *Higgs' Bison*. Her father had laughed out loud. No one else in the car got it. Usually 'Dad' jokes were groanworthy, but at least understandable.

It wasn't until she was in high school that she got the joke and was able to groan about it. She'd wished her father had still been alive to let him know.

The ups were talking to the downs. In a way.

Now Georgia got it. Her world had become smeared with the bioquantum material.

Better than they could have imagined. Faster, more powerful, farther reaching.

Jacobs had been right.

Stretching again, Georgia tapped at the charms and sleptons.

One seventh of a second.

She could see the spark coming. Darting from the rupture tank. Electrons were so cantankerous. She knew that now.

Huge ungainly things, blundering along, like some great bovine through a flower field. Pushing and shoving things aside.

"All right, little guys," she said-thought. "Let's shove them back."

But they wouldn't. The sleptons shivered. The photinos shimmered.

She couldn't stop the charge.

Poor Katie. Georgia would miss the dance grading.

"Jacobs," she said-thought. "Little guys?"

It wasn't like they were *sentient*, but they responded anyway. Shivering and shimmering their way, they vibrated to their sisters and cousins throughout Jacobs's body.

Easy enough to shunt the protons into line, to tinker with the molecules.

To restart his wounded heart.

One fourteenth of a second. Time moved in slices.

"Hello?" someone said. "Kerridge?"

Jacobs. Brought back to life. By her hand.

"It's me," she said. Not speaking so much as letting these tiny shards of reality carry meaning. Preons and quills, smaller even than the miniscule leptons. Even they had their own building blocks. Particles without names.

"I see what happened," Jacobs said.

One twenty-eighth of a second. Fleeting.

"You brought me back to life. You didn't have to do that."

"Of course I did. Look at these things."

"Fourth of July," he said. "Overlaid with Guy Fawkes."

"And Chinese New Year." She liked the fireworks idea. Bursting and bristling with colour.

"Well," Jacobs said. "This bioquantum idea was right."

"I need you to do something for me."

The lance tip of the discharge was only inches from her.

"What's that?" Distracted. "Look at all this. It's fractal. Immeasurable."

"Tell Katie I'll be there. In spirit. Wish her well."

One fifty-sixth of a second. How much smaller could she slice time?

"Katie. Your daughter? Why do I need to…that arc. I see it."

"I won't survive. There's but a tiny fraction of a second left to me."

"But you brought me back. I can see all that. History unfolds."

"And the future."

She saw her death on the horizon. One one hundred and twelfth of a second.

"Let me reach."

"Tell her."

"I—"

One two hundred and twenty-fourth. 1/224. Georgia saw flowers and sparkles. The arc's blade was but a fraction of an inch from impact.

"Tell everyone about it," she said.

No time left.

"Thank you," Jacobs said. "For bringing me—"

Rhododendrons and pansies. Phosphorous and copper. These brilliant tiny particles. The cosmos expanded down forever.

Georgia let her body go.

She drifted. For one seventh of a second she spun around the world. For an hour she basked with dolphins off Morocco. For a day she slipped out to the sun and watched as the particles crowded together, just for the fun of it.

For a week she rode the waves back into the world. Right into Redding, right by the lab, right on to Classic Dance Studios.

There she was. Radiant, beautiful Katie.

Dancing, spinning, smiling, but eyes downcast. Tears.

"Honey, I'm here," Georgia had the particles murmur.

Katie looked. "Love you, Mom," she whispered.

"Love you, too." And Georgia watched her girl hurl herself into a dance that surpassed anything these tiny particles could manage.

EARTHCORE: INITIATION
Grace Bridges

Ko *ahau te taniwha.* I am the taniwha, that legendary beast called dragon by the ignorant. Some call me kaitiaki—the guardian—others call me mythical. Ha! As if their beliefs on the matter make any difference to the fact. I am here. My siblings are many. And you will be hearing more about us soon, very soon, for we have allowed ourselves to be seen by some of your mortal fellows, and given them gifts.

This is not usual.

We kaitiaki generally keep to ourselves unless our interests are at stake. And we have indeed been roused, as you may have already learned.

It has become clear to us that the ephemeral nature of the gifts is a liability to those we wanted to assist. We have argued through many nights and days: how this could be changed, by what ritual, by what authority.

Now it is time to set our plan into motion.

Anira Fraser sat on a pale grey beach near the south end of Lake Rotorua's western shore, gazing out over the water. The late afternoon light and clear sky touched the view with a golden flush, from the bush-clad hump of Mokoia Island to the translucent waves lapping just past her feet, from the distant suburbs across the lake to the higher pasture hills beyond. Even the long, hulking peaks of Mount Tarawera, normally dark and ominous, gave the impression of basking in sunshine.

Her legs were plunged almost to the knee in a steaming pool of hot spring water. She'd dug the hole in the pumice sand until the water had come up to meet her, bubbling up from below. She glanced at the rolling boil of the water bubbling between her toes, wobbling the outline of her feet. She smiled. For her, it was as safe as the cold lake. Not only that—it did things to her mind, made her thoughts clearer, and several other odd effects which she would predictably forget as soon as she'd been out of contact with this spring's water for more than a day or two.

She hung her head over her sand-hole and breathed deeply of the mineral steam, closing her eyes and enjoying a moment of clarity as the effect pushed into all the corners of her mind. The pumice shifted under her hands, falling in from the side of the hole and partly burying her feet. She'd dug her hole too deep for it to remain stable.

Then the whole beach jolted. More than the beach—she eyed the next bay, where she'd once seen a geyser erupt out of the water. It seemed calm enough now, though, and she traced the horizon to the right of the hospital hill. She squinted. Was there more steam over Kuirau Park than usual? Perhaps she'd better get Tiger to come have a look.

As she was scrambling to her feet, the earth heaved again and a dark glut splashed into the sky above the trees. A mud eruption? It wouldn't be the first—the area was famous for it. She crawled out of her hole and pushed upright, almost losing her balance as the ground shook yet again. When it stilled, Anira crossed the beach in three strides, topped the dune, and broke into a run.

Tiger McRae had his curtains closed and the volume on his gaming console turned up all the way, since his mum was out and couldn't complain. Anira had asked him to go down to the water with her, but honestly? He'd just be bored.

There was a low *boom* and he turned his avatar this way and that, shifting his onscreen view. Where had it come from? Nothing. Weird. He flicked up a virtual console, a map that would show enemies nearby—there were none. Great. A glitch in the game. The front door slammed.

Anira appeared, panting, in the hallway, and there was another boom, louder this time. The explosion wasn't in his game. He hit the off button and was on his feet in a moment. "What is it?"

Anira jabbed a thumb over her shoulder. "Mud eruption—at Kuirau—I think. But I can't see it clearly." The whites of her eyes gleamed in the dimness of his room. He stepped past her and hauled the front door open again.

From here, trees close by obscured the view to the south, but his powerful vision caught the droplets of grey mud fountaining out into the open sky. "You're right," he said. "Let's get over there."

Manaia Martin bundled her squirming one-year-old into the sling and struggled to get it securely fastened so he wouldn't escape. He was really too big for it now, but she'd be less mobile if she had to push a pram instead. "Would you keep still, Wiremu!"

She frowned at the window, now flecked with tiny drops of ash-laden volcanic mud. In the street, steam pumped from the crack in the road—it was usually just a wisp. Her trembling fingers fumbled with the knots. If that was Kuirau erupting again…it was just a couple of blocks from here. They had to get out of the danger zone, even if only on foot.

Manaia finally got the stiff fabric in place and bent to wrap a kerchief over the little one's mouth and nose. He complained loudly at this and tried to yank it off, but she tied it at the back of his head before rigging a similar mask for herself.

She opened the door, stepped over the threshold, and locked the house behind her. When she turned to the street, the air was already gritty and dense. The rising steam called to her irresistibly as she passed the vent. She'd never seen it this strong before. Just for a moment, she covered Wiremu's head with her arms and leaned her face into the fumes.

Whoa. The minerals—the heat—it was almost too much. It pushed into her lungs until nothing more would fit, and she staggered back a step, gasping. She'd been so sure she had to get away, but now she wasn't convinced. At all.

"Manaia!" Tiger and Anira came apace on their bikes from the direction of the lake, coming to a halt a safe distance beyond the billowing fissure. "Did you feel it too?" Anira called out.

Manaia nodded. "At first I wanted to get a safe distance away. But then I smelled this steam. We're wanted over there."

"You'll be all right walking?" Tiger indicated the sling.

"It's not far. Go ahead, I'll be right behind you."

"See you in a minute, then." The two cycled away into the increasing gloom. Manaia straightened her back and set off as fast as she could, Wiremu giggling at the burst of speed.

Graeme Guptill sat fishing in his tour boat, the *Funky Pūkeko*, about halfway between the city lakefront and Mokoia Island. He'd finished his day's work of showing tourists around the island, but had resisted showing them his old trick of summoning the birds. Now that he knew it was a gift from a taniwha, he wasn't sure he wanted it. He did miss the sense of belonging when hundreds of little creatures swarmed him, perching on his head and outstretched arms, flying and singing in intricate patterns around him—but only when he stood in the stream fed from the island's thermal spring.

The fish had no intentions of showing him any love today. *Oh well*. He enjoyed being out here on the water, away from the bustle. Everything was silent.

Too silent, actually. He surveyed the surface of the lake, unnaturally smooth, mirroring the golden-blue sky. The summer air hung heavily over the shore, the town. He'd only heard this kind of silence one other time, immediately before a violent eruption in the bay at Ohinemutu: the visible interference of several taniwha in human affairs.

The first *boom* crossed the lake. He stowed his rod and spun to look at Ohinemutu, setting the boat bobbing as he did.

There was nothing happening at Ohinemutu. But beyond it…just past the main road into town…mud gurgled into the sky in a towering stream.

Rumbling echoed from all directions; the lake floor must be shaking. Its identity as an ancient crater held no comfort now. Sudden waves stood up in sharp, choppy edges, only to drop down again and be replaced by others. The *Pūkeko* pitched, and he grabbed a railing.

A flapping and fluttering reached Graeme from the opposite direction. He turned towards Mokoia and gulped. A swarm of birds of all kinds—*his* birds, the birds that lived on the island—headed straight for the eruption on the mainland. They passed over him in the *Pūkeko*. He stared up at the stately kererū, the sleek tui, the tiny fantails and silvereyes, even a pūkeko or two with their red legs stretched behind them. All rushed headlong towards danger.

Well, if that isn't a sign, I don't know what is.

He had to get back to land. Graeme clambered to his outboard motor and yanked the cord to bring it to life. The harsh sputter shattered the atmosphere. He sped towards the dock, thinking ahead: he'd tie up at his mooring and hop in his van. It wasn't far to where he thought the eruption was, but walking would take too long and expose him to ash. He gripped the steering wheel and willed the *Pūkeko* to fly like her namesake.

Bethany Rutherford waved goodbye to her colleague and locked the door of the information office, sighing. The lass had hinted again that Bethany might need to retire soon. Bethany didn't see why; she liked her job and was just as good at it as anyone else. She withdrew the key from the lock and quickly set the alarm using the panel at the side of the entrance.

Turning to walk away, she was stopped short by the pavement jolting under her feet. She scanned the area, her gift not showing any unseen creature here, but they must be close. If she wasn't very much mistaken, that was the song of a taniwha.

People on Fenton Street stopped in clusters, glancing at the sky. Step by step she reached the corner and peered around into Arawa Street; it led all the way to Kuirau Park. With a canyon of clear air between her and the source, the voice became intelligible.

"Haere mai ra, e te whānau o kaitiaki wairua!"

How odd for the taniwha to initiate a ritual welcome without being face to face. In her mind's eye the whole city suddenly became the expanse of a marae. The singer was calling her, Bethany, and the rest of the "spirit family", to its home. Would they know to come? But she was already so close to Kuirau…she'd just drive down and phone them from there if she needed to. She paused and responded with a soft chant of her own: "Karanga mai, e ngā kaitiaki o te tapu," then she slipped around the back of the building and into her car.

Anira and Tiger cycled along Tārewa Street through the ever-thickening clouds of damp ash and skidded to a stop in front of a pair of police officers in paper breathing masks, setting up a barrier.

"Get out of here," said one of them, her eyes stern above the mask.

Anira shrugged at Tiger and they wheeled the bikes away, stopping when the police car was invisible in the whirling ash. They met Manaia at the next corner and explained.

"Let's go round the other way, then," she said. "We can get into the park from the main road."

But when they got there, all was silent and still. Well, as silent as it could be for a large boiling pond with a minor eruption nearby.

"Not much action here," said Tiger. They continued to the parking area opposite the hospital.

A crowd had gathered to watch the spectacular mud fountain. Here too a cordon had been set up, and a couple of officers tried in vain to make people leave.

Manaia pointed. "Look, it's my cuzzies." Ngaire and Rangi were all up in a policeman's face, gesturing into the park. Hanging back a little, eyes downcast, was Hana.

"One guess," said Tiger. "They feel the need to get in there, too."

Gravel pinged behind them. Graeme's black van peeled into the carpark from the north. Moments later, Bethany drove in from the south. Both leaped out and talked at the same time.

"My birds! They came straight here." Graeme pointed at a circling mass above, just out of reach of the ash.

"A taniwha is calling us to come in close." Bethany waved a hand towards the hot interior of the park.

Anira gulped. Had suspected as much. Didn't mean she relished the thought of approaching a live spewing volcano, even if it wasn't the kind with lava. But they were being summoned, and go they must.

"Come on then," she said, and led the troop through the spectators to where Ngaire and Rangi cajoled the cop.

"Please, sir," said Ngaire. "That volcano is caused by a taniwha, and we're taniwha people. We need to get in there."

"Pull the other one," said the cop. "That's the lamest excuse for a rubbernecker that I ever heard." He looked up as the rest of the gang gathered around behind them. "And who's all this then? More volcano watchers? Just don't land yourselves in hospital from inhalation."

Anira surveyed her team. Tiger, Graeme, Manaia and child, her cousins, Hana and Bethany. *Harley's missing.* But Harley hated crowds, so another way in would probably be best. Perhaps they'd meet in the middle. She forced a smile and turned to the officer. "Excuse me, sir, but did you hear what happened in Picton just before Christmas?"

The man's eyes grew round. "The taniwha people. I thought that was a made-up story."

The other cop came over, a well-built Māori even taller than Graeme. "Everything all right here?" At his side stood Koro Wāhi, the elder from Whakarewarewa. The old man nodded at the gathered Earthcore.

"These people say they need to get in," said the white cop. "They're the same folks that did that thing in Picton."

"Ko ngā uri o Māui-tikitiki-a-Taranga," murmured the Māori. *Descendants of Māui.* The legendary demigod, their powers kin to his.

"Ae," said Wāhi. "It is so. They need to go in." He raised his hands over them. "May it go well with you."

The Māori officer lifted the cordon tape and Manaia surged forwards with Wiremu in the sling at the head of the line. Anira shrugged and followed after.

Soft drizzle now pattered onto the park, dulling the sunlight. The trees and fences and rocks blurred in the mist, though Anira couldn't tell if it was because of the rain or rather the volcanic steam that pumped out of the earth somewhere not far ahead, beyond a stand of manuka trees. The earth rumbled gently from time to time. Anira glanced back; Tiger was behind her. Other shapes followed through the sudden gloom—not the fall of night, but ash floating in the air.

Around a large rock, she came face to face with the end of the world. Well, not really. But here, near ground zero of the new outbreak, grey mud hung thickly as droplets in the air, covered every branch of every tree, every inch of path and fence.

She squinted ahead, then forced her unwilling legs to step forward until she stood beside Manaia.

The source. They were still several paces away, but Anira was just fine with staying right here. The mudhole was maybe four metres across, a black tomo that fell to unseen depths where mud blubbered noisily.

Slowly the group assembled, mere shadows in the haze. Harley materialised out of the gloom. "I see we're all the same kind of crazy, then."

Anira was about to reply with something snarky, but was interrupted by silence: the hole stopped bubbling, the steam stopped hissing. Only the mud and ash fragments floated down onto the landscape with a sound like falling snow.

Bethany drew in a sharp breath and pointed at the crater. She grabbed Graeme, who jolted as her touch transferred the gift of seeing the unseen. He reached for Manaia, who joined hands with Tiger, who held out a hand for Anira, but Hana seized it first.

Anira took in the awed faces of her friends and that Ngaire and Rangi were about to connect with Bethany on the other side, then hooked herself into the line.

The air came alive with iridescence. Taniwha of all shapes and sizes whirled around the new volcano; Anira barely noticed Harley taking her other hand as she stared into the intricate dance.

From the centre of the crater rose a huge head, its glittering eyes regarding each person in turn. The shape reminded Anira of a traditional half-bird, half-human figure, but different in some way she failed to grasp. Its body, incorporeal, remained underground.

The creature opened its mouth—or was it a beak?—and spoke in Māori through the sharing of Bethany's gift.

"Kua kite mātou i a koutou." *We have seen you.* "We have seen your steadfastness against those who wish to harness our taniwha power for harm. And we have seen that it is difficult for you when you must stay close to our springs to retain the gifts."

Tiger frowned; Anira hoped he understood the language well enough. He'd only recently begun to learn Te Reo. Noticing her attention, he gave a slight nod and a smile. He was making do.

The immense taniwha rumbled on. "We have decided that you need these gifts at all times. This is not an easy thing. Therefore, we have called you here to fulfil a ritual that will change you forever—not just for a day."

Ritual? Anira gulped. *This is serious.*

"You must complete the circle around me," said the taniwha, turning a slow gaze from side to side. "Have no fear. You will not be harmed. Keep the contact."

The huddled group spread out around the edge of the small crater. The line stretched and almost encompassed the great head. Harley reached for Rangi, but couldn't quite traverse the gap to the boy's hand. They regarded each other helplessly; the taniwha was silent.

Anira regarded the mud-caked grass at the edge of the precipice just beyond her toes. She took a deep breath. "Look, guys, I know you're not going to like this, but if we all step inwards just a little bit, we can do it."

"Faaa," said Tiger. "That's cutting it fine." But he set his jaw and took a step until his toes almost hung over the muddy edge.

There was shuffling as the others followed his example and spread out even more. Anira extended her arms as far as possible while still gripping Hana's and Harley's fingers on either side. She drew her head back sharply as the centre of balance threatened to tip her into the hole.

Rangi made contact with Harley, and as they took hold of each other, the stretch became so wide that Anira teetered. Tiger pulled her back just in time.

Her footing was anything but steady. Every breath jeopardised her balance.

The taniwha inspected them. "Ka pai. You have done well. You are ready to receive what we give. Remember, no harm will come to you. Do not move until I tell you it is done." The head withdrew into the ground.

A torrent of boiling grey mud shot out of the crater. One of the younger kids screamed. Anira wobbled. Heat blasted outwards. Did the taniwha really

123

know what a human could withstand? Had it remembered that Wiremu was here too? She couldn't step back; someone might fall into the hole and be boiled alive. Pure terror washed through Anira from head to toe. No time to think, move, escape, anything.

A few seconds more and the mud fell on her, on them all, from above— a heavy, ash-filled, smothering, burning liquid.

Except it didn't burn. It did not scald or even overheat, although all Anira's nerves told her it was still close to boiling. She grinned behind a thickening layer of it as it piled heavy upon her shoulders, her embracing arms…her heart.

She needed to breathe. She tipped her face down to escape the fall of mud, felt it layer the back of her head, opened her mouth open and sucked in some superheated air. It was probably so toxic it shouldn't even be called air any more. *Nothing will harm me. Nothing will harm me.*

Another rumble. She blinked, unable to see for more than a second before more mud ran down her face, unable to let go of her companions to wipe her eyes. But in that second, the eruption exploded sideways from the hole.

Mud filled her mouth and nose. Hardened over her tightly-shut eyes. Weighed down her outstretched arms. There was nothing except the mud and the firm grip of her friends on either side.

She cleared the mud from her mouth with her tongue, not without swallowing a good deal of it, but the torrent still pummelled her face. She held her breath, hoping the barrage wouldn't last longer than her oxygen.

Just as that thought passed through her mind, the flow stopped. She spat, breathed, and forced her eyes to open.

Mud-splattered, the Earthcore stood immobilised, the ashy mud having well buried their feet and ankles. They looked more like stone statues than people, but for the astonishment in their eyes.

The tallest statue—Graeme?—tried to free a leg.

"No," Anira croaked. "We're not finished yet."

There was another rumble, but of a different timbre, a higher pitch, a hissing, rushing sound reaching her through mud-plugged ears.

"Here we go!"

Anira's cry was drowned out by an explosion of water from below the ground, a clear, sizzling geyser. Steam hit her full on, stealing her breath again, slamming the mud from her body in chunks where it had begun to dry. The steam wormed into her brain, wakening the hidden corners like the stream did, slotting new puzzle pieces into place.

As with the mud, the towering water soon reached its zenith and turned to fall on them. Anira gasped, the weight of water cutting away wet ash, leaving her practically clean again, her feet clear of muck.

The crater became quiet. Then the great taniwha's head reared once more, gleeful laughs pealing out.

"It is done!" he roared. "You may break the circle. Each of you shall now enjoy your own gift at all times, in all places. Such gifts that are able to be transferred by touch are now bestowed on all of you. Bear them well."

The creature swirled back into the ground, only to burst out of the park's pond a short distance away, its enormous mass climbing into the sky carried by diaphanous wings.

"Ae," said Graeme, rubbing his hands together as he stared after the taniwha. "It is done. I still see him even though I'm not holding onto Bethany."

Others nodded, watching until the taniwha had flown out of sight. Little Wiremu turned his head, freed a hand from the sling, and waved.

"Hey," said Harley. "Does this mean I can run on *any* water?"

"I won't need glasses, even out of town," said Tiger.

Anira sighed. The extra memory power would be useful, but would she ever sleep again? She would find out soon enough what the taniwha had decided.

The wind picked up and blew away what remained of the ash cloud. Above, the last light of evening set the sky aglow, a few stars sparkling into view on the dark east side of the firmament, Graeme's island birds circling the park. Fog still clung to the ground. Anira was the first to step out of the ring and back towards the path. Already she heard shouts from the crowd, and caught sight of Harley dodging into the trees to escape. She smiled. Some things would never change.

Tiger came up beside her, nodding at the haze ahead. "Get ready for a media circus. Reckon they're planning on making us famous."

She peered at the bright lights set up beyond the next hillock, and grimaced.

Some things would never be the same again.

MID-LIFE
Matt Cowens

Not knowing what else to do, Scott sank his teeth into the mass of flesh that pressed into his face, grinding and tearing at it as the blood pounded in his ears and his panic grew. Bitter, salty fluid filled his mouth and threatened to choke him. Straining his neck forward, he grabbed another mouthful and tore at it. Somewhere above him, muffled through the water, he could hear screaming.

The thing that was wrapped around his face flinched, withdrew a little. Its grip on his right arm loosened. He tensed every muscle in his body, his lungs aching, and pushed upwards.

He broke the surface of the water and threw his head back, gasping for air. The indistinct screaming resolved into the voices of his husband Kyle and their teenage daughter Kim, shouting instructions to one another. Scott wrenched his right arm free and flung it above his head, fingers splayed. There was nothing to catch hold of. He saw a flash of the river bank, of Kim raising her rifle and aiming it at him, and Kyle throwing something into the water, and then he was under the surface again, in the cold, airless chaos of his struggle for life.

The thing under the water with him was not happy. The hole he'd torn with his teeth was spilling vile green liquid into the river and the tentacles wrapped around his legs were doing their best to tear him into pieces. Scott would never see the surface again if he let this thing pull him any further down. He was reaching for the knife on his belt when a flash of light and a surge of white-hot pain sent him tumbling into unconsciousness.

When he woke, he was on dry ground. He tried to sit up, coughed up a mouthful of bile, and gagged.

"What happened?" He wiped his mouth with the back of his hand.

"Taser," Kyle replied, handing Scott a damp cloth and cradling his cheek. "Knocked both of you out cold. You swallowed some water, but we got you out before you drowned."

Scott pushed himself upright, blinked and looked around, saw the camp fire and the slippery shape on the ground beyond it. Kim was roasting a chunk of tentacle on a stick.

"You tasered me?" he asked.

"No, I tasered that thing. You were just…collateral damage," Kyle replied.

"We got you out, Dad. That's all that matters. And this thing smells like it's going to be edible." Kim sniffed at the lump of meat, took a tentative bite.

Scott rubbed and stretched his jaw, patted his chest. He felt like someone had sandpapered the inside of his lungs, but nothing seemed to be broken.

"The beacon?" he asked.

"Still working, hon, despite your little swim." Kyle held up the emergency beacon, its reassuring green light blinking away.

"It's not my fault, I mean, come on. How was I to know fishing in a river would lead to…" he looked at the body of the creature on the other side of the fire, "a giant bloody horned squid pulling me in."

He didn't mention the twelve-page guide to the planet he'd left on the kitchen counter, along with the map.

"It's your surprise family survival holiday, Dad," Kim joined in. "You booked it. I said we should go to a beach somewhere but you insisted on going off-world to some remote, uncharted planet. And you crashed the stupid sport-ship so we're stuck here."

Scott looked to Kyle for support, but withered when he saw his expression. Kyle had been nothing but kind and supportive but Scott could see that he'd never be allowed to make surprise travel plans again.

"Next time, Kim. We'll go to a beach next time," Scott said.

"No beach," Kyle said. "A resort. Inland, in a nice, safe theme park.

You'll put in the overtime and save up, I'm sure."

"Uh, yeah."

They'd been able to salvage most of their gear before the small, rented ship had sunk into the swamp Scott had chosen as a landing spot. He'd put the top down as they were coming in to land so they could soak in the view and feel the wind in their hair—his own almost as black as Kyle's thanks to a dye treatment. He hadn't expected the ground to give way under the supercharged thrusters or the ship to stall when he tried to boost his way out.

The brochure for the planet had assured him that ninety per cent of the lifeforms on Crysis were human-digestive-system compatible. With a giant horned squid to feast on, they weren't going to starve, and so long as they stayed away from rivers and kept their rifles handy they weren't going to be eaten by local predators. That just left dying of embarrassment or having a fatal number of strips torn off him by his aggrieved husband and daughter.

"I may never go fishing again," Scott said, running his tongue across his slime-coated teeth. "Or swimming. And, uh, if they manage to tow us out, you can drive home."

He closed his eyes, lay back and waited for the rescue ship. It wouldn't be more than a couple of days. At least he'd have a story to tell his dad…and a fine pair of squid horns to mount in the den.

HER GRIEF IN MY HALLS
Alan Baxter

This old two-storey Queenslander creaks and moans, but I never mistake its sounds for *hers*. Its voice is as aged and distinct as the sugar cane industry in the tropical north, but *hers* is different. The house complains of generations, but *she* cries for grief. For loss. Maybe for justice.

Of course, I didn't expect her when I moved here after my wife died, looking for solitude and financial relief. High on the ridge, far from any town, this place was cheap and I could buy it outright. With no debt, I need very little to survive. Selling my paintings once a month at the markets an hour away, and the interest on my savings, together earn me enough.

Hide, paint and mourn my Sarah, that's all I wanted to do. But I'm not alone. I bought a house with an occupant, though I've never seen her. I wonder how long ago she lived. I *must* see her, as much to prove I'm not going mad as to satisfy my curiosity.

Her footsteps beat a melancholy cadence as she walks the rooms and landings above, her silky wail of despair strangely melodic. Each time I've leapt from my chair and run for the stairs, I've been overwhelmed by the knowledge that she's gone before I've taken two steps. I used to be afraid, until I realised that she ran from me, and perhaps it was her fear that should bother me more.

So I've resolved to be more subtle.

My home's entrance is grand. An arched door surmounted by stained glass opens onto a black and white tiled floor. The staircase rises up one side and the landing passes across two walls like a Western saloon, leading to four bedrooms and two bathrooms. The ground level has a library to one side, a large living room to the other, kitchen and dining room directly ahead of the front door. A simple but effective arrangement and far more space than I need.

The ridge the house sits upon is one of many, knifing down to the muddy sea. Beyond the acres and acres of sugar cane fields I'm letting go wild, rainforest surrounds me, abundant with verdant life and myriad creatures that forage and hoot and howl and whistle. Mercifully few people, though. The monthly market crowds are more than enough. So I take care of the too-big house with my echoes and *her* shrieks, and I don't need anything but for humanity to leave me to my grief.

I use the living room as my studio and spend evenings in the library, surrounded by thousands upon thousands of pages. I do love books. That's the only time I hear her, she only ever walks and moans as I read. When I'm still. Never at night when I'm in bed. Never during the day as I paint or cook or cry. Just of an evening as I sit lost in novels.

After some thought, I've moved the drinks cabinet into the library and brought down the mirror from the dresser in the smallest bedroom, which I've set atop the shiny wooden surface. It's angled to the library door, and in the hall by the entrance is the wardrobe where I store my boots and coats. One of its doors is open just so. Its mirror sees the one in the library, and sitting in my leather chair, I can see the reflection of a stretch of second-storey landing, and two doors. Not mine or the smallest room, but the other two which I keep made up as rooms for guests I know I'll never entertain.

I sip rich, sweet port and the novel is forgotten on my lap as I observe my cunning arrangement. The footsteps began some minutes ago, pacing overhead, around my bedroom. It's never bothered me that she starts there, at least, not since I understood she was more afraid of me than I of her. It is the master bedroom, after all. I can only assume she was once the lady of this house.

Sometimes she treads the balcony that skirts the upper storey, a match for the veranda below with its intricately wrought iron curlicues and rails rubbed smooth by who knows how many hands in the last century. But this evening she doesn't go outside and I hear my bedroom door click open. Her sad step moves onto the landing.

It's always hot and humid. The fan turns lazily, but the sweat that beads my brow and soaks my palms cannot really be blamed on the climate. My heart begins to race. Her cry sounds, that desperate *ooooh* of longing. It carries a pain that echoes my own.

The night outside buzzes with life, a gecko somewhere high on the wall *tick-tick-ticks* as it hunts. I'm rigid, barely breathing as I watch the dim reflections. A movement makes me stifle a gasp. Pale, floating lace tickles the edge of my view and she wails again. My hands tremble as the fluttering white resolves into a dress and I can see her plainly. After all I've heard these months, I still find it hard to believe the sight before me.

Her hair is long and dark, falling in soft waves over slim shoulders. Her hands are raised as if to accept a parcel, her skin ivory pale. I can't quite see a face and lean forward to get a better look. She notices the movement in the mirror and startles. Her head snaps around and for a moment our eyes are locked. She's beautiful and terrified and mortified, and her full mouth widens in shock as she cries out and dissipates like mist in a sudden breeze.

And I am bereft.

I saw to the very heart of her anguish, observed her pain laid bare, felt so briefly that her anguish matches mine, and I am ashamed. My cheeks are awash with tears. For her, for my Sarah, and for myself. Loss is a black hole that sucks light and happiness away. That poor woman. Her pain is lodged alongside my own now, transferred in that tormented look.

The rational part of me thinks she looked Victorian. Her dress with its full skirts, its intricate sleeves and high lace collar. Perhaps she came to this home when it was new. Perhaps it was built for her by some adoring husband, or hopeful suitor.

I cannot know for certain. I only know I desperately want to see her again, if for nothing else than to apologise, but I wonder if I ever will. With shaking hands I pour more port and drink. And pour and drink again until a stupor stills me in my wing-backed chair.

Weeks have passed and finally I hear her again, having all but given her up as gone for good. The familiar shuffling across my bedroom floor makes my heart skip. I haven't been able to paint since our encounter. Since I looked into her eyes. I've simply moped, venturing out only a handful of times for supplies. Mostly booze.

Dear Sarah, what would you make of me now?

But I hear her, pacing above. The furniture and mirrors have been returned to their former locations. My cunning merely feels cruel. A clever trick that hurt us both. She paces and I rise quietly, stand slightly uncertain of foot from a fine Shiraz, and walk silently to the library door. There I wait, gaze resting on the landing.

My bedroom door drifts open and she steps out, looks directly at me and her lips part to release that desperate sound. She lifts her hands as though she wants me to place something there, expression twisting. In confusion, I raise my own hands. I don't understand. She cries, her voice a distant howl, then she wafts apart and away. As she goes, she reaches forward one hand, grasping towards the door at the end of the landing. The door to the smallest room.

Then I'm alone with only our combined despair. I finish the Shiraz.

Over the following days I find the will to paint again, but the woman is my only subject now. She inhabits my waking mind and my dreams. I can't shake the sensation that I've interrupted her in the middle of something important, some eternal, unresolved nightly mission, and if I want to learn more I must let her finish her wandering. But how to let her do so, and observe it, without spoiling her progress? I'm drawn to the smallest bedroom, the way she reached for it. Does she travel there when she roams unimpeded?

I fill canvas after canvas with her image, and by night I eschew the library, sitting instead in that smallest room, in a threadbare armchair by the bed, reading by a bedside lamp. The lampshade is of glass panels and beads, dragonflies dancing around its border. Its multi-coloured light is poor. There's no fan up here and the air is close and sticky, but I endure the discomfort for over a week before I hear her again.

I don't notice her footsteps at first as I read, but jump when her moan drifts along the landing. I put my book aside, stare at the closed door. She wails again, nearer this time, and her footfalls seem solid. The door yawns open.

I sit perfectly still as she glides in and her face changes as she sees me. She turns, points urgently to the corner with the small single bed, then reaches for me, supplicating as she tatters, swirls and fades.

Once more I feel her sorrow, and I weep. I can't help but remember Sarah, and imagine her berating me for hiding, for taking on the ancient grief of others as if my own is not enough. She would tell me to get on with my life, but what is my life without her?

What was the woman pointing to? There's nothing in the corner, under the bed or mattress, except polished floorboards, inscribed here and there by long dead boring insects. The walls are pressed horsehair boards inside and painted weatherboard without, a deep burgundy that appealed to me greatly when I inspected the place, but it does draw in the heat terribly.

In a frenzy of confusion I retrieve tools and tear up the flooring and pry off wall panels to expose the bones of the house but discover only wooden trusses and dust and cobwebs and nothing else.

Returning to the library, I sit beneath the fan and think. The smallest room is often reserved for the smallest person. If I can aid my guest will it salve my own misery?

Steeling myself against the scrutiny of others, I travel to the nearest town. The records office is tiny and combined with the local library. There is no microfiche. Everything is kept in carefully maintained registers, defended daily against the march of dust and mites. A woman with large-framed glasses, *Hi, I'm Joan* on her name badge, judges my request with tight lips and seems to decide I'm harmless. She sets me up in a back room with a tower of ledgers, replenishing each as I finish it with another one bigger than the last.

Joan is happy to know someone is living in the old house again. It seems the place has a history. It was built by a very rich man, who intended to continue the growth of his fortune with sugar. He and his young wife moved into the newly built abode, and everything was fine until the birth of their child. The baby was born hale and well, a boy, Nigel Anthony, only offspring of Cecil and Madeleine Wilmer, for the birth killed the mother.

Madeleine. My ghost has a name at last.

Cecil collapsed into inconsolable despair, his family destroyed the moment it was made, and eventually he left, taking his son with him, leaving the house and his grief behind. But Madeleine had no such luxury.

Does she mourn the loss of the boy? Or the loss of a chance to know him, to hold him? Does she know he lived or fear he died too, wondering why his ghost isn't there for her to care for?

Joan brings me new tomes and I learn that Nigel Anthony Wilmer grew into a successful young man. He eventually become a magistrate well respected throughout the state of Queensland. His professional life is documented in several newspapers of the time. He was a good man, it seems, one of whom his mother could be proud.

I make copies of all the articles I can find and take them home.

Her footsteps have been slow along the landing, almost as though she anticipates something. Anticipates me, perhaps. I stand in the smallest room, two particular articles held before me. One of her son's birth, another lauding his reception of an Order of Australia. Surely enough to make a mother relent in her despair.

The door opens and I smile as she slides in, but her lips are turning down in pain the moment she lays eyes on me. I brace against the wash of shared desolation and raise the papers higher. "Can you see..?" I begin, but she yowls and swirls away.

I was foolish before, I know full well that my presence disturbs her. Perhaps I was being selfish. I wanted to see her receive the news I had found.

This is not about mending my heart, but hers.

I have spread several articles celebrating Nigel's life on the bed in the smallest room. Had they chosen a name before he was born? Will poor Madeleine be able to read these scraps of news, see her son's name and know he had the thing that was denied to her, a life fulfilled? He lived to eighty-one years old.

It's another week before I hear her again and I remain in the library with wine and book, the door closed, her privacy assured. She makes her way through the house, her voice a miserable song of loss. The door to the smallest room clicks open and I hold my breath. The entire house holds its breath, it seems, silence descends like a shadow.

But there is no cessation in her cries and tears are dampening my cheeks again. She walks and laments, clearly unmoved by the messages I have left her. Does the strange distance between here and where she truly is blur her vision? I pour more wine and lift my book and try to close my ears to her weeping.

Another week has passed and I have a final plan. The library door has been shut every night while I wait and now she walks again. I hold onto my patience until I'm sure she's out of my bedroom, treading the landing towards the smallest room.

"April 14th, 1881, Nigel Anthony was born to Cecil and Madeleine Wilmer," I say in a firm but calm voice. I speak loudly enough to ensure I'm heard through the closed door, but not so much that I might seem to be shouting and scare her. "Poor Madeleine died," I continue, "but Nigel did not."

There's a moment of stillness and I'm sure she's there, stopped to listen. I have to assume so and I press on, reading aloud clearly and slowly, mentions of Nigel's schooling, graduation, his career and commendations. I mention Cecil too, where I can, and his successes after he moved away with his son. It takes several minutes of oration to snapshot long and celebrated lives to the wife and mother lost in my halls.

I finish and wait, sipping dark Merlot across dry lips and tongue.

Relief floods me as I hear her again, and it's a different sound. Tears, but of relief more than grief. Her wail is replaced by a sigh of something hard to define but I desperately hope it's closure. Then, like air escaping a previously sealed vessel, she goes. Her presence slips away, not like the disintegration I've witnessed, but an utter removal. Without understanding how I know, I am convinced she's truly gone this time.

My own grief surges back as I find myself absolutely alone at last and it's almost too much to bear. Only the knowledge of Madeleine's escape keeps me from falling to pieces, but I let myself wallow, and drink, and bask in solitude.

Almost a month after Madeleine left, I realised that a ghost remained within the walls of my house. Me. Perhaps, I thought, it was time to move, though I've come to wear this home like a favourite old bathrobe. I'm reluctant to leave.

But a journey begins with a single step and so I've decided to attempt to rise from my despair in situ. A gathering of artists will arrive tonight and we'll discuss things and eat canapés and drink fine wine. I'm frightened of the possibilities, but excited too. And more than a little guilty. I'm sorry, Sarah, it's time. I know you would have told me that before I even came here, but I was ever the obtuse one.

THE MUSIC OF THE SPHERES
Debbie Cowens

The first time my daughter had the dream was the night of the supermoon. She had watched, wide-eyed and full of questions, as the huge golden moon followed us on the drive home from dinner at my parents'. Afterwards I, a fount of Googleable knowledge, did my best to share my freshly acquired understanding of elliptical orbits and syzygy to sate her curiosity. Looking back, I wonder if I should have noticed something. Perhaps she was more than usually excited. Perhaps her six-year-old mind was brimming with more questions than normal. If I observed any change in her behaviour I dismissed it as too much of her grandma's chocolate pudding or the usual Friday night's nervous excitement before a weekend with her father.

"Read me *Hey diddle-riddle and the jumping cow*," she giggled as I tucked her in, her legs wriggling and scissoring under the blanket.

I raised my eyebrows.

"Please?"

I bent and kissed her forehead before retrieving the book from her bookshelf. I had hoped to have seen the last of *Hey diddle-riddle* some months ago. It involved a shambolic cast of farm animals and nursery rhyme characters posing riddles to the reader about planets and stars. The puns were painful and the verse didn't scan, but as a bedtime story its worst flaw was that Erica couldn't resist shouting out the answer to every riddle and inevitably finding herself less sleepy at the end of the story than she had been at the start. I'd learned the hard way with *Astro-cat's Blast Off* that to show obvious disdain for a book could lead to it becoming the most requested bedtime story for months, so I smiled, sat on the edge of her bed and read the first riddle.

Two books later, she drifted off to sleep. I brushed aside the pale curl of hair that crept across her cheek and regarded her peaceful face. The garish yellow moonlight seeped around the edges of her bedroom curtains, unnaturally bright. With one final kiss goodnight, I tiptoed out and headed to my own bed.

I woke as though jolted by a sudden, violent sound despite the undisturbed quiet of the night. In the near darkness, my alarm clock glowed twelve forty-two in red segmented digits. My mouth was dry and tasted metallic and stale. I slid out of bed to grab a glass of water, and by the time I reached the door, I had decided an aspirin was also required to ease a dull headache.

In the hallway, light came from underneath Erica's door. I rammed the door open to bust her in the act of illicit post-bedtime reading or play, but her bed was empty. Erica stood facing her window, the curtains wide open to reveal the leering yellow moon, floating over the sickly shadows of our garden. Moonlight flooded around her like a giant searchlight.

"Erica!" I scolded, my voice weak and hoarse. "Get back in bed right now."

She didn't flinch or turn. I marched to the window, grabbed her arm but stopped when I caught sight of her face. Her eyes were wide open but unfocused, her pupils two pale orbs, reflecting, though not seeing, the moon. Her expression still haunts me. Erica was not simply sleepwalking. Her posture was too rigid; her breathing, though deep, was not peaceful. She was locked in frozen awe, caught in the monstrous moonbeam like a rodent dazzled by a car's headlights, her mouth agape, the veins in her neck bulging and luminous.

"Erica!" My voice was weaker in my ears than it had felt in my throat. "Erica, wake up!"

I grabbed her by the shoulders and pulled her into my arms. Her small body, though tense and rigid, did not resist. With her face buried in my embrace, the pull on Erica was severed and she softened into deep sleep as I held her. Gently and without daring to exhale, I carried her to my bed and lay beside her, watching her steady breathing and peaceful face until exhaustion dragged me into fretful dreams.

The next morning, Erica was only three spoonfuls into her rice bubbles when Kurt arrived a quarter hour earlier than usual. At the sound of the doorbell, she bounced from the breakfast table.

"Daddy!"

"Princess!"

I remained in the kitchen but her giggles and patter of feet fed me the image of the greeting in perfect clarity: her bounding into his arms and him lifting her to spin her round the hall, her hair bouncing in a fountain of curls. He entered the kitchen, carrying Erica on his hip, her arms clinging round his neck and her smile threatening to split her cheeks wide open. As I'd pictured, he was wearing the bright blue T-shirt she'd picked out to buy for him on Fathers' Day, though his suede jacket and her leg obscured part of the "Number 1 Daddy" phrase emblazoned on it so that it read "Numb 1 Dad". His height, though not unfamiliar, startled me when I saw him framed by the doorway. He took up so much space.

"Morning, Cass," he said. He glanced around the kitchen but said nothing.

"Sorry, we slept in a little." I gripped my coffee mug, silently ordering myself not to put my used plate in the dishwasher or wipe the bench in front of him.

"I guess I'm a little early, but the sunrise looked so awesome on my run that I couldn't wait to pick up my Eri-berry and get started."

He shoehorned some mention of his new-found love of exercise into every conversation as though he was a paid spokesmodel for the perks of divorce and an early-onset midlife crisis.

"Daddy, did you see the supermoon last night?" Erica chirped in his ear.

I felt my stomach lurch. I hadn't decided yet whether I should try to tell Kurt about last night but the fervour in her voice suddenly made last night's unsettling events real again.

"Supermoon?" He turned to face her, cocking an eyebrow and adopting a cheesy Movietone American accent. "Was it faster than a speeding bullet? Able to leap tall buildings in a single bound?"

Erica giggled. She leaned back and tilted her head with a matter-of-fact expression. "No, a supermoon is when the moon comes close to Earth in its orbit."

"Wow, sounds pretty neat. Did you see the man in the moon?"

Erica shook her head and slid down onto her own feet.

"Maybe we should go to the Observatory today? You could look through a telescope. See if you can see spot the man in the moon."

"Yeah!" Erica bounced on her feet and pressed her hands together in tiny applause.

"What a waste of a sunny day. Besides, Erica you've been talking about how excited you were about going to the zoo."

"But I want to go to the observatory," she insisted.

"Cassie, come on. What does it matter?" Kurt put on his reasonable face.

I glanced at Erica. "Would you like a cup of coffee? Erica needs to finish her breakfast."

"But Mum, can't I just go with Daddy?"

"Not until you've finished your breakfast."

"But I'm not hungry." She glowered at me.

"Time to fuel-up, kiddo." Kurt lifted her up onto the chair by her bowl. "Most important meal of the day and I can't have you running out of energy on me, can I?"

"Okay, Daddy." She smiled, grabbing her spoon and resuming her soggy rice bubbles with all the smug satisfaction of Goldilocks discovering the perfect bowl.

I poured Kurt a coffee and took him aside out of earshot. "I'm not sure the observatory is a good idea. Erica got worked up about the moon last night. It unsettled her. I found her watching it middle of the night."

"She's a curious kid. What does it matter if she got up to watch the supermoon? It wasn't a school night."

"But she didn't *get up* to watch it, she was sleepwalking. It was weird."

Kurt's brow crinkled and his mouth curled leftwards in his sceptic's grin. "Maybe she did sleepwalk. Maybe she was pretending to be asleep when you caught her so she wouldn't get in trouble. Either way it's not worth getting wound up about."

"She wasn't pretending, Kurt." I lowered my voice to an angry whisper. "She wasn't blinking, her breathing was shallow, she didn't wake up when I called her or touched her. It really scared me. Now you can believe me or you can tell yourself I'm over-reacting all you want, I don't care, but I'm asking you to check that she sleeps safe tonight, okay?"

Kurt took a mouthful of dark coffee. He'd given up dairy start of the year. He nodded. "Sure. Whatever, Cass. Of course I'll keep an eye on her. Maybe just try and relax. Take it easy this weekend, eh?"

I clenched my jaw and swallowed a sarcastic response. In Kurt's mind he was doing me a favour by looking after his daughter for a weekend.

"You ready to go, kiddo?" Kurt strolled over to Erica and launched her off her chair like a giggling rocket before she had a chance to answer.

"Yay!" Erica cheered, her feet scarcely touching the ground. She scampered off to grab her backpack.

They left in a flurry of goodbyes and laughter and I found myself alone in a silent house. It seemed no trace of her remained but her bowl with a scattering of rice bubbles in a shallow pool of milk.

At the weekend's end, Erica came home, bursting with smiles and stories, and proudly showing me her new purple sneakers adorned with glittering stars and moons.

"And they even light up when you move!" she explained, dancing an excited jig around the hall, her heels flashing a vivid purple.

"They're lovely, honey," I told her, shooting a look at Kurt who either didn't notice or pretended not to see.

"And we went to the observatory. It's ah-maz-ing. There's a giant telescope, like super big, but you have to go up all these stairs. And there's a bit where you can play like you're flying a spaceship and another bit with these films but they play on an oval screen, only it's at your waist and you can pick which planet in the solar system you go to. And you can throw these little balls down into the big bowl-thing with two holes, only you have to guess which one gravity will suck it into, and I got it right every time, didn't I, Daddy?"

"You sure did." Kurt grinned. "We had a great time, didn't we?" He tousled her hair, putting her backpack and the silver gift shop bag just inside the front door.

"Why don't you go and unpack your bag now, Erica?" I suggested, folding my arms.

We waited until her flashing purple heels had skipped down to her bedroom before commencing the old argument.

"How many times do I have to say this? You shouldn't be buying her toys and presents every time you see her."

"C'mon, you're making too much of this. She just wanted a book she saw in the observatory so I got it for her."

"That's because you've set up the expectation that you'll buy everything she wants."

"It was just a book about the moon, for crying out loud. I'm meant to tell her no, I don't want her to read a book because her mum wouldn't like it?"

"You shouldn't have to blame me in order to establish reasonable boundaries. You need to tell kids no on some occasions, Kurt. It's called being a parent," I snapped. "Besides, it wasn't just the book, was it? It's the shoes as well."

"So I'm the bad guy now? For buying a book and a pair of sneakers?" He shook his head and leaned against the doorframe.

"Don't act like you didn't know what you were doing. I told you I was worried about her getting over-excited about the moon and not sleeping, so what do you do? Take her to the observatory, buy her a book on the moon and a pair of glowing moon sneakers as well? Such a deliberate move to get at me."

"No, Cassie, it wasn't. It wasn't about you. It was about Erica. It was about me wanting to spend some time with my daughter, doing something she's interested in. She's like the smartest little kid and you're acting like it's something to worry about. When I was her age all I did was watch TV but she's not like that. She soaks up everything. She learns it all—planets, asteroids, black holes. You should have heard her in the car, chatting away about the moon's gravity compared to Earth's. She's amazing."

"I know that. Don't you think I know that? I just don't want you to screw it all up." I said, half-joking. "I mean, I should say us. I don't want us to mess it up. To mess her up."

"I get that, but you have to stop worrying over every little thing. You're a great mum, you're a total pain in the arse, but a great mother." He grinned and I almost forgot how awful he could be—and had been.

"Did she sleep okay?"

"Fine. Like a baby."

"She was terrible sleeper as a baby." I grimaced. "Not that you'd remember. You slept through any amount of crying."

"Trust me, she was fine. There's nothing to worry about."

For the next few weeks, at least, it seemed Kurt was right. Erica had no more sleepwalking episodes in the night. Her enthusiasm for space continued. On Thursday trips to the library after school, she selected more books from junior non-fiction and had nearly demolished the astronomy section by the next full moon.

Then it happened again. I woke up violently, my body jerked forward, snapped awake from the sensation of falling just before I hit the ground.

I found Erica bone-white, glistening and frozen, at her bedroom window. Silvery moonlight flooded the room, casting a Medusa spell on all it touched. Long brittle lashes framed her eyes. Had she been petrified in awe?

"Erica?" I whispered.

She didn't flinch but her jaw fell open in a mechanical seamless movement like the mouth of a rotating clown waiting for a ball to be thrown into it. Wordlessly, she began to sing. It was a strange, unnatural music unlike anything I had ever heard.

The melody was indistinct. It jarred with discordant anguish one moment, then swelled into the most triumphant joy the next. Had I half-heard this angelic song in my dreams or in some forgotten memory? It was beautiful and terrifying. One note promised the sublime, the next horror. I was caught in its rapture.

I listened and wept at its beauty. I had no sense of time passing. Had she sung this unearthly song for minutes? Hours? Finally, she stopped. A cloud cloaked the moon and the room fell dark. Silent and wordless, Erica walked back to bed and fell asleep without waking. I felt as if I had suffered a terrible loss. The sense of foreboding was overwhelming. I dared not touch her lest I wake her. I crept to her side and watched the steady, peaceful rise and fall of her chest before retreating to my own room. The red broken arms of my alarm clock read three thirteen. I sunk beneath my sheets and lay trembling in the dark, aware I had witnessed something more terrible than my fears. Real horrors lay waiting in the wide, silent darkness beyond our house, beyond our world.

I could not protect her from the night, the immense terrors lurking in the shadows and shrieking in the moonlight.

Not while she slept.

I did my best to keep her from that strange dream. The next day, I made her nap in the afternoon.

"You need to rest for tonight," I told her when she complained about the indignity of being expected to have a nap at the age of six. "We're having a special treat—Mother and Daughter Movie Marathon. We'll stay up all night watching movies and eating popcorn."

We sat up in my bed watching all her favourite cartoons and movies. She drifted off many times and I had to nudge her awake. Finally, at three o'clock she was too tired.

"Please don't wake me if I fall asleep, okay?" She yawned only five minutes into *Labyrinth*. "I don't mind. I've seen this one." She snuggled against my arm and shut her eyes.

"Okay," I whispered, stroking her hair and watching as her breathing deepened.

I couldn't have brought myself to wake her, even if I'd wanted to. She looked so sweet, so peaceful. There wasn't any danger now, I told myself. Not while she was next to me and I watched over her.

It wasn't until my alarm woke me at six-thirty that I realised I'd nodded off myself. Erica lay against me still.

Over breakfast Erica was remarkably unaffected by the late night. My body was stiff and slow and my head ached. Coffee helped, but I could barely keep track of Erica's rapid conversation.

"Time, our time, is just one line of notes in the music. What do you call that? You know the music that you sing while all the other instruments play different tunes that go with it?"

"The melody?"

"Yes, that's it. We're singing our own melody. It's like we're singing our time melody so loudly we don't hear all the others but they're there, playing their own music in the stars. Sometimes when our orbits sync up, the music folds together." She swirled her spoon through her rice bubbles, creating an outer ring with a hole of milk in the middle. "If you followed the music, you could go into another song."

"Like the Pied Piper." I frowned.

"Huh? Who's that?"

"It's from an old children's story about a man who played beautiful music on his pipes to lure all the rats away from a town and drown them."

"Poor rats. That's mean."

"Well, when the townspeople didn't pay the piper, he played his music again and all the children followed him."

"Did they drown, too?"

"Yes, I'm afraid so. So the moral of the story is don't go following strange music, okay?"

"I don't think that's a very appropriate story for children," she informed me. "Mrs Henderson told Liam Jefferson he shouldn't be watching *Throne of the Damned* because it has people being killed in it and it wasn't appropriate."

I smiled. "I guess you'd better not tell Mrs Henderson that story then."

Erica shook her head earnestly and took a massive spoonful of rice bubbles.

"Erica, I don't know if reading about wormholes and black holes and all these timeline theories is appropriate either," I began. "It think it might be better for you to start learning about something else perhaps? You can leave all the astronomy until you're older?"

Her face wrinkled in disappointment and confusion. "What's wrong with reading about astronomy?"

"Nothing, nothing." I felt guilty, like the worst kind of knowledge-stifling, small-minded, controlling mother. "Learning about the planets in the solar system, constellations and galaxies, that's all wonderful. I'm very proud of how much you like to learn, it's just that when I found you sleepwalking and staring at the moon in your sleep, it scared me."

"I'm sorry, Mummy."

"Don't worry, honey. It's not your fault. But when you told me just now about the music in the stars, it scared me in the same way."

"I didn't mean to."

"I know, Sweetie, but you know these things you've read about time travel or parallel dimensions or whatever, they're just theories? Nobody even knows if they exist. Maybe you should be reading more about the facts we do know about space and leave the theoretical astrophysics for when you're older?"

She stirred up her remaining rice bubbles in a jumble and ate a spoonful of mostly milk. "I guess so, but it won't stop it."

A few days later, Erica's teacher called me into school with concerns.

Erica had scrawled strange equations, pages of them, in her writing book. When Mrs Henderson had asked her to tell her about them, Erica had only said they weren't equations, but music. The music of the stars. She hadn't seen the symbols, she heard them. The stars had told them to her.

The school's counsellor repeated the same story after her talk with Erica. Then the child psychologist, although he recommended more tests and observations and requested to take a copy of all of Erica's writings. There was an exercise book full of them by the time we had our appointment three days later. Kurt, who I'd had to involve by this stage, was delighted when the tests pronounced Erica as profoundly gifted. In fact, he seemed proud more than concerned that the psychologist believed Erica had told the stars' music story due to understimulated imaginative intelligence. I didn't even see a trace of guilt at the suggestion that possibly Erica had made up all of it to shift focus away from parental conflict. She was highly intuitive as well, apparently.

Doubt and guilt make a convincing combination. After all, her stories about stars began not long after I'd argued with Kurt about her trip to the observatory. But it hurt to believe Erica would lie to me like that, that she'd been faking the strange singing in her sleep, that she'd seen my fear and played on it.

"Erica wouldn't lie. She's not like that," I told Dr Buxton.

"All children her age lie, Ms Hooper." He took off his glasses, polishing them on an eggshell blue handkerchief before putting them back on. "Even the good ones, especially if they think they're helping."

I said nothing, but Kurt oozed smugness. Fine. At least he won't argue about the expense of a private child psychologist, not if it means hearing what he wants.

"You must understand that in many ways Erica is not an ordinary child. The equations in her books are highly complex," Dr Buxton continued.

"You mean they're real equations? Algebra, science, that sort of thing?" Kurt asked.

"Not exactly. There are fragments of known equations; everything from Einstein's field equations to orbital velocity formulae and quantum mechanics but none are completely accurate. I've checked. There are other symbols, childish squiggles really, scattered throughout. Some characters resemble known symbols—Sanskrit, Norse runes, pictograms, but there's no consistency." He leaned back in his chair. "I even sent a copy through to one of my linguist friends, but he couldn't identify more than forty percent of the symbols. She simply made most of them up. This demonstrates an advanced imaginative capacity, which would be remarkable in itself, but coupled with the ability to remember and reproduce the sheer range and quantity of such advanced formulae with even half the accuracy she has... Well, I've never seen this kind of mind in a child her age."

We followed all the psychologist's recommendations immediately, Kurt and I. Weekly therapy session for Erica, one-on-one and family counselling. She began attending mixed age gifted and talented lessons at her school, which she enjoyed and related in full to me every day on the drive home. She seemed happier, if not happy, and her sleeping was back to normal. At least, at first...

The song woke me not long after one o'clock on the eve of the next full moon. I ran into her room and once again she stood by her window, the curtains thrown open and her arms hanging limp at her sides. She sang that wordless tune, cold and beautiful.

I grabbed her by the arms. "Erica, stop it! I know you can hear me. I know you're pretending. Stop it!"

But she kept singing. I clamped one hand over her mouth. Her lips were like ice and the muffled hum of her song grew louder, coursing through her whole body, through mine.

"Erica! Stop!"

I shoved her back from the window. She shifted plank-like towards her bed, and toppled like a helpless domino. The moonlight fell across her face and I saw the symbols scrawled in shadow over her skin. Like ripples in the ocean, tiny indecipherable figures ebbed across her face, cresting then vanishing without a trace.

Still she sang. I scooped her up in my arms and carried her to my room. I laid her in my bed, pulling my cover up over both our heads until finally, in the safety of darkness, she fell silent in my arms and we both sank into a restless sleep.

The next evening, I covered her window and mine, nailing old tarpaulins hauled from the garage to the outside of the windows. I felt certain that if I could keep the moonlight out, I could keep her safe.

I dozed off not long after two, the red digits of my alarm clock blurring and merging into imperfect words in my mind: thirteen past one was "lie".

I woke at the sound of the music. Her voice was soft, yet the song thundered in my ears, reverberating through the walls and floorboards. I'd drifted off to the music. It had penetrated and shaped my now-forgotten dreams, and suddenly, its violent crescendo had wrenched me awake, startled and frightened. My nightdress was clammy and clinging to my sweat-soaked back. I was cold, shivering and Erica had vanished.

I leapt out of bed and raced to her room, following the sound of her voice, though my instincts recoiled in terror at the unnatural beauty in the discordant music. My ears throbbed at the immensity of the sound as though the strange pitch, the sheer purity of those notes was not destined to be heard by human ears.

But I couldn't resist. I wish I could be certain that it was my love and maternal instincts that forced me to run to Erica and not some terrible flaw in human nature that compels us to our destruction, like a moth to the flame.

I found her shaking by the open window of her room. The tarpaulin had been ripped from its nails and the upper corner of it flapped like a silver wing, beating against the glass.

The moonlight, brighter and more ominous than ever, flooded the room like a searchlight. And my Erica, my little girl, seemed too small and delicate to be making that deafening, glorious sound.

The shadow-ink symbols scuttled across her forehead. I didn't attempt to identify them or look for similarities with her drawings. They vanished too quickly and the very sight of them sent a prick of repulsion down my spine. All I knew was I had to get her out, release her from the terrible thrall of the moon and the music.

Made stronger and heavier as though anchored by some unseen weight, I could not lift her from where she stood. I had to drag her from the room, inch by inch, and my muscles ached from the exertion.

It was only once I had her safe back in my dark bedroom, submerged under the covers, no fragments of light invading, that the singing stopped.

She slept soundly after that, but the adrenaline and fear were too strong for me to rest. I lay in the dark, listening to the soft rhythm of her breathing, trying to block out the silent echo of her squalling song.

It wasn't until the next morning that I saw blood on my pillowcase and realised my left ear had bled. I washed the crusted blood off my earlobe in the bathroom before Erica woke.

"Why am I in your bed, Mummy?" she asked when she finally opened her eyes.

"You had a bad dream."

"Was I looking at the moon again, like you said?"

I nodded. "You were singing, too. Do you remember any of it?"

"No," she blinked, and her eyes shone with unfallen tears. "But I can hear it, the song. It won't stop. It's in my head."

"Me too," I whispered, folding her up in my arms.

We spent the morning painting the outside of the windows. The leftovers of fence paint in the garage ran out after Erica's and my bedroom. We drove to the hardware store, car radio blasting and chatting all the way. It was as though we had an unspoken agreement to drown out the music with our jokes and talk. Erica chose a bright blue paint, Summer Cobalt, for the rest of the house. We ate the café-bought ham sandwiches in the sunshine of the back garden, admiring our handiwork with our stereo, dragged onto the deck, bleating a stream of cheery pop songs. The neighbours, let alone Kurt, would think I had lost my mind when they saw the blue windows, looking like the abstract oblongs in a child's drawing of a house. But I didn't care. I wouldn't let the moonlight into our home, not tonight, not ever.

We had fun that day in the sunlight. Though our arms ached from the effort, Erica insisted on fetching her poster paints and adding a mural to the exterior of her own bedroom window. When I'd finished swathing the ranchslider in a thick coat of blue, I returned to her side to admire her work. She had painted us, two figures standing side by side. Though I was the taller of the two, we were otherwise identical with our red triangle dresses, purple shoes and bright yellow hair that matched the giant sun hanging over us.

We ordered pizza for dinner and ate on the deck, enjoying the final scraps of daylight before heading into the sanctuary of the artificial lights in our shrouded home.

We watched TV until bedtime and, without comment or questions, Erica got into my bed. I read to her and stroked her hair until she fell asleep beside me.

I don't know what woke me up. On some days I think it must have been the shriek of tyres. Others, I think it was the music, that terrible, ceaseless song that plagues my every moment, sleeping and awake, just on the knife-edge of hearing. But I don't remember the moment of my waking any more than I can recall when exactly I had fallen asleep. All I remember is the moments after—the breathless panic when I found the empty space beside me; the churning, sickening dread when I didn't find her in her bedroom. Or the study. Or the kitchen. The horror at seeing the open front door. I must've been screaming, but I heard nothing as I ran down the driveway. The jagged gravel stabbed the soles of my feet, sprinting desperately to a soundless rhythm.

I ran to the end of the street, towards that terrible golden light. The car's headlights glared like two monstrous yellow eyes even as it stood motionless in the road. The driver's door was open and a figure silhouetted, crouched in front of the car, frozen in the beam of light. Traces of the words stammered breathlessly down the phone. None of it mattered. I ran to the crumpled child in front of them.

It was Erica—cold, broken, gone.

Beneath the blood pounding in my ears, the ragged catch of my breath, I heard the music. I hear it now, though it's over a fortnight since she was buried in the darkness of the earth. Daylight no longer banishes it. I must listen to its call always, alone.

Her painting is still on her bedroom window, though it's fading and beginning to crack after last week's rain. I fear I am, too. Perhaps I could grieve, could sleep, could hold on to the torn threads of my sanity if it were not for the music. The endless tide of the indescribable song grows louder as the next full moon draws near. Maybe it will lure me into the moonlight. I have scoured the paint off all windows except hers, and wait. If the moon does not lead me to my Erica again, I will make my own light.

I will find silence again.

DIGGERS
Sally McLennan

They lived scattered about the shore line and, although they were really grave robbers, they called themselves Diggers. Long after a barnacle died they crept to the sealed door of its shell dwelling and dug their way in. Prising, pulling, wrenching at the door of the shell house, they tore its two halves apart. There, Diggers would make their homes. Curled up in their barnacle shells they felt as safe as sea snails.

By day, they slept, moist and warm, within their stolen shelters. Or, if the tide was in, they waved tiny fronds of sea-grass in the water, doing their best imitations of barnacles as they sieved for food. But by night the Diggers played. At low tide, there were Digger dances around the tidal pools. The Olden Diggers held their council sessions: sometimes talking, sometimes watching with sad, wise eyes as the Young played chicken with crabs, gambled for food or a better shell, bickered, or danced and sang songs to one another as they ringed the pools.

Thinkers, who lived in shells on their own, sat musing as the moon crossed the clouded sky, their eyes growing soft and thoughtful. They carried head-high staffs of driftwood with strange spirals and whorls carved upon them. No one knew if their musings were wise, for they were not shared. The Young would say they were not great thinkers—for no Digger can grow wise alone.

One young Digger, Kari, liked to dance more than any other. She let her feet lead her in measured treads around seashells and wild dances across the sand beds. On the night her adventure began, the dance steps were quick and the songs happy. Kari wore red seaweed twined in her hair and pieces of sea-polished glass that shone wetly under the moon. Kari whistled and hummed with the others. She stamped and whirled, drawing in towards the gull feathers stuck in the sand, then bowing low, she fled outwards. Kari raced round the pools in tight circles. The tune soared and then died out as the dancers stumbled. And as the moon slipped to touch the surf, it was Kari's turn to sing. She turned outward to the sea and sang into the silence:

Where does the moon send
her light when she leaves us?
Why do horizons end
there where she sleeps?
Why can we not go
into the waves with her?
I want to know
the company she keeps.

The Young stood behind her, their eyes round, as the light faded from the water. Some were frightened by Kari's song and others felt a craving they couldn't understand.

A group of Olden Diggers broke through the dancers' ranks and walked straight to Kari. An Olden Digger scrubbed at the sand with his feet, as if he would say something, but it was the youngest council member who spoke: "Kari, your song is beautiful as always. But you know what you sing of is wrong." The Councillor frowned.

Kari turned reluctantly away from the sea to face the Digger who had spoken. "What do you mean, Kaikeri?" she asked her older friend steadily.

"Kari," said Kaikeri, "there is nothing I can say that has not been said. By day, Diggers sleep in barnacle shells on Digger Rock. By night, we play near our homes. To leave Digger Rock would be foolish. We know of no other safe place."

All the Young nodded agreement, and turned to drift shellwards, with sombre faces.

Kari stood alone, watching the sea as pink began to streak the sky.

Although her tummy was full, Kari felt empty. Confused, she walked past the puddles to the shell home she shared with Lali Digger. It was a long time before she curled up and fell asleep.

For the next four nights, after the waters receded, Kari sat alone thinking. She hungered to know what lay beyond Digger Rock. The Olden Diggers worried about her, but decided it was best to leave her in peace. Their meetings continued as before; the dancers still danced, and the bickering Young still fought among themselves.

On the fifth night after Kari's song, however, there was a full moon. Once the water drifted away, Kari and Lali opened their doors and went to join the other Diggers. Kari danced and sang more wildly than ever before. She waved bunches of seaweed above her head, and leapt high over the sand. Her friends smiled to see her happy again. But when the sea slipped to the bottom-most edge of the beach, Kari stole away. Only Lali Digger saw her leave the circle and skirt Digger Rock.

"Where are you going, Kari?" Lali asked.

"I'll be back, Lali," said Kari, "You go enjoy the dance."

And Lali did, although now and then the young Digger turned back to see where Kari had gone.

At the end of the rock, Kari looked left and right to make sure she was out of sight of the dancers. Then she ran. She ran past glistening heaps of seaweed and ghostly towers of driftwood. She ran past gaping, empty pipi shells and bubbling holes in the sand. Though her heart pounded with fear and her legs ached, she kept running. Soon she was far, far away from Digger Rock.

Kari slowed to a walk. Her breath rasped her throat and her sides ached. Kari looked over her shoulder, and though she could see a long, ragged line of Digger toe marks behind her, she could not see Digger Rock. While uneasiness tickled her spine, Kari made her feet keep walking just as fast as they could.

A long time later, Kari was forced to rest again. Sand fleas chirped at her, but she ignored them, and sat on the sand to bind seaweed round her feet. Though they had been toughened by nights of dancing, her footpads were blistered and torn. Kari knotted the last piece of seaweed at her ankle and stood up. She grimaced to see how much closer the water was. Although Kari longed to swim in the black bubbling surf, it frightened her, as it did all

Diggers. It was impossible to tell whether any of the blurred shapes ahead were rocks, where she could shelter from the oncoming tide. Her throat tightened with fear.

After she passed a fourth large clump of seaweed, Kari began to lose hope. Perhaps none of the ridges in the distance were rocks. Kari pushed herself to reach the next mound on the sand. As she neared it, she saw the shine of wet seaweed. She would run no more; the sea was approaching and Kari was exhausted.

But there was something underneath the seaweed. Kari climbed between the thick dark strands, her hands held out in front of her, and felt something hard beneath her feet. In the dim light, large blotches of white shone against a pinkish surface. It was rough under her fingers. Kari chortled. A rock!

Kari climbed up till she found an empty barnacle shell with half its door missing. She poked her head in first, to be sure it was empty, and then crawled inside, exhausted. Though it was not padded with feathers like her home-shell, within moments Kari was asleep.

She stayed at New Rock for two nights. Once the sea swept the seaweed away, she saw that there were many empty shell homes, and no Barnacles at all. Kari wondered what had happened to them. A Thinker at Digger Rock had once said that too much algae in the sea might hurt shellfish. But no one had listened for no one knew what to do about it.

New Rock was much smaller than Digger Rock. But now there was a place besides Digger Rock where Diggers could make their home. No Digger would have to sleep two to a shell again. She had to return to Digger Rock. Kari thought about this as she sang herself to sleep.

On the next night, low tide was late in the evening. Because of this, and because she wasn't trying to hide her departure, Kari was able to leave New Rock early. She ran at a fast trot and was home before light coloured the sky.

As Kari reached the Rock, she wept. Though all the others believed she was dead, Lali had been keeping watch for her return. "Kari! Kari! Welcome home!"

Diggers thronged around Kari, laughing with delight, like the bubbling sea. Kaikeri and Lali cried with joy and the Olden Diggers smiled their relief.

Through the rest of that night, and all the next, Kari spoke to a full council of Diggers. She told them all of New Rock. Some didn't believe that she'd been as safe there as at Digger Rock. All were curious. Diggers questioned her as long as the moon's light lasted.

Finally, it was decided that the next night Kaikeri the Councillor would lead a handful of fit and brave Diggers to New Rock. The only blight upon their farewell was that Kari, the hero of the Rock, did not join them or come to wish them luck. It was Lali Digger who told them which direction to run in and what they should look out for. They waited for Kari a moment longer, then they chanted farewells, and the adventurers left Digger Rock forever.

Kari sat far, far down the beach. She was completely still as she watched the Diggers leaving, growing distant and then fading into the grey night. Kari toyed with her hair. She wouldn't go to New Rock. It was the same as Digger Rock, really, just in a different place. Kari was still empty inside although she was proud she'd left Digger Rock. She'd taken a risk, and helped all Diggers. But Kari had to work out if she could be contented at Digger Rock. Kari thought about how she had found a safe place when she really needed it.

The moon rested low on the horizon. Kari got to her feet and walked to the water's edge. The sea splashed loudly before her. Its waves swelled darkly forward before they pulled away again. Suddenly, her throat was dry. Bubbles ringed the foaming sea. They reflected Kari's face back at her many times over. She looked at them for a long time. She wondered that Diggers had gills, and could breathe when their shells were under water, when most were scared to actually swim.

The sea shone silver white. It seemed there was a great path of light leading straight to the moon. Kari bent to touch the water and it was warm. Kari knew then what she wanted. Unafraid, Kari walked steadily into the water. With the froth making her skin tingle, Kari set her face to the light and swam out into a new life, into the arms of the welcoming sea.

Kaikeri and the others paused to rest. They should almost be there. A soft wind from the sea touched their faces and took their hands. For a moment, they heard a snatch of song drifting on the sea breeze.

TO THE CENTRE OF THE EARTH
Robinne Weiss

Three scientists sat in a meeting room on a drilling rig in the middle of the Indian Ocean. They were hunched over the chemical analysis of the latest core sample.

"This must be what broke Bryant's drill—the stuff that has stymied everyone else," remarked Kaitlyn.

"But what is it?" asked Emily.

"Cooled magma. What else could it be?" said Rolland.

"Well, if it's magma, then we've been completely wrong about what magma is," said Kaitlyn. "Look at this." She pushed the paper toward Emily. "What do you make of those numbers? Go from this week's first sample to the most recent one."

Emily, the team's biologist, read aloud. "One, seven, twelve, twenty-three—yes, we'd expect carbon to go up as we got closer to the mantle—forty-two, seventy... two thousand nine hundred and thirty. This must be a mistake. There can't possibly be that much carbon in those rocks."

"It's not a mistake. I ran the sample twice. Do you think we're hitting living organisms again?"

Emily's brow furrowed. "We haven't seen life in our samples for over two kilometres." Her eyes widened. "If these are microbes, they're like nothing we've seen before. I'll run the sample again, to separate the organic carbon from the carbonate. If it's organic..." she left the sentence hanging, but her eyes gleamed with excitement.

"Looks like you've got something to do again, Emily," said Rolland. "No more complaining that we're beyond the zone where life can exist. Could be a paper in *Nature* here."

The prospect of life this far down in the earth's crust was exciting, and not just from a scientific point of view. The team from Woods Hole Oceanographic Institution needed a breakthrough to keep their funding going. They'd been drilling for over a year and still hadn't reached their goal—the Earth's mantle. Their rivals, from the Chinese Academy of Science, were drilling in the South Pacific. Rolland's attempt was only funded because the Foundation for American Leadership decided America had to get there first—an Earth Race instead of a Space Race. His funding was contingent on his team being the winner of this race. If the Chinese reached the mantle first, Rolland's money would be pulled from under him, and years of work would go unfinished.

Rolland climbed to the top of the Russian oil rig they had outfitted for research. The observation platform terrified most visitors to the rig—forty-three metres above the churning waves, the rusted metal grating underfoot and flimsy railing didn't inspire confidence. Rolland loved it. It cleared his mind and calmed his nerves to stand on the platform with the wind flapping his jacket and whipping through his hair.

And it was the only place on the rig with decent cell phone reception.

His first call was to his wife. "Have you heard from the girls this week?" He always tried to steer the conversation away from work. He got enough of work, living it twenty-four hours a day on the rig. He could count on his wife to fill their conversations with the latest news of their daughters, now both at college.

"I suppose you haven't heard about the earthquakes yet," she said.

"What's happened?" He couldn't keep the fear out of his voice, but whether fear for his daughters' safety or for his research was greater, he didn't know.

"The girls are fine," began his wife. Rolland released the breath he was holding, and knew the fear had all been for his children. The dread he now felt, though, was for his research.

"The first was centred off the Carolina coastline. We barely felt it here. Maren's apartment building collapsed, but she was at class, so she's okay. They cancelled classes for a week until an engineer assesses the classroom buildings. She's home now."

"That was *the first?*"

His wife took a deep breath. "The second hit New York City. We felt that one—magnitude six point four."

"Six point four! And Jess?" Jess was at design school in New York.

"She's fine. She's still there, but the city is devastated. The military is organising evacuations for those who want to leave and have places to go outside the city. She's trying to get a seat on one of those flights."

"And you?"

"I'm fine. Maren has been a big help. Especially now that the protesters are camped outside the door."

"They're at the *house?*"

"Well, after the third quake—"

"Third?"

"It struck well out to sea, and no one was hurt. But...Roll...they're blaming this all on you." Her voice was strained.

Rolland struggled to calm himself. He knew the public exposure had been necessary to secure his funding, but a vocal segment of the public had decided that since they didn't understand his work, it was evil. How could those yahoos think his little hole in the floor of the Indian Ocean thirteen thousand kilometres away was causing earthquakes in the North Atlantic? That was just it—they didn't think. They were witch hunters who only wanted someone to persecute. And now they were persecuting his family, who deserved none of this.

He reined in his anger. His wife didn't need to listen to a rant. No doubt she'd performed her own when the protesters showed up.

"Have you talked to the Institute? Call Billie—she should be able to pull some strings, have the protesters removed by the police—she's good at things like that."

"Hon, the Institute is besieged, too."

"Aw, fuck. Honey. I'm so sorry you have to deal with this. I think we're just days away from finishing the drill. I'll be home by the end of the month. Call the Institute and see what they can do about the protesters. I'll give Billie an earful, too. Pay whatever it takes to get Jess home. I'll be there as soon as I can. This will all blow over."

His second call, to James Markham, director of Woods Hole, was even less cheerful.

"Rolland. I was hoping you would call. We have a situation."

"I know, the protesters—"

"I don't give a damn about the protesters. It's Chao I'm worried about."

Dr. Chao Kwan, the lead scientist of the Chinese team.

"What's he up to?"

"The more important question is, what's he *down* to? *China Newsday* just reported he's reached six kilometres."

"Six…but has he hit mantle? I know where he's drilling, and he's going to have to go a lot further than us to reach the mantle. We're almost there. Today's core sample was way off the charts for carbon. Emily is reanalysing it now to see exactly what's there. We'll be sending some samples back for DNA testing. If we've found life this deep in the crust, it won't matter what the Foundation does with their funding."

"If you've found life down there, so has Chao. We need that paper written and published. Now. Never mind sending samples here for testing. I'm sending you the equipment to analyse them yourself. It'll be there in…" James paused and Rolland heard keys tapping on his computer. "…three days. I want to see the papers flying out of there within a week. We can't let ourselves be scooped on this one. We need to be first in *Nature* or *Science*."

Rolland stood for a while on the observation platform after hanging up. Three earthquakes on the east coast. There was no way his drilling was responsible for it, but until both his daughters were safe at home, he was more worried about that than about Chao.

And the protesters on his doorstep…that, he felt responsible for. He didn't advertise his home address, but anyone could have found it—he didn't hide it. Didn't think he had to. Now he wished he'd been more careful.

He sighed. There was nothing he could do except finish this drill as quickly he could and get home.

He headed down to the drilling deck to talk to the crew. Maybe they could drill round the clock if they worked in alternate shifts.

When Rolland walked into the lab hours later, Emily was bent over the microscope. She straightened up at the sound of his footsteps.

"My eyes are bugging out," she said, rubbing her face.

"No surprise. You've been at it for ages. Got anything?"

"The carbon is organic—amino acids. But they're just floating around in the slurry. There are no cells, no structures of any kind. I'll send samples back to the lab for—"

"James is sending the equipment for DNA analysis. Chao's team is at six kilometres. We need to find something and publish it, fast."

"Well, I've got the data on the tardigrades we found at 1.7 kilometres. I'm already writing that up."

"No. It's got to be something from the lowest sample. We've got to beat Chao to this—he's likely to make it to the mantle before we do."

Noise on the drilling rig rose to nerve-wracking levels as the Russian drilling crew doubled their efforts. For once, Rolland was thankful for their military-style precision and respect for authority—he only had to suggest they needed to increase their speed.

"Of course, Sir. How fast, Sir?"

Maybe they'd beat Chao to the mantle after all. He smiled at the thought that the Foundation for American Leadership didn't know he was drilling from a Russian rig with a Russian crew. American ingenuity was one thing, but for this sort of thing, there was nothing better than a good old Communist regime, even the remnants of one.

The DNA sequencer arrived on a supply helicopter, along with forty kilos of potatoes, a case of frozen chicken, and two dozen cabbages. Rolland sighed when he saw the cabbage—the Russian drilling crew was great, but the cook didn't have much imagination, and Rolland was sick of cabbage soup. First thing he'd do when he got home was take his wife to that fancy new Italian restaurant, Mario's, and order everything on the menu.

Emily wasted no time getting the equipment set up and running. Three hours later, she called Rolland and Kaitlyn to the lab. "There's no DNA there," she said.

"There has to be," countered Rolland. "What else could be making all these amino acids except a living organism?"

"I don't know, but there's no DNA in those samples. Kaitlyn, you're the chemist—could these be produced by any non-biological process?"

"Theoretically, yes. But all those reactions require water—lots of it, to produce this concentration of protein." She frowned. "And all the processes we know of require near anaerobic conditions. The increase in carbon dioxide in these samples says to me there's just too much oxygen down here."

"Amino acids, carbon dioxide… It's got to be life. So where's the DNA?"

"Let's draw another sample. There has to be something there."

"We've reached 5.8 kilometres, Sir. I think we're in, Sir." Vanya, the drilling foreman had climbed to the observation platform, where Rolland was trying, unsuccessfully, to phone his wife.

"We're through the brittle rock?"

"Yes, Sir. We've hit something… soft."

"Magma!" whispered Rolland. "The mantle. Has Kaitlyn taken the core samples?"

"She's down there now."

"Excellent." Rolland slapped the foreman on the back and smiled. "Hold at 5.8 kilometres and get ready to lower the observation pod." The foreman suppressed a salute, then started down the ladder to the drilling deck.

"Vanya!" Rolland called. The foreman stopped and looked up. "Congratulations! You're the first guy to drill to the centre of the earth."

Vanya responded with a rare smile, nodded his acknowledgement, and returned to his work.

It wasn't really the centre of the earth, but it was the first drill to hit the mantle—if they were lucky, and Chao's team hadn't made it there yet. Rolland clattered down the metal steps to the operations centre.

This day had been a long time in the making. The first plans were laid out in 1957, and people had been trying—and failing—to drill through the earth's crust to the mantle ever since. Rolland had gotten involved in 2020, when a tanking global economy made research funds all but impossible to get.

But in 2040, global warming defied all the models. There was a sudden spike in sea temperature and atmospheric carbon. Human-induced changes had brought the earth to a tipping point. Something was happening deep within the earth that was speeding up climate change beyond even the worst-case scenarios. The daily news showed chunks of the Antarctic ice shelf calving off. Small Pacific Island nations were negotiating their wholesale evacuation to mainland neighbours. Suddenly, everyone wanted to know what was going on inside the earth.

Still, it hadn't been easy to secure the nine hundred million dollars they'd needed for this project. Nine hundred million dollars could build a lot of sea walls.

"It's not magma, whatever it is," said Kaitlyn.

They'd been poring over the chemical analysis of the first sample from the mantle. Kaitlyn and Emily were seated at the table in the lab. Rolland was pacing.

"Amino acids, carbon dioxide, water? It's…" Emily's voice trailed off.

"It's what?" prompted Rolland.

"I know this sounds crazy, but I recognise this chemical signature. I used to work with this stuff as a lab tech for Merck."

"So, what is it?" Rolland stopped pacing and turned toward his colleagues.

Emily looked up with bewildered eyes. "It's albumen—egg white."

The rig shuddered.

"What the hell?" cried Rolland as he steadied himself against a cabinet.

They scurried out of the lab and up to the drilling deck, where the crew was swarming like ants. Barking an order in Russian to one of his crew, Vanya strode over to Rolland.

"What's going on?" asked Rolland.

"Earthquake, Sir. We're attempting to withdraw the drill."

The rig shuddered again, and a cry went up from the drilling crew.

"Eto slomano! Eto slomano!"

Vanya turned and ran, leaving Rolland, Emily and Kaitlyn gripping the deck rails.

Rolland was on the observation platform, shouting into the phone above the racket on the drilling deck below.

"We've reached the mantle. There's been an earthquake, and the drill is broken. We're trying to salvage one more sample."

"There have been earthquakes all over the globe. We're pulling you all out," said James tersely.

"But, we're not responsible for the—"

"I know that! But now is not the time to be in the middle of the ocean drilling into the earth's crust. I'm organising a flight out. Be ready to go. Bring all your data."

"What about Chao?"

"Chao and his team are dead. Their ship sank yesterday. Freak wave or something."

"Shit," muttered Rolland. "Okay, we'll be ready."

His wife didn't answer her phone. He left a message on her voicemail.

They packed the bare essentials for their evacuation—if they were going by chopper, they wouldn't be able to take much.

"Do we just sit around and wait?" asked Kaitlyn. "When are they coming for us?"

Rolland shrugged. "I suppose it depends on how hard Sri Lanka was hit by the quakes, doesn't it?" Sri Lanka was their supply point and nearest landfall. "I doubt we'd be high priority if they had a natural disaster on their hands."

"Well, I can't just sit around," said Emily. "I'm going to run another PCR on the last sample—see if I can't scare up any DNA."

"Good idea. Kaitlyn, let's go check with Vanya—maybe we can squeeze one more sample out."

"It would be great if we could deploy the observation pod, too, even if we only get a few hours of data before we have to go," added Kaitlyn.

Three days later, no helicopter had arrived for Rolland and his crew, but they'd managed to extract another core sample, thanks to Vanya's clever but, "very foolish... dangerous" hack of the broken drill.

Everyone else had gone to their bunks for the night, but nervous energy kept Rolland, Kaitlyn and Emily in the lab.

It was oddly quiet on the rig, now that the drill was still. Rolland's chair creaked as he shifted. The sound of Kaitlyn's fingers tapping on her keyboard filled the room.

Emily sighed loudly and leaned back in her chair.

"This DNA matches *nothing.*"

"It's not archaea?" asked Kaitlyn. "That's the most logical, isn't it?"

"It's not archaea."

"What about tardigrades? Those things can survive anywhere."

"Nope. Seriously, if it wasn't for the fact I can sequence it, I'd say it's not even DNA."

"Do you think the conditions in the mantle have damaged it?"

"If it were damaged, I shouldn't be getting these long sequences. It's just not—"

"Guys," interrupted Rolland. "I think you need to see this."

Kaitlyn and Emily gathered around Rolland's computer screen.

"I was analysing the sonar data from the observation pod. It's completed about half its field of vision. Look at this, and tell me what you see."

The women were silent for several long minutes as they stared at the screen. Rolland didn't dare look at their faces. He almost didn't want to know.

Finally Emily whispered, "It's a head. The head of a... a..."

"What *is* that animal?" finished Kaitlyn.

Rolland let out the breath he didn't know he was holding.

"You see it, too."

"But, if that's half the field of vision, then that thing must..."

"Fill the entire earth. Yes."

"I don't understand."

"Think about it, Kaitlyn. Brittle outer layer, *egg albumen*, DNA we can't match," said Emily.

A tremor shook the rig.

Rolland looked at Emily and Kaitlyn. Their faces mirrored his own shock.

"We're not going to make it home, are we?"

BIG ENOUGH FOR TWO
Piper Mejia

A t the sight of home, a little thrill lifted the corners of Diana's mouth. She slowed to admire its symmetry against the forget-me-not sky. Small, but big enough for two. The 1950's wooden bungalow was painted in pale grey, with off-white trim around the windows and a steel grey door. The colour scheme wasn't her idea, but Steve had said keeping it neutral would increase its resale value, not that they'd sell, he'd assured her when she protested.

Painting the outside had been the first task. A newlywed project. Steve thought they could get a few more years out of the old paint job, but when she showed him the hand sander and overlarge pair of painting overalls she'd found in the cellar, he'd agreed to go half on the paint. He'd even bought her a face mask to protect her lungs from the dust and fumes. With her hair covered in one of Steve's battered ball caps and her feet clad in a pair of his cast-off boots, she systematically tackled each surface while he stayed indoors with the windows shut and the curtains drawn. He would've helped if he hadn't been so busy making a good impression at his new job.

The progress was satisfyingly steady; section by section she remedied small wounds; filling holes and replacing rotten timbers, before protecting the house from further harm with even layers of semi-gloss paint. When he helped to put away the leftover paint into the cellar, Steve agreed that the final results were worth the effort.

Diana turned into the pebble driveway with a practiced turn of the wheel, pleased, not for the first time, she'd gone with stones the size of a baby's fist over flat concrete. The warm grey tones enticed the eye from road to house like children to a candy shop.

On the day the larger river stones had been delivered, Steve had arrived home early. Diana had been chatting with the Clays, nearby neighbours, who were still living in the house they'd purchased as newlyweds.

"Steve, you look worn out," Diana commented as he struggled out of his car, his arms full of files. "Why don't you take a break? I can finish laying these."

"Don't be such a tease, Diana." Mrs Clay gave her shoulder a playful punch. "You promised to help prune my roses."

"I'd give you a hand there, Steve, but I'm afraid my days of strength and vigour are beyond me," Mr Clay offered. "Home improvements are a young man's game."

"I'm fine, Diana, don't fuss," Steve responded, his face a little pinker. "I'll drop these inside to go over later, and change. Besides, you look too good to mess up." Though his tone was right, his smile did not reach his eyes.

When Diana returned, the edging was incomplete and Steve was gone. The unused stones formed an unattractive rock cairn at the end of the drive. Diana chose the ones with the most pleasing shape, evenly distributing them up one side of the driveway and down the other, admiring how their linear progression drew perpendicular lines with the road. Inside, Steve was waiting for her in his usual place at the dining table, pencil in hand, notebook and calculator laid out in front of him.

"I've gone over the numbers." He chewed on the corner of his lower lip, a sign she took to mean he was happy with his calculations.

"And?" Diana saw he'd underestimated the hours she'd spent digging and levelling the driveway in preparation for trailer after trailer load of stones.

"Well, I still think it could've waited, but by doing the job ourselves we've saved a small fortune," he said, smiling up at her.

The sharp edge of a broken river stone cut into her clenched fist. She shoved it deeper into the pocket of her jacket. "I guess that's why they call it a labour of love," she replied.

After dinner, Diana left Steve busy with his numbers and went downstairs. The cellar shelves read like a time capsule of home improvements; the cleaning equipment, paint, and now a handful of pebbles and the broken river stone. Each new contribution was a shrine to the tasks completed, with the remaining space on the shelves a promise of more to come.

Diana pulled into the carport, barely wide enough for two cars, even when she parked far to the right. Steve had complained that he struggled to open the doors wide enough; though as far as she could tell her stack of marking was just as great as the pile of papers he lugged home each night.

From the carport, the quickest way inside was through the laundry room, but Diana preferred to check their mailbox first. The short trip to the grass verge gave her a chance to smile and wave at the local dog walkers and pram pushers. Often someone would stop to compliment her on the improvements being made to the house. In the brief time they'd lived here, she'd met most of her neighbours and knew the rest by sight.

"Diana, I'm glad I caught you." Mrs Stillwater cradled a Bichon Frisé in her arms while her Dachshund sniffed and scratched around the base of the mailbox. "It's really late notice, but I wanted to invite you over to meet our informal neighbourhood watch group."

"I'd love to. When?" Diana knelt and rubbed the small dog between its ears, gently pushing it off her lawn and away from the temptation of peeing on her mailbox.

"Tonight? About seven?" Mrs Stillwater put the Bichon on the ground, clipping a lead to its collar.

"Thank you, that sounds great. But it's our anniversary tonight. Perhaps another time?" Diana tilted the box in her hand to display a store-bought cake decorated in yellow and white sugar flowers.

"Happy anniversary! I'll give you more notice next time. Everyone wants to hear what you've been up to, but they can wait." Mrs Stillwater pulled her dogs to follow. "You have such good ideas."

Diana waited until they were out of sight before bobbing down to check there was no damage to repair, another reason she would never have a pet.

Along the path to the front door, Diana stooped to free late daffodils trapped within the hedged hebes and pluck unwary weeds threatening to disrupt her careful arrangement. Steve had argued that the plants were an unnecessary cost, and maintaining a garden would take more time than mowing a strip of lawn every couple of weeks. It had taken her a fortnight of gentle persuasion to convince him that with the cuttings and bulbs from the neighbours, and the use of some old pavers she'd found in the cellar, there wouldn't be any additional costs to their household budget. She'd even suggested that she do the mowing so there'd be no extra burden on his time. Besides, the regular exercise saved her a gym membership. Putting in the vegetable garden and small orchard in the back yard had been an easier sell. After all, hadn't they already reaped the benefit to the total of their weekly shop from what little they were gifted from her mother's garden?

At the sound of ringing, Diana scrambled through her purse, hunting for her phone and house key. The key was attached to a silver fob in the shape of a needlepoint with the words 'home is where the heart is'; a housewarming gift from her mother. She loved the weighted feel of it in her hand, a reminder of what waited for her at the end of every day.

"Hello? Can you wait a sec? I just got home." Diana carefully closed the door, putting the key in a glass dish on the hall table and her purse on a hook in the hall closet, before returning her phone to her ear. "The paint? Oh, the interior paint. Yes, thank you it was just as you promised. Fast-drying and no smell." She carried the cake through the living room towards the kitchen. "The colour match was brilliant; my husband didn't even notice the difference. He probably thought all they needed was a wipe down with some sugar soap." Her laughter froze in her throat at the sight of the dining table revealing that Steve had not been as considerate. Under the spotlight of the afternoon sun pouring across the table, Diana saw a score of pen strokes marking the softwood like hieroglyphics for the blind. "Yes, I'm happy to recommend your services. Thank you." When she hung up, she thought of Steve telling her that he was glad to have married a teacher; that every holiday she worked on the house was like getting a refund on his taxes. It was clearly evident that he was careless with his praise as he was with everything other than his career.

Diana's mother was a great source of information for any improvements which required more skill than she had. Even so, Diana knew that major changes, a new kitchen and bathroom, would have to wait, but that didn't stop her from changing the colour of the cupboards or replacing tiles on walls and floors. On the weekends, when Steve insisted on sleeping in before spending the day watching TV, she would visit second-hand stores and reclamation depots. Along with furniture she refurbished, she found beautiful handcrafted tiles, works of art, which with little effort made her kitchen and bathroom look brand new.

"Haven't you started dinner yet? I'm starving." Diana winced as Steve kicked the laundry door closed and dumped his laptop on the vandalised dining table. "I need to get a head-start on this lot, so I can't help." He gestured towards the piles of papers spilling out of his briefcase.

"In a minute." She resists the urge to point out the damage to the table top; tonight is a celebration. "I stopped to pick up the grout and the rest of the tiles on the way home. Could you bring them in for me? They're really heavy."

"Guess that's why you married me; to tote and carry." He headed for the front door, scooping up her car keys on the way.

"Oh, that was definitely one of the reasons," she whispers. "I'll get started on dinner while you put them in the cellar for me."

The cellar had been an unexpected bonus. The real estate agent had started the tour with the benefits of being close to public transport, shops and schools, but had quickly realised that those wouldn't be selling points for Steve. The low maintenance, square footage, and the large yard with a possibility of subdivision if the housing crisis continued, were the real drawcards. When the cellar was mentioned, Diana knew this was the house she could make into a home. While Steve went outside to visualise a shared driveway and space for a second dwelling, she climbed down the stairs into the cellar. The railing wobbled under her hand and the third step creaked— a weakness requiring attention—but it was dry and warm, lit by narrow windows that needed cleaning. Against one wall, a set of shelves housed leftover odds from the previous owner. Along the other wall, pale outlines of missing tools hung like the two-dimensional ghosts waiting to be brought back to life. Under the stairs, a well-oiled door led to the back. Once outside, she saw it was built into a slope that fell away from house towards one of the neighbour's; hidden from both the back and front yard. When she returned upstairs, Steve had been interrogating the real estate agent on his commission, lawyers' fees, insurance. The realtor wore a look of defeat and all it took was for her to quietly remind Steve that her mother had given them the deposit and they could easily afford mortgage payments between them with his new job. She'd even pay the insurance herself. After all, it was easier if one person was responsible for all of the incidentals that came with owning a home.

The window over the kitchen sink gave a great view over the extensive backyard and the surrounding neighbourhood. The subdivision had been put on hold when the costs came in. Steve had fumed about red tape and council interference. She'd agreed with him that it was a shame. They'd just have to make the best of it; they could always subdivide later. They were still young. Besides, the yard was great for entertaining now that the deck was finished.

"Do you want one?" Steve gave the beer a little shake in her direction. "We still have a few left over."

"Thanks. Dinner won't be ready for an hour." She waited as he unscrewed the lid and poured the beer into a glass. She would have preferred to drink it straight from the bottle, but Steve didn't know that. "I'll just go pick some flowers for the table."

Steve had never explained why he had invited the men from work. He had sprung his invitation to dinner leaving her to throw something together at the last minute. The three men had driven over together with a designated driver, having brought a box of beers each and one for the house.

"This is great," the one called David said. Diana winced when he scoured the deck as he dragged a chair closer to the picnic table. "So, you've done all the work yourself?" His question was aimed at Steve, who just nodded.

"We'll you've done a great job on this furniture. Must've saved yourself a bomb." Diana can't remember what the other two men were called: Mike and Phil possibly. They were the ones that insisted on seeing the cellar, *the man cave*; all four of them tromping down the stairs while she finished dinner and set the table. She could easily her hear their raised voices through the floor boards.

"Nah mate, you've got it all wrong," one of them had said. "Too bloody tidy by half, and look at these tools, you want to rough them up a bit if you want people to believe you've done it all yourself."

The breadknife slipped, its serrated teeth biting into her finger and leaving a trail of blood across the loaf.

"You know what they say about that man who dies with the most toys." That had been David. She whispered the expected response under her breath as she washed the blood off the cutting board and applied a band aid. "They win."

Steve's laugh didn't match the others' and he spent the rest of the evening forcing the conversation away from the house, the food, his marriage. That was the last time they'd had guests over.

"Too busy," he'd told her. "Besides, I think it's unprofessional to be too friendly with the competition. I could be their boss one day soon."

The sun was setting when she returned to the kitchen and poured the rest of her beer into the sink; the thick head spoilt the taste.

"Dinner's ready. Can you make some space?" She arranged the lilies from the garden into a vase and carried them into the dining room.

"What's the occasion?" Steve shuffled his papers over, making room for the placemats and flowers.

"It's our anniversary." She set down the plates and returned to the kitchen to grab him another beer.

"No, it's not." He saved his work and leaned his laptop against the wall.

"Of when we bought the house. One year today," she reminded him.

"Oh, is that all?" He caught her frown and added, "This looks great. Thank you."

"The broccoli's from the garden. I couldn't decide between that or the marrows. We have too many really. I'm going to ask my mother if I can bottle them…and the tomatoes. Make a store of them in the cellar." She found it difficult to keep the conversation going. Steve never wanted to hear about her job or any of the changes she'd made to the house.

"That all sounds great. As long as I don't have to help." Steve stuffed in one forkful after the next while his eyes twitched compulsively from his food to his pile of work.

"No. Of course you don't." She stood and took his empty plate, placing it on top of her own half eaten dinner. "Would you like dessert now?"

"Maybe later. I've really got to get this work done if I don't want to be up all night." He swiped the crumbs from the table and redistributed his work, taking up every space.

"Okay, later then." She made a note to wash the floor in the morning, after he was gone. "I've got a couple of jobs to do; so just call out when you're ready."

She'd gotten used to skipping the third step and using the wall to her right rather than the railing, but now that the second bedroom was finished they had her full attention. So focused on the job in hand, she hadn't realised Steve had been calling her name for some time.

"Diana, where the hell are you?" he yelled from the top of the stairs.

"Coming," she replied, setting her tools down and stepping out of her sawdust-covered overalls. She found him pacing in front of the second bedroom, his face almost purple with rage and his hands clenched at his sides.

"What do you mean by this?" He swung open the bedroom door revealing the bright yellow wallpaper, bordered with a frieze of daisies and ducklings.

"Why are you so angry? We talked about it." She watched warily as he paced from one side of the room to the other.

"Yes, we talked about this and you agreed we weren't ready." He slammed a fist against the crib, shunting it into the dresser and knocking over an artfully posed trio of farm animals. "This isn't like choosing curtains and then changing your mind because they didn't look right once you hung them up."

"Stop shouting at me, Steve." Diana stepped in front of the toys to save them from further harm.

"Diana, this decision will affect both our lives. Forever. You're just going to have to get rid of it." He stares pointedly at her still flat stomach.

"I made the crib." Her voice trembled as she stroked the smoothly-sanded baby bed.

Steve's voice softened. "I didn't mean get rid of the crib. We can put it away, for later. When we can afford it. Besides, this house is barely big enough for two."

"I'm sorry, Steve. I thought you were ready. The house is done and you're doing well at work." She rearranged the soft toys; clustered together for comfort.

"I'm not doing well enough for this," Steve said. "Why don't you go to bed and I'll put this stuff in the cellar? I'll even help you repaint the walls and after...well, afterwards we'll doing something, just the two of us."

"No, it's okay. I'll help." Diana picked up one end of the crib, letting Steve walk backwards towards the cellar door. "I've been doing some work down there, too."

"Great. I'd love to see it." He took the first two steps without looking. It was just a little push, but his foot didn't find the third step, the one she'd removed for repairs. He dropped the crib and reached out to grab the railing; the one that was lying on the workbench drying from a fresh coat of paint.

He might have survived the fall if the workbench had been further away, but Steve was not the only one good with numbers. His head hit the corner with a sickening crunch.

Diana smiled. "You're right as always, Steve. This house is only big enough for two."

WHY I HATE CAKE
Paul Mannering

Kids do the stupidest things. Dares are a sacred rite of passage for all children. Do something insane to prove your courage, improve your cool and stand out from your peers. I did all kinds of stupid things growing up on the farm. I jumped off shed roofs, crossed bull paddocks wearing a red T-shirt, rode boars and rams, I even peed on an electric fence.

I don't recommend the last one.

We ate things on dares too. Particularly the larvae of a winged beetle called the Huhu (sounds like who-who). These grubs grow to about the size of your thumb and they eat dead wood so they taste almost exactly like peanut butter doesn't. I always liked to fry mine first, having seen a friend run around screaming with one of these blind maggots attached to his lip by its wood-munching mandibles when he tried to eat one raw.

Being on a farm, both my parents worked from dawn till well after dark. Us kids got used to looking after ourselves and were pretty adept at cooking and most chores from a very young age.

Mum did have one tradition, each Christmas season (in the middle of summer down here for us) she would make a Christmas cake. A huge, rich, heavy slab of spiced cake, filled with nuts and dried fruit and other things. The cake would then be iced with marzipan and royal icing, two layers, so when you cut it, the cake looked like a cross section of a cliff face. This cake was indestructible, and almost indigestible. It would sit in the darkest corner of the cool and shady pantry stored in a wooden cupboard on a large tray, then it would be hacked at for months until it was finally gone, leaving nothing but the smell of cinnamon and spices and candied fruit in its wake like a cake ghost. Mum always refused to make these cakes at any other time of the year. She was usually too busy to bake so we looked forward to Christmas for this treat.

One year, I was around seven years old, and the cake had been made. I was a growing lad and had fallen in love with the soft chewy consistency of the thick double layer almond and marzipan icing and the storm of nutty-fruit flavours of the moist cake. On a child's whim, I snuck into the dark pantry, leaving the light off to hide my criminal intent. I opened the cupboard and reached into to touch the iceberg of a cake that sat there. Picking a small piece of marzipan off, a tiny piece, not likely to be missed. Oh it was good…sweet and chewy and fine. Fearing discovery, I fumbled the cupboard door shut and slipped out of the pantry.

The next day I went back and with my fingers I tore a piece off and ate that too, then the next day, then twice the day after that. Soon I was visiting that cake regularly. There in the dark of the pantry, I would reach in, squish a handful of cake together in my fist, and then gorge on it, crunching and chewing, the nuts and fruit and heavy cake goodness.

It was my guilty pleasure until one day we had visitors. Mum prepared coffee and went to the pantry to get the cake. Her cry of "Bloody Hell!" tore through the summer air and chilled me to the bone. I knew I was in for a hiding when she found out it was me who had nibbled the cake to ruins.

Biting my lip and clenching my buttocks in preparation for the spanking that would come, I fronted up. Mum was red-faced with anger. She was holding the cake platter, upon which the cake lay broken and torn like fallen masonry. I waited for the hammer to fall. Her face was taut with rage and disgust. This was going to sting.

"Bloody mice!" she raged. "Bloody mice chewed through the cupboard and demolished the cake!"

I felt elation. Yes! An alibi! A suspect, a fall guy someone else to blame! I brightened considerably. "Really?" I came closer for a curious look. Mice were one of those fascinating phenomena to young boys.

A small round hole had been gnawed through the corner of the cupboard. The mice had been quite at home there; an abandoned nest at the back, and the area around where the cake had stood was awash with tiny mouse droppings. Mum took the tray out of the pantry and went to find store-bought biscuits for the visitors instead. I stayed in the pantry, Mum had turned on the light of course, and that showed a scene of carnage.

Among the scattered clumps and crumbs of torn cake there were the small pink jelly remains of several baby mice. None of the tiny corpses were complete, each had been at least half eaten. So small and hairless, juicy and crunchy with a consistency like dried fruit and Christmas cake nuts.

THE MYSTERIOUS MR MONTAGUE
Jane Percival

I never eat pork. It's not that I'm vegetarian, or Jewish or Muslim, it's all to do with something that happened in the 70s, when I was fifteen years old.

As a kid, I had a fascination with meat. I have an early memory of accompanying Mum to our local butcher's and being given a fat, pink saveloy. She lifted me up onto the counter and I sat there munching on the sausage, looking around wide-eyed. I liked the smell of meat and sawdust. There was a plastic ribbon curtain dividing the shop front from the rest of the premises, and I caught glimpses of strange shapes when the strips moved in the breeze.

My uncles, Eddie and John, owned a butcher shop in Kilbirnie. On a visit when I was about ten, they took me through to the back to show me the other two rooms—a workroom where they processed the meat, and a walk-in cool room. I wandered around, careful not to slip, absorbing every detail...

In the middle of the workroom there was a rectangular wooden block, scrubbed clean and scored with the marks of countless knives. There were also a couple of circular wooden chopping blocks; one had a small hatchet embedded in it. A range of gleaming knives and hacksaws hung from the left-hand wall. There were lidded bins containing mysterious pieces of raw flesh. Strings of pale sausages, looped like intestines, were hanging from the ceiling alongside fat black puddings. On the benches there were shag-pile carpets of tripe waiting to be trimmed, and a huddle of glossy sheep kidneys. Through another door was the cooler and I could see a row of carcasses hanging from huge hooks attached to the ceiling.

There was that 'fleshy-bloody' smell that I now identify with the butchering of meat. I didn't find it repelling. The floor was covered with sawdust, which added a subtle, pine smell to the room.

Later, when I was a teenager, I hung around long enough to be offered a job helping keep the workroom and cooler tidy, and sweeping up the sawdust. After a while, it became accepted that when I'd finished school I'd be taken on as my uncles' apprentice.

One afternoon, I was left alone to mind the shop while my uncles made their deliveries. I was fifteen and in my last year at college. In fact, I'd been trying to drop out for some time, but Mum had insisted I stay on until the end of the fifth form. It was just after 4:00 p.m. and quiet. Most of the housewives had finished their shopping for the day, and it was too soon for the after-work rush of people looking for a last-minute chop or piece of steak for that night's tea. I was in the workroom, trimming some hard fat off a piece of brisket when I heard the ring of the front door bell. I returned to the shop, wiping my hands on my blue and white striped apron. The sprung door slammed shut behind me, but the guy didn't raise his eyes. He was looking intently at the various items displayed in front of the window.

He wasn't someone I'd served before and looked to be roughly the same age as my uncles, in his forties, I suppose, with the kind of thick hair that is dark but fading to silvery grey around the edges. He had olive skin and a neatly trimmed beard, and was wearing a grey three-quarter length woollen overcoat, despite it being a warm November afternoon. His shoes were a well-polished black and he wore matching leather gloves.

His glance rested on the tray of plump black puddings sitting on the counter.

"Do you make your own blood sausage?" His voice was smooth, with the merest hint of an accent.

"Of course. Well, not me, but my uncles do," I responded, thinking this was a stupid question. In those days, butchers didn't sell anything they hadn't made themselves. "It's their shop."

"And they are made using…pigs' blood?"

"Yes, and some barley and oats, herbs…" my voice trailed off. The guy had an odd look on his face. "Why?"

"Are your uncles…in?"

"No, they're out making deliveries. They'll be finished after 5:30 p.m., but we'll be closing around then."

The man stood for a moment, tapping his fingers on the counter. He looked out the window then checked his watch, before turning towards me.

"I'm short of time today, but I'd like to talk to them about their methods." He withdrew a small, white rectangle from his wallet and placed it on the counter. "Can you give them my card?"

With those words, he left.

I watched him walk briskly along Kilbirnie Road until he'd disappeared from view, then retrieved the card from the counter. On it was inscribed 'Saul Montague' in black, with the word 'Facilitator' written below in a cursive script. There was a local phone number. I propped it up on the shelf behind the counter next to the jars of pickled onions, then immediately forgot about it.

It wasn't until I was sitting in class the following afternoon that I remembered the card. I felt bad that I hadn't given it to my uncles before finishing the previous day. Perhaps they'd found it already.

After school I hurried to the shop. Opening the door, I was relieved to see that the card was exactly where I'd left it. I went over and took it down from the shelf. Eddie was serving a woman with a couple of kids. When they'd left, I walked over to him.

"This guy came in yesterday and asked about black puddings. He was a bit odd, but said he'd be in touch with you. He left this."

Eddie read out the word 'Facilitator' then turned the card over. The reverse side was blank.

"Black pudding, did you say?" he queried. "Is that all?"

"Well, he asked if we made it ourselves and if it was made from pigs' blood. But that's all. Sorry I forgot to tell you yesterday."

I had barely finished speaking when the shop doorbell rang again and there he was. I glanced at my watch. It was just after 4:00 p.m. Eddie looked at me with eyebrows raised and I nodded.

Montague went straight up to Eddie, "I see you have my card." He stepped forward and extended his gloved hand. Eddie wiped his palms on his apron, then shook hands with the man.

"I have a proposition for you," said Montague. "Is there anywhere we can talk without interruption?" He didn't acknowledge having met me the previous day, directing all his attention to my uncle. I could hear chopping sounds from the workroom.

"We can go to the back. My brother's out there, too. Are you able to mind the shop, Joe?" Eddie looked my way and it was then that the man turned and stared directly into my eyes. He had an odd expression on his face and didn't avert his gaze when I answered, "Sure."

They left me alone for a decent amount of time. Then the sprung door opened and all three came back into the shop. Montague walked through swiftly and left. Eddie and John stood by the window and watched as he walked down the road.

"Are you still okay in the shop?" asked John.

"Yep," I replied, and my uncles returned to the back room where I could hear them talking. Finally, my curiosity got the better of me and I went through.

"What did he want?" I asked.

John looked at Eddie before responding. "We're not exactly sure."

He explained that Montague had initially enquired about the black puddings; about how often we had deliveries of pigs' blood and how fresh it was, how many puddings it was likely to make, and so on. My uncles had at first thought that he wanted a regular supply of the puddings, perhaps to on-sell. But as the conversation had developed, Montague had seemed more interested in the blood itself.

"He asked us about supplying blood to him on a regular basis," added Eddie. "We said we'd think about it. He told us it would be worth our while, whatever that means. Anyway, he's coming back on Monday, after we've had time to think about it and to come up with some options."

As I helped my uncles with the end of day tidying up tasks, I couldn't help wondering about Montague; what exactly he wanted and what on earth he'd use the blood for. It was a Friday and I had a whole weekend to reflect on it.

By Monday I was still thinking about him. It wasn't just the blood thing that had captured my attention, but the strangeness of Montague himself. After school, I hurried to the shop. Both John and Eddie were serving customers behind the counter. What I really wanted to know was whether Montague had returned and what had been decided, but I didn't know how to broach the question. In the end, I didn't need to. As with his previous two visits, he turned up at the shop just after 4:00 p.m. I was sorting the different meats in the front-of-shop display and made an effort not to stare at him. When I finally raised my eyes, I was disconcerted to see that once again he was looking straight back at me. He had a very direct gaze. I quickly glanced away and focused on re-arranging the mock chicken legs.

Eddie and John finished their sales and ushered Montague through to the workroom. On his way past, Eddie looked at me, raising his eyebrows. I nodded back. The three spent a good twenty minutes talking. At one point, I stood by the sprung door, straining my ears. When I had to go through to fetch Mrs O'Grady's order, they were sitting around the desk where John worked on the accounts; they stopped talking when I came in. Avoiding eye contact, I collected the brown-paper parcel and hastily retreated. It all felt very secretive. Finally, their discussion drew to a close and they came back into the shop. They shook hands and I could see that an agreement of some kind had been reached.

John turned to me. "Mr Montague here is going to be taking collection of some products from us. He has requested that you make the delivery to his premises in person, twice a week after school."

"Okay…" I said.

John went on, "He has a shed down by the bay. Can you go with him now so that you know where it is?"

I was surprised and looked at Eddie. "You go, Joe. It's not far away, it won't take long."

Montague was already half out the door. He barely acknowledged me, so I removed my apron and followed as he walked briskly down the street towards the harbour. In ten minutes, we were at the waterfront area where a scattering of small boats and yachts, and two or three fishing vessels were moored.

The slight curve of Evans Bay was dotted with small boatsheds and a couple of larger, covered dry docks. Seagulls wheeled overhead as we approached, and some kids were fishing further down the wharf. There was the tangy smell of salt water and rust. Barnacles clung to the wharf posts, just below the water line.

Montague led me to a boatshed positioned at the end of its own small jetty. Green paint was peeling from the walls in several places and the windows were grimy and didn't offer a glimpse of what was within. The door was shut tightly and locked securely with three large padlocks. Montague withdrew a decent-sized keyring from his coat pocket and, using a different key for each padlock, unlocked them. They were well-lubricated and opened easily.

"Wait here." He went into the boatshed and returned almost immediately with a one-gallon steel milk pail, complete with lid. He handed it to me. "This is what I want you to use. You can bring it here after 4:30 p.m. on the agreed days. I'll be here to collect it from you." He turned away.

"Mr Montague…"

"What is it, boy?"

"Nothing." He was locking up the door and raised his head to look at me.

"That's all right, then. I'll see you next Tuesday." He returned the keys to his pocket, turned, and walked away in the opposite direction.

Carrying the bucket, I made my way back to the shop. I knew I'd look stupid walking along the road with it and hoped that I didn't run into any of my classmates.

Reading this, you may well think that so far, my story is of no great interest, but it is difficult to convey in words the strangeness of Mr Montague himself. I was only fifteen; my mind was alive with ideas of adventure and strange happenings. I had recently been reading Edgar Allan Poe and Bram Stoker, and my brain was humming with questions and suspicions.

My uncles didn't really expand upon the arrangement they'd come to with Montague. And because of their reticence, I didn't raise it either. So, it became something of a secret.

When that first Tuesday came around, the pail was full and ready to be delivered when I arrived at the shop after school. At 4:30 p.m. I collected the pail from the workroom—the blood was so fresh that the outside of the bucket was warm to the touch—then carried it down the road to Montague's boatshed. It was heavy and awkward to carry and kept bumping into the sides of my legs. I had to change hands several times and was left with red marks on my palms after the delivery. I could see that I'd have to find a different way to carry it if possible.

Montague was waiting outside as arranged. I greeted him, handed over the bucket then stood awkwardly, waiting for his response.

"Thank your uncles from me," was all he said. His look told me it was the end of the conversation so I headed off, but after a few steps I turned back.

"The bucket…I'll need it for the next delivery."

"I dropped off another at your uncles' shop. When you bring the next one, I can exchange it for an empty one."

"Oh." I headed back along the road. The sun was beginning to drop behind the hills and it was cool in the shade. When I looked back, the boatshed was in shadow, the door and windows tightly shut.

Delivery days were Tuesdays and Fridays. It was December and getting close to Christmas. School had closed for the year, and I was finished with it for good. John and Eddie had talked to Mum and it had been decided that I'd start work 'officially' in the third week of January. I still came in to the shop for a few hours each day, usually in the afternoons, and had attached a wooden crate to the front of an old bike for the blood deliveries. As long as I avoided bumps, this seemed to work okay. It wasn't long before my curiosity about what Montague was up to got the better of me. I decided to do a bit of investigation of my own.

On the last Friday before Christmas, after delivering the blood and returning the empty pail to the shop, I quickly retraced my route on foot. It was summer and would still be light for a couple more hours. I ordered some fish and chips from the shop across the road from the wharves, then sat to eat them on a park bench in the adjacent children's playground, partly hidden from Montague's shed by a couple of straggly trees. A bunch of seagulls appeared as soon as they saw me and vied for a position at my feet. There I sat, partly in the shade of the trees, watching, savouring the hot, salty chips.

I didn't have to wait long. After about ten minutes the door to the boatshed opened and Montague came out. As usual, he was wearing his woollen overcoat, suit trousers and shiny black shoes. I could see him quite clearly through the vegetation. He'd closed the door and was about to lock the padlocks when he stopped, opened the door again, and peered in. He seemed to be talking to someone. This I didn't expect. I wondered who or what on earth was locked inside. It didn't make sense and I felt a prickling on my spine.

I sat there for a bit, not sure what to do next. I weighed up asking my uncles about him again, but knew there'd be no point. I finished my meal and shook out the paper. The gulls fought over the last scraps, and a cool breeze started up. I gazed northwards along the bay towards Wellington Harbour. The road wound around the suburbs and back towards Oriental Bay. I was almost certain that this was the way Montague had walked, but I wasn't one hundred percent sure. I had the feeling that he wouldn't be pleased to find me poking about near his boatshed...but after seeing him talk to someone behind those padlocked doors, I was more intrigued than ever. I decided to double-back along the road a bit, then turn around and walk back to the shed, as if I was arriving for the first time. That way, if Montague did reappear, he'd think I'd only just arrived. I was sure I could invent some reason or other to explain my presence.

Five minutes later I was on the wharf, surveying Montague's shed more closely. I realised that despite its run-down exterior, it was actually in really good shape. The items lying on the wharf around it—the heavy metal hooks, rusted chains, even an unravelling fishing net—now seemed contrived, as if added for effect. A shiny steel flue rose from the left front corner of the roof above the curling red paint of the corrugated iron. I surveyed the area. The kids fishing at the other end of the wharf were packing up their gear, and traffic was building up on Kilbirnie Road. At that very moment, the sun slipped behind Mt Victoria. Across Evans Bay, a golden light rose up the hills behind the Shelly Bay Air Force Base, leaving the harbour edge in dusky shade. A gust of cool wind swept along the wharf and the seagulls rose in unison and flew squawking into the last of the sunlight.

I walked around the three sides of the shed. The fourth side had a ramp leading down to the water. It was high tide and the water lapped halfway up the ramp. Unlike the remainder of the shed, the ramp was clearly in disrepair, its door nailed shut with battens. Someone had used white paint to roughly write the words 'The Larch' diagonally across it.

I was about to peer through one of the windows when I felt a hand grip my shoulder. I jumped involuntarily then half-turned.

"Looking for something?"

"I…" My face flushed hot with embarrassment.

"Have you ever heard the phrase 'curiosity killed the cat'?" Montague's accented voice was cool.

"Yes. But…that's all it was. I was just curious. I didn't mean any harm."

Still gripping my shoulder, Montague twisted me around to face him. With a frown on his face he slowly looked me up and down. My shoulder hurt and I was afraid. I was tall for my age, but Montague was taller, his figure imposing. I could sense a muscular frame beneath his coat. Of course, now I see that he was in the prime of life, but at the age of fifteen, anyone over thirty seemed old.

I was weighing up whether I could escape from his grasp when he finally spoke. "I was going to drag you back to your uncles, but perhaps you can be of use. Can I trust you, boy?"

"Yes. I—I think so."

His face relaxed a little. With a sigh he let go of my shoulder, giving me a small shove as he did so. "Well, we'd better have a talk. Inside."

He reached into his pocket and passed me his keys. "Open the locks. Use the three Yale keys."

With shaking hands, I tried to unlock the first padlock. After a couple of unsuccessful attempts, Montague took over. He indicated that I should go in first, but I was no longer that keen to see what was inside. I cast my eyes along the wharf, and across to the street beyond. There were no actual people, kids or otherwise, in sight—just cars driving past. No-one would hear if I called for help.

I turned the handle and pushed open the door.

It was dark inside. The glass in the windows was opaque and little of the early evening light could penetrate. It was uncomfortably warm and I noticed the glow of a pot belly stove in the corner to the left of the door. Montague switched on the light.

The sight that met my eyes was totally unexpected. The interior had been completely refurbished. The walls and ceiling were shiny white, and the floor, also white, was tiled. The corner diagonally opposite had been partitioned off, the interior hidden by a single blue curtain hanging from a metal rod. I could hear the regular beep of a monitor of some kind, and there were several items of unfamiliar equipment in the room. One of the buckets was on the floor by the partition, empty. I looked around.

It reminded me of a hospital ward. The wall facing the harbour, where there once would have been large doors leading to the ramp, was completely sealed. A wide, waist-high bench ran around two-thirds of the room, into which a stainless-steel double sink was set. There was a small, white refrigerator and a large wooden desk positioned against the sealed doors, and a couple of chrome and vinyl swivel chairs. The desk was stacked with a few books and some tidy piles of papers. I noticed an open spiral-bound diary, covered with lines of tight writing in black ink.

"What do you think?" Montague was looking for a reaction. I tried to remain calm, but he would have seen my surprise.

"What is this place for?" I couldn't help but ask the obvious. It was a lot to take in.

"This, dear boy, is my laboratory. It is equipped with the latest medical and scientific equipment. My work involves the study of life itself."

Our conversation was interrupted by the sound of coughing from beyond the blue curtain. As it died away, the beeping of the machine seemed even louder.

Montague scrutinised me. "I'm about to reveal something to you, boy. I want your word that what you are about to see will be kept between ourselves."

I looked him in the eye. "My name's Joe."

"I know your name. I want your word."

"You have it." It had been so easy to agree, but I hadn't known what I was agreeing to.

Upon this, he walked briskly to the curtain and drew it aside. I stepped closer and saw a high, single bed, made up with snowy white linen. Beneath the covers lay a young woman. A large, dull-green enamelled machine of some kind, set on casters, was positioned next to her supine form. A clear plastic tube rose up to the top of a shiny metal stand, then down again, all the way to the invalid. Halfway along the tube was a clear, plastic cylinder, three quarters filled with bright blood, which fed directly into a vein on her bare right forearm.

I had taken all this in with my first glance, but my eyes were drawn to the sleeping figure. She was tucked in securely, with only her right arm exposed. Although asleep, she appeared restless; her lips moved as if she was having a conversation in her dreams. A tangle of long, auburn hair spread across the pillow, framing her face. There were purple shadows under her eyes and translucent skin pulled tightly over her cheekbones. She didn't look well.

"What's wrong with her?" I asked.

"This is Maria. She has a…rare disease…and I am in the process of implementing a cure."

"If she's sick, shouldn't she be in hospital?"

"A hospital cannot help her, boy."

I looked back at Maria. I couldn't help thinking that there was something very wrong with the whole situation.

Montague replaced the curtain and walked to the other side of the room, indicating that I should sit down beside him. It was then that he offered me a job. He explained that he was run off his feet with collecting and delivering the various items associated with his projects and could use the help.

At first, I refused, but he was very persuasive, explaining that it would only take a few hours a week, perhaps ten at the most. I could fit the errands around my butcher duties, once I started my apprenticeship. Additionally, he offered me a very good hourly rate. He reiterated that his work was sensitive and I understood that this wasn't the type of work I'd discuss with anyone else, not even my uncles.

And so, it began. On Tuesdays when I dropped off the blood, he would tell me when he needed me to call by during the following week. On the occasions that he had an errand for me to run, he'd invite me in, but only briefly, and I didn't get another chance to see the girl, Maria, for many weeks. By then it was too late. As for the fresh pigs' blood, I felt certain it had everything to do with Maria. I often found myself wondering if she was still gravely ill, or if her health was improving.

After I'd been running Montague's errands for more than a month, he provided me with a set of the padlock keys, emphasising that they were only to be used in a case of *extreme* emergency. I realised that he trusted me.

Around the third week in March, everything changed. It was a Tuesday evening and I turned up at the boatshed with the bucket of blood. When I arrived, I was surprised to see that the padlocks were still in place. I knocked on the door, then looked around, to see if Montague had left a note, but there was nothing. I took out my keys, aware that my heart had begun to beat faster.

I pushed open the door. It was dark inside, and cooler than usual, the only glow coming from a lamp beyond the curtain. I turned on the lights, placed the bucket of blood on the bench, and walked over to the desk, looking over my shoulder, expecting Montague to show up at any moment. There wasn't a note there, either. By now my heart was racing and my one thought was that this was my chance to check on Maria.

With trepidation I walked over to the curtain and drew it back a little from the corner. There she was, propped up a little in the bed studying a picture book held in her left hand. She looked up, clearly startled to see me. I was struck by the colour of her eyes. They were a very dark brown, almost black, but with a ruby hue. Her skin had a pinkish tinge, as if she were feverish.

"Hi," I said. "I've brought the blood for Mr Montague. He's not here so I've left it on the bench."

She didn't say anything.

"You must be Maria. I'm Joe."

Maria's eyes were fixed on me, watching every movement. She seemed to be glued to the bed, with her right arm still attached to the transfusion tube. I was absolutely sure now that this was what it was.

There was no way to tell how much blood was left in the machine, but it appeared that it was fed in from the top through a stainless-steel funnel type arrangement. I noticed a small glass bottle of transparent liquid also feeding into the machine, inscribed with the hand-written words 'antigen suppressant'.

Maria opened her mouth as if to speak, but the effort must have been too much for her as she fell back upon her pillow, breathing in short gasps, her body trembling. I realised there was no point in asking her any more questions as my presence seemed to be making her agitated. She had started to quiver uncontrollably.

I wasn't sure what to do, so I scribbled a note on the back of an envelope and left it on Montague's desk. Other than that, I could only wait for him to get in touch with me. If nothing else, he'd need to give me the list of days he wanted me to come in for the next week. As I made my departure, turning off the lights on the way, I touched the pot belly. It was quite cold.

When Thursday arrived and Montague still hadn't contacted me, I was starting to wonder. I decided to visit the boatshed during my lunch hour on the off-chance that he might be there.

When I drew nearer, my heart sank as I saw the padlocks were still in place. I let myself in. There was no sign that Montague had been back, and the air was stale and smelt of decay. I could hear the machine beeping urgently from the corner. Almost too afraid to look, I made my way over and drew aside the curtain.

Maria was lying in the bed, barely conscious. The transfusion tube had dried up and the entry point in her forearm was inflamed. The bottle of clear fluid feeding into the machine was empty. I stood there, paralysed with uncertainty. Finally, I wet a rag under the tap and wiped her brow, but she barely moved. The bucket of blood was still sitting on the bench where I'd left it. I lifted the lid and wasn't surprised to see that it had started to go bad. I emptied it into the sink and rinsed it out.

I went over to Montague's desk, hoping to find some clue as to what he was up to with Maria. My note was still there, of course. Sifting through his papers I noted that his correspondence was mostly associated with orders for medical supplies and an exchange of ethical ideas with (what I assumed was) a colleague in Germany. The spiral notepad was nowhere to be seen.

It was then that I noticed an old book Montague had left on his desk. It was lying open and had thick yellowing pages, with lines of ornate Gothic script. The page to the left had the heading, *'Blōd, Pigge and Seolf'*. On the right was a simple illustration depicting three figures—two men and a pig. One of the men was standing over the other, who was lying on a bed. The unfortunate pig was strapped to a bench alongside. It appeared that the pig's throat had been slit; the blood was squirting out and being collected in a container. I had no idea what it meant and quickly shut the book.

When I returned to Maria's bedside, her eyes were open, but she didn't seem aware of her surroundings. I decided to straighten up the bedding and, as I did, the sheets came away from the side of the bed. I pulled them back to smooth them out and was concerned to see that she was restrained by three leather belts, at the chest, waist and hips. Looking further, I noticed two red rubber tubes leading from beneath the hem of her simple white gown to a couple of bags similar in size and appearance to hot water bottles, tucked into a bracket at the end of the bed. They looked full. By this time, I was shaking all over. Then my eyes focused on the unfathomable. Maria's gown had risen up a little. Instead of feet peeping out below the hem, I saw two pig's trotters. I thought my heart would leap from my breast.

I quickly pulled the bedding back and tucked it in securely. It was time to leave; I had no idea what to do.

That evening I went to the library to check the newspapers from the previous few days. I found what I was seeking on page three of the Wednesday edition of *The Evening Post*. It was a brief item about a man's body having been found washed up at Shelly Bay. It stated that the deceased was bearded, aged around forty to fifty and had been clad in a heavy woollen coat. There was no indication of wrong-doing and it was suspected that he'd fallen out of a boat or off a wharf and had been weighed down by the coat and had subsequently drowned. Police had requested that people come forward if they had any information.

The next day I told my uncles about Montague's non-appearance and the item in the newspaper, leaving out any mention of what I'd found in the boatshed. I needed time to think everything through. They suggested that if he still didn't show on Friday, we should contact the Police.

On Friday when I biked down to the shed with the fresh pigs' blood, I was almost certain it would be for the last time. I unlocked the door and was hit with an overpowering smell of stale bodily fluids. Horrible grunting noises were coming from the corner and I had to force myself to investigate.

When I pulled back the curtain, I saw that my worst fears had been realised. The creature that had once been Maria had diminished in size. The head and face were distorted. A few coarse, white whiskers had sprung up around its jowls and the teeth were exposed behind a scary grin. The tube had come away from its front leg—for a leg it clearly was—and the picture book was lying partly-chewed on the floor. The creature had been thrashing around on the bed and what was left of the beautiful auburn hair was a matted mess, most of it lying in tangled clumps on the pillow. The rubber tubes had disconnected and the bedding was badly soiled. The creature was emitting plaintive grunting noises and clearly wanted to escape. Its dark eyes looked at me wildly.

This time I knew what I had to do. It's not that I *wanted* to do it, but the creature was obviously in severe distress. God only knew what Montague had done to it during the course of his experiments.

With a heavy heart, I left Montague's boatshed and made my way back to the shop. Once there I collected my new set of butchering knives, honing my best boning knife until it was razor sharp, before packing them up in my leather satchel. Then I walked back to the harbour, all the while thinking about the image in the old book I'd seen on Montague's desk.

It was a simple matter to dispatch Maria. She was already restrained, after all. Before attempting the task, I removed all the bedding from under her body and positioned the stainless-steel bucket beneath the bed to collect the blood. As I gripped her head to hold it still and raised my knife, I swear that her eyes looked as human as they had before her body had reverted to its original self.

Before I left, I retrieved the old book from Montague's desk and screwed up the note I'd left for him. I put both into my satchel with the knives.

Later that day, I asked my uncles to sit themselves down, explaining that I had something serious to discuss with them. I updated them on how Montague had asked me to run errands for him, and how he'd been conducting experiments on a pig in that boatshed.

They weren't as surprised as they might have been. I suspected that Montague had been paying them *extremely* well and that despite their reservations, they'd appreciated the money. I also told them about how the poor pig had been strapped to a bed and neglected since Montague's disappearance. I then explained that I'd taken it upon myself to kill the poor animal and that I needed to dispose of the remains.

The three of us took the butcher's van down to the boatshed. I let my uncles in and they carried the carcass out to the back of the vehicle. John commented that it was a poor specimen of a pig, and would only be good for making sausages. I stuffed the bedding into a large plastic bag and we took the mattress, too, as there was a fair bit of blood on it. I locked up the shed for the last time.

And that should have been the end of the story.

After about a month had passed, I rang the police to report Montague as missing. A couple of constables came by to interview me, with my uncles sitting in. We showed them Montague's card and I explained that I had delivered blood to Montague twice weekly and that I sometimes ran other errands for him. I left out the bit about having access to his shed, or about seeing the pig. I told them that we hadn't seen sight or sound of Montague since sometime in February. That we'd had to throw out three buckets of perfectly good fresh blood that we hadn't been paid for.

After the interview, I accompanied the police to Evans Bay to show them the boatshed. They called for help and were able to break the locks on the door. Inside, the room was exactly as I'd left it. I could see that the constables were more than a little surprised at the interior. I stood by as they gaped, until one looked up, saw me, and told me I could go.

The police contacted me again a few days later. They felt certain that our description of Montague matched that of an unidentified person who'd been found drowned in the harbour in March. I feigned surprise. They thanked me for coming forward as they were glad to have that mystery solved. They were now hoping for information about his next of kin.

Two months later, I had my final call from the police. They'd located Montague's next of kin, a sister in England. She had only just reported him missing after not having received any correspondence for a couple of months. They asked me if I'd ever seen anyone else with Montague.

"No. Never. Why?"

"It seems that Mr Montague was taking care of his niece, Maria. She had a serious ailment. He was apparently working on a cure and she had been placed in his care. Her mother is desperate to hear from her."

"Oh…" I said, my voice weak. "That's terrible."

"Yes. It is. You definitely didn't come across Maria?"

"No. I wouldn't have," I stammered. "I mean, I only made deliveries and ran the odd errand."

"That's a shame. We have no other leads. Well, it seems we are finished here. Ring us straight away if you do think of anything."

"Yes. Of course." As I hung up the phone, I felt bile rise in my throat. That batch of pork sausages had been a great favourite with the customers.

THE NINEVEH
Mouse Diver-Dudfield

E ven before the airlocks to the cryo-sleep chambers disengaged, Jocelyn Parker had smelled the decay in the air. In a daze she sat up, fingers shaking as she pulled the life support pads from her arm and stared about the quiet ship.

Seven days prior to waking, the onboard computer had flooded the ship with oxygen in anticipation of the twenty-five crew members of the Nineveh reaching their destination. What the system had failed to register was that Jocelyn, who was the ship's computer technician, by some miracle, had been the only one to survive the voyage. In that time, the oxygen stabilisation had activated the decomposition in the others' bodies, and finally getting the strength to look, she found her crew, her co-workers and friends, were nothing more than rotting flesh inside their cracked methane gas cryogenic units.

In shock, Jocelyn concentrated on her training. She dressed and, feeling the residual weakness from the sleep process, she made her way to the ship's command-board and ran a diagnosis.

A preliminary search of the ship's logs told her that a hundred and ten years into the Nineveh exploration voyage to the star cluster Pleiades, a corrupt line of code had re-routed life support from her crewmates, leaving only her pod functional. For ninety years, she'd slept with her dead friends at her side, the only spark of life enclosed in a slow-moving tomb.

But all that paled in comparison to what awaited her. Now as she sat, numb, her eyes staring blankly out the large bay windows at the green and grey swirling planet of Tilottama, their mission, she fought to keep her attention on the screen. It was playing the last message from Earth, received sixty-eight years ago, its message clear and simple.

'Do not return. The Earth will be gone.' The stranger, no doubt a third generation operation manager, gave a teary-eyed plea. He instructed the Nineveh to continue with her mission to study Tilottama, make it their new home, and rebuild humanity.

They were all that was left of Earth.

A tear welled in Jocelyn's eyes and she blinked away her building emotions. The operation manager had explained how harnessing the energy from the Earth's core, a process in its infancy when the Nineveh left, had doomed the Earth. The core had split, the man had told her desperately, and their planet had nothing but days left.

The irony was, taking one look at the ship's preliminary search of Tilottama, it was immediately obvious their new home was an uninhabitable gas giant.

From 1.98 billion miles away, the blue haze of water, the pulsation configuration and sound emissions insinuated an atmosphere identical to Earth. So they had assumed. It was a lie, a mirage, and they had fallen for it.

She searched for more communications from Earth, but there was nothing; over half a century of silence. Her resolve faltered, the unbearable smell from her dead friends soaking into her skin, the silence, the death, the utter isolation.

A silent tear fell and she lightly touched the compression injection device laid out neatly in front of her. Two minutes and 35 seconds would be all it would take. The toxic mixture would end her suffering before she'd have time to fully grasp her loss.

Taking the device in hand, she went to the cryo-pod three down from her own and knelt as she wiped the moisture aside from its surface. If she was to administer the lethal dose, she couldn't do it alone. Not without him.

His name was Leo Huáng and he had been a beautiful possibility. The ship's navigator and sole representative of the New China Territory, he and Jocelyn had clicked from the start. Lingering glances and comfortable silences had been a pleasant spark of what was to come.

Through the smeared unit she could make out his hand, resting stiffly at his side, and she placed her palm against the glass. There was so much that could now never be. But they would be together again soon.

With a surge of emotion, she gripped the device, her attention lingering for just a moment on her own reflection in the glass, and slowly, meeting her own sad gaze, she found her hand unconsciously lowering.

Jocelyn could still remember the faces of her parents, disapproving, devastated, mournful. No one had understood her choice to volunteer. She had given it all up, not only her friends and family, but time itself. Four hundred years in total. How incredibly sad that her sacrifice would come to nothing.

It took all her strength to drop the device. The desire to end her torture was unbearable but, for the sake of the others she refused to give in. She could not be the person responsible for the end of all humanity.

Jocelyn didn't know how long her journey would take or if there was anything, or anyone waiting for her at the end. But she had to try.

She stood, stronger now, and with a simple recalibration of the computer, she returned to her cryo-unit. A lot could happen in another two hundred years.

WHAT YOU WISH FOR

I. K. Paterson-Harkness

"Y"ou're not normal," she said.
"And I don't think your father and I
can be held responsible, either."
I said nothing.
We were on our way to visit yet another doctor.

Up ahead the road was blocked.
Orange-vested council workers slouched on shovels,
while some guy holding a stop-go sign
dictated who could go and who could not.
Mum kept looking at her watch, while I
shielded the side of my face from the sun
with the palm of my hand
and lazed back in the seat.

"What? You've done it again!" she exclaimed.
I shoved the beer that had suddenly appeared in my hand
behind my back.
Jeez,
it's not like I'd intentionally conjured the beer;
I'd just felt like it, and there it was.

"Don't try to hide it!" she cried.
"You need to get control of this!
Yesterday you wanted a kitten.
Today you felt like beer.
God, I hope you never want babies!
Rachel, it could be classed as stealing."

I shrugged, and popped the beer's lid.
Mum scowled as I took a swig.
It tasted good.
"How can it be stealing," I asked,
"if I haven't taken anything from anyone?"

"Oh Rachel, please!" Mum blasted her horn as a
motorcyclist raced between the lanes and cut in front of us.
"Use your brain, won't you?
Something can't come from nothing. It can't just be
magicked into existence.
That's a basic law of physics.
You have taken it from somewhere."

I tapped the side of the beer can with my nails and
thought of my kitten.
He was black with white paws and fluffy all over.
He'd even come with a bell on his collar.
"Well, if you got me the things I actually wanted…"

Up ahead the lights went red
like Mum's face when she looked at me.
I think she hated me right then, she basically
spat as she talked.
"Honestly, Rachel." Her voice dropped low.
"How old are you? You know how hard we work for this family.
Do you think we're made of money?"

In reply, I just swallowed, and
shook my head,
but as I did I felt a weight in my lap.
Mum and I both stared at the thick wad of
hundred dollar bills,
folded in half and bound with a thick rubber band
that had just materialised there.

We shared a look.
A long, long look.
"Perhaps we should cancel the next appointment,"
she said.

DANCING WEST TO EAST
Simon Petrie
and Edwina Harvey

Bright-eyed, curly-haired, coffee-skinned young Boland comes bouncing through my door with the insatiable energy of a wallaby. "Can I ride the music bike for you, Nanny Elsie? Can I?"

I pause from the pastry I'm rolling to consider his question, or seem to. "I suppose so," I tell him casually.

He clambers up on to my salvaged exercise bike like Hillary climbing Everest, and I drop the needle of the reclaimed stereo onto the old vinyl record as he starts to pedal.

The dulcet tones of Tim Curry swell out from the speakers and fill the room as he croons "The Brontosaurus". I close my eyes, swaying to the music, remembering a better time lost so long ago. I was younger then, the world was a better place... or so I used to think.

But Boland can't contain himself, he pedals faster and faster, until poor Tim Curry is imitating a chipmunk.

"Boland, no!" I admonish him, but his little face is cracked by a cheeky smile. "Slower! You know how it goes!"

It goes at the speed of light—or almost—until by the third track Boland has expended his excess energy and the song emerges from the speaker at the speed it was intended to.

Back at the kitchen table, I cut pastry circles and line my tart tin with them, add spoonfuls of thick, tangy blackberry jam and put them in the oven to cook.

Funny how Boland always seems to arrive when I'm baking.

Time for a sit down, I think, until the tarts need to be taken from the oven. I've had years to get used to the idiosyncrasies of my fractious wood-fired stove. I'll know when.

I rest back in my lounge chair and close my eyes, letting Tim Curry float me away, wondering when Boland will grow tired of pedalling, hoping it's not until this side of the LP is finished. Though I suspect, knowing him, that it'll be about the time the tarts come out of the oven.

I'm right on all counts.

He scampers off the music-bike and beats me into the kitchen, knowing better than to approach the oven with its dragon's-breath tongues of heat.

We share a love for dragons, he and I. It cements our relationship. Well, that and my music bike. And my cooking.

Blackberry tarts go onto the windowsill to cool, their aroma wafting through the community, letting everyone know Nanny Elsie has been cooking again. All is right with the world.

I blow to cool a scrap of pastry wrapped like a sleeping wombat around a droplet of jam, and offer it to Boland. "Careful, it's still hot." It disappears into his grateful mouth before the words have left mine, and then he smiles his sunshine smile.

"Would you like a glass of lemonade to polish that off?" I invite him, extracting the big ceramic jug from my stone pantry where, hidden from the midday sun, it stays cool.

He nods so hard his head might fall off. I pour us a glass each.

Taking up two still-warm tarts and my glass, I retreat to my chair. It isn't long before he's climbing into my lap, his glass precariously balanced as he wriggles like a puppy to get comfortable. I give him one of the tarts to eat and we nestle, young and old, two ends of a rainbow.

"How old are you now, Nanny Elsie?" he asks me, with the nonchalance of youth.

I have to consider this for a moment, as I tend to ignore my age and just get on with living. "I'm one hundred and five. I'll be a hundred and six next birthday."

"And I'll be six on my next birthday!" he announces proudly, though his last birthday was barely two months ago. Fancy a century separating us two best of friends!

A century and two totally different worlds.

He wriggles his shoulders against my chest, and I know what he's about to ask me. "Tell me a story, Nanny Elsie?"

"Which story would you like, Boland dear?"

"The one about the metal birds."

I sigh, and smile at the memories. I used to live close to the airport once, and I loved to watch the planes take off and come in to land. I've tried explaining airports to Boland, but the closest we get is a field full of birds.

"All right then. Once upon a time, in a world that existed before you were born, there was a field of metal birds not far from where I lived—"

"Were they big?" he interrupts, in a time-honoured tradition—always prompting to make sure I haven't forgotten any part of the story.

"Yes, Boland. They were big as big as big! As tall as the hill that runs behind the commune, and as long as the beach. And with stiff, outstretched wings." I pause, but my memory has passed his test and he allows me to continue. "And people travelled inside them in comfortable seats, and watched movies, and ate meals as they flew." We've never quite come to terms about watching movies either, but he takes my word that it used to be possible in the old days because I'm Nanny Elsie and I'm older than anyone else in the commune.

I remember flying business class once. Oh! It was divine! All silver service up at the pointy end of the plane. It was a frequent flyer special bonus, and I'd thoroughly enjoyed being treated like a queen as we'd floated above the clouds. The trip from New York to London could have been twice as long as far as I was concerned; I was enjoying myself so much!

Boland wriggles, insinuating himself and the present between myself and the past.

"And they'd fly through the air and land in other fields in other countries all around the world."

I've shown him my spinning globe of the world, and Samantha has a big atlas, but for Boland at five, I suspect "World" just means "as far as the community boundaries". I'm sure it'll get bigger as he gets older. Boland is an adventurer, and boats still sail from one country to another, even if the sky has been lost to us.

Boland's blackberry tart has been gobbled down and I catch his empty glass before it slips to the floor. He's napping, and it's not long before I join him in sleep, dreaming of riding home on a jet.

Dinner is almost always a community event. There's a big open square in the middle of our village, with a fire pit in its centre. Tonight we have a pig already roasting on the spit. Everyone brings a plate of food to share: the blackberry tarts are my contribution. We eat and drink and laugh as the kids skip and play around us, eat their fill and go to bed when full night falls. Then we adults stoke the fire again and tell our stories, firelight flickering from face to face.

I read Moana's mind before the words can escape her lips. "Tell us again, Nanny Elsie, how the world you knew ended."

How many times have I told them this tale? They should all know it by heart by now. Yet they never tire of it. Most of the elders of the community were only children when it all happened. Many don't even remember the world I was so madly in love with. The younger ones…well, I'm filling their heads with fairy tales, aren't I? They'll never experience the world I lived in, and many can't even begin to imagine what I've seen. It's important that they know my stories though, and pass the knowledge on to their children's children when they are old like me.

So I draw a deep breath and begin: "The old extinct volcano beneath the Vatican erupted, and the Pope got consumed by the fires of hell." Not exactly true, but it makes a good beginning. "That terrible, terrible year we had everything thrown at us: floods, famine, earthquakes, tsunamis, and volcanoes all compounding one atop the other. Villages, towns, cities all wiped out. Hundreds of thousands of people dying with each disaster, then the diseases that came as an aftermath. I think we survivors got immune to the death tolls. We were too busy concentrating on staying alive. The old world that we knew shifted and altered daily all around us, and those few of us who were left just had to cope the best we could. There was no oil any more to heat the cities, feed the cars, buses, boats, the planes."

Maybe there's still oil in the ground, maybe some countries have hoards of it stashed, but they stopped drilling for it when they couldn't refine it any more.

I glance around my audience, all spellbound in the firelight. I could be speaking about angel's wings and pixie dust for all they know of cars and planes. We have our own two feet, donkey traps, horse carts, rafts and fishing boats, but we've relinquished the skies and not many of us remember what planes were any more.

"The solar flares were the final straw. That's when the global communications fried," I say in a hushed tone, and as one they all suck in their breath. "Computer networks collapsed, mobile phones died the death. Planes plummeted to earth like gassed birds. The people in the space station…" I glance up and all their eyes follow mine to look at the heavens. Some nights we still see the station pass overhead. "What became of the people in the station, I'll never know. A quick death, hopefully; preferable to suffocation or starvation as you look out through the portals at the planet below, knowing you can never go home."

"Tell us again about the planes," Vincent asks me across the shadows. A robust fellow in his sixties, he's old enough to remember them, while all the younger ones have to rely on are their imaginations.

"I used to live close to the airport. I used to love to watch those big metal birds fly in and fly out, daydream that I was on one of them floating above the clouds, making my way to another country."

Collectively my audience sigh as they picture my dreams.

"You came from the clouds," Elijah reminds me.

"I came from the Land of the Long White Cloud," I correct him gently. "Time was I used to fly home every year for Christmas, sometimes twice a year if I could afford it. Or my family would fly to me."

"In the big metal birds."

"In the big metal birds," I assert quietly, and feel the wave of sadness build within me. "But like those astronauts trapped in the space station, I can't go home again."

"Boats still link us to New Zealand," Moana reminds me, seeing the sadness in my eyes as I recall my long lost family and friends.

Salvaged fishing trawlers retrofitted with masts and sails, old-style wooden sailing ships, outriggers fitted with solar sails, repurposed tankers fuelled by biodiesel all ply a trade between our two countries, their numbers growing every year. But the sea's not for me. Safe enough when you're flying over it maybe, but I fear travelling through those angry waves.

"I know I'd be sick as a dog the minute I set foot on a boat. Better to stay here where I know I'm loved."

"If we scavenged fabric, melted rubber tyres to seal it, and filled it with hot air, made a wicker basket for you to ride in, you could fly home again," Elijah tells me.

"A hot-air balloon. How ingenious!"

"I have a book about it," he says, like it's a pot of gold.

When the electricity ran out and the internet died, books printed on paper were treasured again. Elijah dug half his library out of the ground in the hill behind the community, books dumped as landfill when electrons overtook paper for storing knowledge.

"It's a very generous offer, but I don't know how to fly a balloon. And anyone who came with me—well how would they get back? The winds all blow from west to east."

"They could pack the balloon up and put it on a boat and sail back to us when you're safely home, Nanny Elsie," Elijah states. Obviously, he's thought this through.

"And they can get sea sick instead of me?"

We all break into giggles at the thought.

I'm heartened that Elijah thinks so much of me to come up with a solution to my problem, especially when I'm not even sure if it *is* my problem. While part of me longs to return to the land of my birth, part of me knows how lucky I am to have survived the end of the Old World, and be part of this close community in the New World. I'm needed here. It keeps me young. My age is respected as experience, wisdom. I contribute to the community in any way I can, and know I can rely on the support of the others should I need it. Old people aren't discarded here. Like the books Elijah has dug up, we're treasured, treated with respect.

"Tell us another story of the past, Nanny Elsie," Jack says across the darkness.

"No, no, you've had your fill for the night. Someone else can have a turn."

I listen to other tales by the firelight. The Southern Cross is setting when

I finally excuse myself from the circle and drift off to my little house to sleep.

The wings of my dreams take me back to Christchurch in the time before it was scarred. When I wake up I can still smell the roses in the city where I was born. It would be good to see it again.

About mid-morning, a herd of small boys, Boland in the lead, come charging into the open square where I'm helping peel sweet potatoes. He runs straight at me, shouting, "Nanny Elsie! Nanny Elsie! I've seen a dragon! I've seen a dragon!" He's panting heavily as I scoop him up into my arms, happy to enter his fantasy and play along.

"Was it a green dragon with big thick scales, Boland?"

"It was sort of grey," he pants.

"With patches of red," Kelvin offers.

"And blue," Finn adds excitedly.

When there were no forms of electronic entertainment to provide the imagination for them, little brains bloomed again like flowers in the desert after the rain.

"Well fancy that; a patchwork dragon! Did it have big wings, Boland?"

"Funny little ones on its side."

The rest of his troupe agrees with his description.

"A long swishing tail then?" I ask.

He concentrates for a moment and says, "It was more like a tail of a fish, Nanny Elsie. It flicked from side to side."

Again the others agree with him.

"Doesn't sound like a dragon to me, Boland." We have a code of what dragons should look like. He's seen my pictures of them, and drawn his versions in return. "What makes you think that's what you saw?"

"Because it flew through the air, Nanny Elsie. And it wasn't a bird."

"Can you boys draw it for me in the sand?" I let Boland drop to his feet and they all fetch nearby sticks and find a piece of dirt to be their canvas. They don't conspire, in fact they face away from each other, and yet they all draw something that looks oddly like a fish. I've seen that shape before, but it can't be…can it?

"Where did you see it, boys?" I ask.

"It was flying away from us over the ridge when we were collecting the snails in the vegetable patch."

So whatever they saw was over a kilometre away.

"I wish I'd seen it," I lament. If only to confirm what it was.

"Maybe it'll fly back this way."

"We could leave food out for it, make a big net and catch it for you, Nanny Elsie."

"It would have to be a pretty big net," I tell them, but they're already on a mission, plotting among themselves how much vine they need to collect to weave a net to catch a dragon.

Moana smiles and shrugs, dismissing the report as the latest kids' game, but I ponder what it is they've seen. Like pearls, imaginings usually have a grain of truth to wrap themselves around.

Late afternoon all the community's children are called in for early dinner. It's not long before Boland and his friends come thundering back into the square on their little feet.

Boland spots me among the dinner makers and heads straight for me shouting, "Nanny Elsie, Nanny Elsie! The dragon's flying this way now. It's coming straight for us! It's even bigger than I thought!"

"Just as well you're safe with us then, isn't it, Boland?"

"We should send all the men out with arrows and spears to shoot it down. I'll lead the way," he announces, and I reflect he's five going on twenty-five. He snaps from child to man then back again in the blink of an eye. "Don't you want to go see it, Nanny Elsie?"

"Maybe we should eat dinner first?" I suggest. "We've got pork and corn and fresh bread and jam tonight. All your favourites."

That's enough to sway him from his dragon hunt.

Night falls as the community gathers around the fire in the square, eating, drinking and swapping stories.

"The space station looks very bright tonight," Moana comments, pointing to a spot in the sky, and my eyes follow her finger.

It's too low and bright to be the space station, and I haven't seen lights in the sky like that for more than fifty years. As we watch the one light gets brighter and splits in two like two big shining eyes.

"I told you the dragon was coming back. Believe me now?" Boland challenges me.

A few in the community get to their feet, startled by the display.

"It sounds like it's roaring," Elijah says.

My hearing isn't what it was, but I can detect a rhythmic rumble getting louder as the dragon gets closer. I'm aware that some of the others are looking to me for guidance. I remain calm. While I don't know what Boland's dragon is yet, there's something familiar about that regular thrum.

Like a moth, it seems drawn to our fire, and as it looms closer we can make out its shape.

"It's as big as a whale!" Boland is awestruck by this behemoth.

"Bigger," I assure him. "But the shape is similar."

"You know what it is, Nanny Elsie? You've seen it before?" Moana is reaching for my hand as if she's a little girl again.

"I've only ever seen photos. They were before even my time. It's a dirigible, an airship, a zeppelin."

It's maybe 200 metres away when a human voice shouts down at us.

"Can we land in your fields? If we throw down ropes, will you help us bring her down?"

Torches are plucked out of the fire and we all head off to the fields to help bring down the airship.

Well, I wasn't expecting to do this tonight!

The kids have all overcome their fears, and are leading the way, ignoring calls from their parents to come back and stay close. They have no concept of danger.

"Keep those flames away, or the ship could go up!" we're warned in a strangled shout. Our torches are doused and by the light of the moon we see ropes thrown out to dangle like jellyfish tendrils. People grab hold and pull, and keep pulling as what looks to be an ancient campervan descends from the sky bringing the whale-like balloon with it. When the van touches the ground, we're asked to tie the ropes off so the airship is tethered between two trees like some massive floating beast.

The air-riders emerge from their craft and Vincent and Elijah welcome them to our community, invite them to share our fire and our food. As they reply, I break into a smile at hearing the accent of my old country.

It's not often we have company to share our meals and tell us new stories of the wider world. There's a buzz of excitement as our guests are led into the square. But the formalities of introductions must come before food and talk. Their names are Edgardo, Katsuko, Mark and Hemi, and they've come from Christchurch, my old home town.

Elijah looks around for me and announces: "This is our matriarch, and

217

one of your countrywomen, Nanny Elsie."

Not regal like a Queen, more like a flustered school girl, I welcome them to our community and suggest that they sit as others offer them food.

Boland insinuates himself next to me and asserts quietly, "See? I told you I saw a dragon, Nanny Elsie."

"And I didn't doubt you for a minute, Boland dear."

I have a feeling Boland is going to offer every excuse to stay up and hear our guests speak tonight, and I'm right.

At first the conversation is dominated by questions and exchanges on how the airship works. Elijah can't believe his luck! I don't follow the technicalities, but understand about the salvaged canvas, the inner balloons, the hydrogen and the reclaimed paper-thin solar panels that drive the propellers of the navigation motors that fought the westerly air currents so they could reach Australia. It took them three days to get here, and it's not their first visit. These are things I absorb as I listen. The rest of the details splash off me to be caught by others who better understand such things.

All I can think of is that we have taken to the skies again. Not like the planes I rode in or watched, but it's a start. Maybe we can build more airships and have a regular run between our two countries. Maybe I can even make my way home?

When talk of the airship eventually subsides, I see my chance. "Tell me, did Christchurch slide into the sea as I've heard? Or is it viable still?"

Hemi puffs out his chest. "Christchurch was pretty badly shaken, like a lot of places, when the big one ripped up through the Southern Alps like a flame up a fuse, but that was years ago now. There's been nothing worse than rumbling these past few years. Touch wood. Now we're getting people coming south to escape the volcanic hotspots like Ngauruhoe and Taupō. So, yes, Christchurch is pretty much back on her feet now—but a lot has changed since you would've last seen it."

"That's true everywhere," I say, and Edgardo, who seems to have travelled further afield than the others, takes this as an opportunity to expand upon the dramatic shifts he's noticed in the societies of the Philippines, Malaysia, and Fiji. But I'm not ready to give up on hearing of my home town, so I steer the conversation back. "Did they rebuild the cathedral again?" I ask. I have to know.

Hemi frowns, so I instantly know the answer. "Like your community, we concentrated first on food and shelter. It's only been in recent years with regular bountiful harvests that we've been able to spare the time to scavenge the Old World places for things that we needed for the airship's construction."

"Same here," I answer. "But the rose gardens…?"

"Roses still bloom in Christchurch," Katsuko tells me. "We just can't spare the time to keep formal gardens any more."

I shrug, seeing the wisdom of her words. "No one sings opera in the Sydney Opera House any more either, but we still have songs."

Someone else asks a question, and the conversation is carried along on a new path as I'm caught up in the memories of Christchurch in all her glory.

After breakfast the next morning we're all invited to take a tour of the airship.

A patchwork quilt of different-coloured lined canvases, it's like Vincent's balloon, but with a blanket of flexible solar panels stretched over the top of the canvas quilt.

The dirigible sways in the breeze, giving it a friendly demeanour, like an elephant at a zoo shifting its weight from one leg to another, awaiting children with peanuts.

As I thought the previous night, their gondola is a battered old campervan slung below the balloon. It has a few surprising comforts like a toilet, a compact fridge, reclining seats and a couple of fold-out beds.

"We take shifts and share the beds, but otherwise there's plenty of room, if anyone wants to join us," Hemi tells us as if we're all potential passengers.

"How would we pay?" Moana asks.

"We've come here to barter."

They'll be taking some of our produce home with them, and leaving some of their technology with us—solar lights, and the knowledge of how to make them. But a trip to Christchurch must be expensive, like it was when the jet age first begun.

"Imagine it, Nanny Elsie," Moana whispers to me. And I am imagining it.

"We want to travel here regularly. Maybe as often as three times a year."

219

Not quite the three times a day service I remember from the Old World.

"And if you build an airship of your own, we could double the trips between our two countries."

It sounds like a dream, but then flying to New Zealand sounded like a dream before last night too. Well, I like to dream...

The others drift off back to their chores, but I'm still looking at the airship when Mark sidles up to me.

"I was wondering if you had any family in Christchurch?" he asks me.

"I haven't had any contact with any of my family, so I presume there's no one left."

"Your last name is Russell, isn't it?"

"That's right." I idly wonder who he's been talking to in the community about me.

"My great-aunt is Jane Russell."

I'm tempted to tell him that Russell is a common enough surname around the region, but I did have a niece called Jane, and I remember the year she was born.

"I don't suppose you know how old she is?"

"She's seventy-six now, but still going strong." And there's a twinkle in his eyes that suggests I'm something that he's been looking for.

"And her birthday?" I press.

"That would be the sixth of December."

Same as mine. If it's not my Jane, it's a surprising coincidence.

"So do you think we're related?" he asks in my silence. "Because one of the sailors who made the trip over here a few years back told me he'd met a lady called Elsie Russell. I'd been kind of looking for you every time we've come over. Never expected to meet you, though."

"Nor I you. I thought all my family had gone."

He embraces me as if I'm as fragile as glass and asks me, "Would you like to come home?"

"For a visit perhaps, but not to stay," I say without hesitation. "My home and family are all here now, but it would be good to connect to my people over there again."

"We could get you back here before summer's over if that's what you want," he assures me.

"How long have I got to pack?"

The news that I'm going spreads through our community like wildfire. There are tears and sorrow, but also acceptance and joy. At first Boland, my best friend, cries—but his tears dry when I tell him I'll most probably be back and say he can use my music bike and play my records whenever he wants.

In the predawn everybody in the community walks me to the airship to see me off in style. I feel honoured, but wonder how could I have impacted on so many lives?

Moana approaches me with a posy of brightly coloured feathers that she carefully pins to my coat. There are tears in her eyes as she says, "Feathers float back. We'll always be here for you, dear, dear, Nanny Elsie." She kisses me on both cheeks and I glance around the one-hundred-and-fifty-strong members of my New World family where I am old, but I am active, and a valued part of the community.

I am going to another place where I'll still be old, but I'll still be valued, and I reflect that's how it should always have been.

I take my seat in the campervan gondola, assured that because the winds are with us, I should be seeing Christchurch this time tomorrow. The airship's tethers are untied and it rises majestically up into the sky. It's no metal bird, but it's taking me home.

SELFIE

Lee Murray

Was I dead?

I peered through the fog.

I was dead: I had to be, because I could see an angel. But if I was dead, why was my head throbbing like the inside of a nightclub? People were shouting and moaning. Somewhere nearby a car alarm was blasting. I smelled petrol.

I blinked. Blinked again. Slowly, my eyes cleared.

Not an angel, then. Just a man with a pigeon flapping on his shoulder, the soft grey insides of its wings like an angel's at his back.

"Miss? Can you hear me? Are you okay?" the man shouted over the din.

Was I okay? I frowned. I felt…different. My back was sore. Probably from landing on the ground. I'd got off the tour bus with the others. The tour my sister had insisted I go on to 'take me out of myself', the one she'd paid for before practically shoving me onto the bus.

Day three. I remember we'd stopped in this little square…I'd been about to take a selfie with the statue—not for me, I didn't give a shit about the stupid statue, that was for Julie's benefit, so later, when I was dead, she wouldn't blame herself so much.

Anyway, I'd been lining up the photo and then…nothing.

"What happened?" I croaked.

The man shook his head, the bird's flapping wings framing his face like a halo. "I don't know. An explosion. A nuclear event. Something big." He extended a hand. "Here, let me help you up."

I curled my fingers around his. "There's a pigeon on your back," I said. Of course, he knew. He must know. It was a pigeon.

"I tried shooing it off. It won't go." He pulled me upwards.

Pain shot through my back and I gasped. "Stop!" I shrieked.

He let go and I lay back, breathing deeply, the way women do when they're in labour, at least the ones on television. Maybe it wasn't really like that. I didn't know. Another pain, a different sort of pain, sliced sharp and deep in my chest.

"Get her off me!"

Ah, I was lying on someone. So that was why Pigeon-Man had been helping me up. I tried to roll to one side to release him, but the pain in my back was excruciating. I sucked in a breath.

"Oh shit." Pigeon-man flapped in agitation. "You're fused, aren't you? It's not just your hand."

"Get off!" the person beneath me—a man—complained. He shoved at my shoulders, pushing me off. The small of my back burned. It was crippling.

"You're hurting me," I wailed.

"Well, you're crushing me."

I recognised the voice. It was a guy from the bus. The one three seats behind the driver, who'd chatted with everyone and shown them pictures of his kids. He'd tried to catch my attention, start up a conversation, but I'd avoided him. Whatever he had, I wasn't interested. But it hadn't stopped him trying to photo-bomb my selfie. He'd been standing behind me: I'd seen him on the screen.

"Move!"

"I can't," I protested. "My back hurts."

"It's because you're fused," the Pigeon-man said. He giggled, a hysterical cackle that sent a shiver through me, and pointed at my right hand.

I lifted it to see what was so funny. My stomach dropped. For an instant, all sound melted away. I closed my eyes. Opened them again. "But—"

"I already told you. You're fused."

My fist had been reduced to a club, my selfie stick welded to a swollen blob of purple flesh. Molten metal seeped between my tendons. Suddenly, the wings on the man's shoulder made sense.

Pigeon-man gave a stiff nod, then lifted his chin indicating the man beneath me. "You're fused to him, too."

My eyes fluttered and the sky disappeared.

The guy underneath woke me, his voice in my ear. That, and the searing in my back. I wasn't sure how long I'd been out. Maybe only seconds.

"We've got attached somehow," he said.

Dazed, I lifted my arm and looked at the lump. My hand was a selfie stick, and I was fused with someone. I twisted my head, and took in the ruined monument, the grimy cracks between the cobbles, some drifting litter.

"If you're looking for the bird guy, he pissed off and left us to it. We need to get up," the guy attached to me said. "We need to find out what's going on." He paused, huffing.

I'm not big, but I must have been deadweight on his chest.

"I'm going to roll onto my left side. I need you to roll with me," he said.

I did as I was told. We turned together, like an old married couple spooning, and then sat up. It took some manoeuvring. I put my good hand down on the pavement. His went out too. Eventually, we struggled to our feet.

"Fuck," he whispered.

I wanted to stagger backwards, but he held me in place with his weight. The newlyweds from the tour were fused together, along with four passengers they'd been posing with. They were sprawled on the ground in a mass, writhing like an upturned cockroach. The bus driver hadn't been so lucky—or maybe he was, depending on how you looked at it. He was fused to the bus, slumped forward, the side mirror welded to his skull like a set of weird antlers. He'd tried to free himself because his shoulder was dripping blood, half his face torn away to the bone.

Across the square, there was a whoosh.

"Shit! It's going to blow!" screamed the man at my back.

All I felt was a dull resignation. I was going to die. I couldn't run; he was attached to me. We were a couple of kids lined up for the three-legged race, and no time left to practise.

My companion had other ideas. He slipped his hands under my thighs, lifting my feet off the ground, and ran, carrying me out in front of him like a sack of potatoes. I thought my head would come off. My back and hips screamed with pain as he jostled and jerked us forward. He ducked around a corner and curled his body around mine, his heart thumping against my back, his breath in my ear. The world rocked. Even out of the line of the explosion, debris rained on us: bits of metal, rocks. I coughed, choking on dust.

Then, everything went quiet. Even the car alarm stopped squawking.

Using the wall to brace us, we got to our feet and looked back. The blue-black smoke cleared. The bus was a chewed carcass, a large piece of it thrown across the square. I squinted at the misshapen hunk of metal, a child's bloodied arm emerging from the green paintwork. I swallowed hard. And the photo group? What about them?

"This way," I urged, shambling forward, dragging my new body-double with me. I rounded the remains of the bus and stopped dead in my tracks. The cockroach was still on its back, its flesh roasted black. A curl of blue smoke rose from the blistered corpse.

"Bend," I hissed.

"What?"

"Bend over. Just do it!"

We barely made it. Even so, some vomit splashed onto the cuffs of my jeans.

When I was done, I pushed myself upright.

"You okay?"

"No." I wiped the back of my mouth with my forearm. "You think it's like this everywhere?" I said.

Behind me, I felt him stiffen. "Maybe."

An old man shuffled past us in a daze. He'd been walking his dog. The leash was melted about his arm, the chain hanging like a warrior's flail, except instead of a spiky ball on the end there was a black terrier. A *blackened* terrier. The dog's tongue lolled out the side of its mouth. Dead.

The man stopped. "Which way to the hospital?" he said.

"I don't know," replied my companion.

The old man dropped his gaze to look at me, eyes watery. I shook my head for no. He nodded, and wandered away.

"We should get going," the guy behind me said.

"Go where?"

"We need to find a phone. I need to find out if my kids are okay, and you probably have people to call, family…"

For a second, I wondered if Julia and Errol were okay, but even if she hadn't known it, I'd said my last goodbyes three days ago. As for Paul, he'd already moved on. I'd heard he was dating someone else.

"Look, we'll find a phone, see if our families are okay, and then we'll decide what to do. You okay with that?" he said in my ear. I nodded. "Good. Right foot first."

Like drunken friends leaving a party, we shambled to the edge of the square, staggering around bricks and bodies. We shuffled for an hour. Until my back felt like I'd slept on a bed of nails and my wrist was throbbing. My nostrils were full of the stench of burning flesh.

I stopped, my shadow forced to stop too. "I can't," I said.

"You can't what?" he said.

"I can't do this. Be fused to you."

"Believe me, it isn't what I had in mind for my post-divorce holiday either."

"How long do you think we can do this?" I whispered. "A few days. A week?"

I couldn't see his eyes, but his voice softened. He gave my shoulder a squeeze. "Look, you're tired and you're in shock. Things look bleak now, but we'll get help. There has to be someone. That old man was looking for a hospital. We'll find it. There'll be people there; doctors who can help separate us."

He was right. Doctors had contributed to splitting up Paul and me.

Shaking my head, I let my body slump, forcing him to take all my weight. My spine blazed with pain.

"No way," he said, his voice angry. He grabbed my arms and pulled me to his chest. "You don't get to give up."

I shrugged.

"Get up."

"No." Technically, I wasn't sitting down. Just hanging off him. That poem about the albatross and the mariner sprang to mind.

He didn't do me the courtesy of arguing. Just lifted me by my legs again and hauled arse. I let him do it. By the time we spotted the sign for the hospital, my shoulders and arms were damp with his sweat.

He put me down. "You have to walk," he puffed. Calmer now, I nodded.

We followed the street signs, walking on the road. Apart from the abandoned cars, there were fewer obstacles. Any people we found were dead or dying, fused to their vehicles. Everywhere metal seeped into purpled flesh, raised lumpy tissue like a keloid scar. Where we could, we checked the cars. There were plenty of cell phones; melted into dashboards, welded to people's palms, their thighs, the sides of their skulls. None of the fused phones worked and the only other phone we found had been smashed.

People spewed from the office buildings like a gross procession of cyborgs. They were hybridised: to their phones, their coffee cups, a printer. I saw one guy scooting along in a computer chair, his arse bonded to the seat.

No one seemed to know much. The power was out. Television stations down. A few radio stations were still operating, but they didn't know any more than us.

At one point we came across a line of kindergarten kids. Lined up on the sidewalk like gingerbread men, the kids were tethered by their teacher to a traffic signal. A group of adults, the ones who still had limbs, were trying to free them by hacking the woman's body away from the pole with a hacksaw, carving her off in pieces like ham off the bone. The kids were screaming. Had the woman been dead before they'd started carving?

"Nothing we can do for them," my companion said, hurrying us away.

There was no god. At least, not one I wanted anything to do with. What kind of god allowed babies to be strung together like plastic beads? Flambéed into car parts? Dissolved in a mother's womb before she had a chance to know them? If there was a god, he was a spiteful and vindictive bastard. Why else would he take all these people and leave me still alive?

Wait. I didn't have to be alive. I put my left arm across my body and felt in my pocket. They were still there. Smiling, I retrieved the silver blister pack. There was always a silver lining. Holding the pack flat against my stomach with my selfie stick, I punched out a pill and swallowed it. Punched out another.

"What have you got there?"

I didn't answer, just shoved the next pill into my mouth. I was gobbling the fourth one, when he yanked my arm backwards, wrenching the blister pack with it. The muscles in my back spasmed and I gasped.

"Hey, give them back!" I twisted as far as I could, swiping wildly, but the pain was too much.

"Stop struggling," he demanded. He held the packet beyond my reach and read off the label: "Valium. What the fuck? You just took four of these."

"My back hurts."

"I hurt too, but Valium isn't a pain killer."

"No kidding, Einstein," I mumble.

Something went off inside him. I couldn't see it, but I could feel it. Trembling with rage, he roared into my ear, "We survive an apocalypse and you want to *off* yourself?"

My lip quivered. "What difference does it make?" I'd been planning to check out anyway.

He gripped my shoulders, his fingers digging into my skin and shook me. "You'll be dead, that's what!"

"So?" I sounded pitiful.

He slammed a hand against a wall. "You selfish fucking cow. So you don't want to live? Well, that's too bad. Until we can find a way to separate, we're in this together." He was breathing hard, his heartbeat thumping against my back. I said nothing, but a fat tear rolled down my face. I brushed it away.

After a while, I felt his heartbeat slow. He straightened. I straightened with him. He sighed. "What's your name?" he said.

I hiccupped. Scuffed my foot against the curb.

"Come on. I'm already in your pants, you can tell me your name."

"Eve."

He snorted. He had a problem with my name? I pulled away from him, pain shooting through my back. "No, stop. You don't understand." He gave a laugh. "I'm Steve. My name is Steve. Get it? *Steve.*"

It took me a second to catch on.

Even our fucking names were fused.

We weren't the first to arrive at the hospital. Cars littered the street leading up to the building. An ambulance blocked the entrance, its back doors hanging open and its contents spewed over the blacktop. We made our way around the swinging doors, shuffling wide to avoid a pool of blood.

"Don't look inside," Steve said, so of course I did.

It was a woman and her baby. They'd been attached like us, but now they were separated. Maybe she'd done it herself. Or maybe a paramedic had done it. It didn't matter who, because it hadn't worked. I clutched at the ambulance door to steady myself. Blood everywhere. Dark, greasy coagulated blood. It had seeped into blankets and bandages, dribbled to the floor, then run along the aisle of the vehicle and onto the ground.

The woman's arm hung over the side of the gurney, the ragged sinews dangling. A fly buzzed over the tattered limb. Had she been reaching for her baby on the opposite gurney? She needn't have bothered: her fingers were still embedded in the infant's thigh.

"Come on," Steve said.

I flinched as he patted my arm.

Inside, the lobby was dark. A bloodied doctor, a scalpel fused to his fist, was slumped on a bench. He waved his scalpel at us as we approached.

"Back off! Just back off. I don't care how easy you think it'll be, I'm not doing it okay? I'm not separating you."

"But we need help," Steve said over my shoulder.

Wiping his good hand through his hair, the doctor scoffed. "Do you know how many people I've *helped* today? Sixteen people. Know how many have lived? Only three."

"You saved three," Steve said. "Three people are alive because of you."

The doctor shook his head. "The only able-bodied nurse is overwhelmed. With no proper aftercare, what do you think the chances are for those people?" He waved his scalpel again. "I did it all with this. Just rinsed it between patients." He sighed. "At best, I gave them enough time to say goodbye to their families. They'll all be dead from infection the day after tomorrow."

He got up and stumbled away.

"Wait!" Steve shouted. "Do you have a phone?"

Turning, the doctor fished in his pocket and took out a cell phone, throwing it at us. "It's almost flat."

He took off at a run as more people-hybrids shuffled in in search of aid.

We huddled in a corner, Steve holding the phone out in front of both of us, while he punched in his ex's number.

"Pick up, pick up," he mumbled.

No answer. He dialled again.

"I'm sorry," I said.

He gave the phone to me. I had no one to call.

"I have to go home," he said abruptly.

"Where's that?" I said.

"Bridgeport."

"But that's 400 kilometres. The road will be blocked."

"I have to."

We didn't leave straight away. We raided the hospital canteen first, helping ourselves to muesli bars, bottled water, and packs of Ibuprofen, which we stuffed into a canvas paramedic bag. You'd think with the two of us, it would've been quick, but the irony was everything seemed to take twice as long.

"We should take the ambulance," I said, as we exited the hospital. "I reckon the gas tank will be full. If we need to, we can sleep in it."

I didn't say it was because the ambulance's seats were deep and the windscreen had better visibility. We both knew I was going to have to sit on his lap and steer while he worked the accelerator.

"Okay," Steve said.

The keys were in the ignition. Obviously, paramedics didn't think anyone would steal their ride. Leaving the woman on the gurney, we pushed her out of the interior, but, all arms and legs, we lost control and it took off like a kid on a waterslide, the gurney skewing sideways. The woman tumbled bodily onto the grass. I felt terrible. We hadn't done it on purpose, but it was as if we'd disrespected her somehow. I picked up her baby, cradling her as we struggled down from the ambulance. I laid the infant beside her mother on the grass verge, and covered them both with a blanket, the bloody blotches making them look like the overlarge cocoon of an exotic butterfly. Then we sluiced out the interior of the ambulance.

It was an hour later and mid-afternoon before we were on the road, heading south out of town.

Our first attempt at driving was pathetic. Like a learner driver, we lurched onto the curb. I had to talk Steve through it, telling him when to accelerate and when to brake, while I watched the road, swerving left and right to avoid the abandoned vehicles. Even worse, were the hybrids who tried to accost us, balancing on the running board, and hanging off the window, pleading for help. I wanted to stop, but Steve was working the accelerator and he reminded me we couldn't help everyone. We weren't doing so well ourselves. When we'd got the hang of driving, Steve tried the phone again. Still nothing from his family. "You didn't call anyone," he said.

"Brake slower," I replied.

"You don't want to call your parents? Siblings? A boyfriend maybe?"

"Even slower."

"Eve."

"I had a miscarriage. Paul left me." Running over the curb, I drove a few metres, then found the road again.

"Your boyfriend left you because you lost a baby? What an arse."

"I cried a lot…accelerate now."

"That's not why he left," Steve said.

"No. He said I was too clingy."

Steve chuckled. 'Too clingy, huh?" I glanced up and caught his brown eyes twinkling in the rear-view mirror.

I dragged my eyes back to the road. "So, what about you?" I said. "Why did you and your wife split?"

He sighed heavily. "I don't know. We grew apart, I guess. I got busy with work, she was busy with the kids and her yoga practice, and in the weekends there was the garden, kids' sports; we never saw each other. It's been two years. We're friends because we have to be. I can't lose the kids, they're like a part of me."

I knew what he meant. Since I'd lost the baby, I hadn't felt whole.

We drove in silence until we came across a milk tanker blocking the road. There was no way the ambulance would get through.

"You're squashing me, anyway," Steve said.

Grabbing the paramedic bag, we tumbled out and walked. It was slow. Like the longest sack race ever. The afternoon was gorgeous: a sunny blue-skied 'great to be alive' day, as if the gods were apologising for the morning's catastrophe. We stopped to crack open one of the bottles from our hospital stores and shared it between us. Walked some more. My back started to ache again from the exertion. Steve couldn't help kicking stones into my shoes.

Out in the middle of a field, a man fused to his tractor, called to us. "Hey, help me."

"We could give him some water," I said, but neither of us deviated from the road. We had days of walking ahead and limited supplies.

"He's dead, anyway," Steve said quietly.

On the outskirts of the next town we came across a line of people sitting at a bus stop. Joined at the hip—literally—the five of them were like the fingers of a glove. They stared at us listlessly as we passed.

"See, *they're* moving," one of the men shouted. "We should get up too. Go somewhere."

"What's the use?" another replied.

"We should at least take a vote!"

They were still sitting there when Steve and I rounded the bend, proof that nothing ever gets done by committee.

We slept that first night under a tree on the side of the road. Wrapped in a foil blanket from the ambulance, his heart beating next to mine, Steve told me about his kids: Marion, his little girl, and his son, Arty, just five. Later, I rested with my head on his shoulder, strangely comforted by his snoring.

The second day, the bodies started to bloat, flies crawling over them.

Steve called his ex for the last time—the phone rang and rang and finally gave up the ghost. "Doesn't mean anything," he said. "They could all be fine."

In the next town, a pair of men were beating a hybrid in the middle of the street while another man, dragging a big screen TV melded to his arm, leaned against a power pole to watch. We skirted the towns after that, slipping in and out of outlying houses in search of water and food. On the fourth night, Steve found a farmhouse with an outside generator.

"I'm going to have shower," I said, pulling forward, the pain in my back now a permanent ache. Well, I was hardly going to be coy, was I? The past few days he'd been right behind me when I'd peed. Exhausted, we staggered up the driveway past a car, a dead woman in the driver's seat. We left her there and went inside. There was food in pantry, clean clothes in the laundry basket, and in the back room, we found a baby in its crib. The stench of ammonia was enough to make my eyes water. It wasn't fused, but without its mother, the poor thing had starved to death.

We'd seen plenty of shitty stuff, but the sight of the baby was the last straw for Steve. He sank to the ground in front of the crib, forcing me down with him. His body shook. "Lisa was taking the kids to Hawaii. I don't know exactly when they were leaving. They might have been on the plane…"

"You don't know that."

"I do. I know it. They've probably been dead for days, but I've dragged us across country on this wild goose chase just in case…We've both seen what's going on. It's hopeless."

"We'll have some food, get showered," I said. "We'll feel better."

"You don't get it. How am I supposed to be a father to them? Have you even looked at us? We've turned into some kind of two-headed monster."

"We're not a monster."

"No? Well, I'm not a *man* any more either."

I twisted, but even straining my neck the angle was impossible. "Of course you're a man. Don't be ridiculous."

He laughed. "I've got a bird's eye view here, Eve. I'm telling you it's gone."

I didn't know what to say. My hand was gone.

He blew out slowly then, ruffling the hair off my nape as he leaned close. "You know, before all this, if you'd asked me, I'd have given my right arm to be buried in you."

I held up my selfie stick.

"Yeah, so you lost your arm. You've got two," he said bitterly.

"Steve, look, there'll be—"

I didn't get to finish. He put his hands on either side of my head, turning my head from one side to the other until I saw stars. "Look around, Eve. You see anyone? Civil Defence? The military?" He paused. "You know what? You're right."

He dropped his voice then, the resignation sending a shiver up my spine. "Nothing will ever make this right. Let's just call it a day. We're going to die anyway, we may as well get it over with."

He was fumbling with something. I heard a faint crackle.

"What are you doing?"

He didn't answer.

I craned my neck back, but I couldn't see. "Steve, what are you doing?"

He laughed. "I'm doing what you wanted, what I should have done all along."

My heart sped up. The pills! I'd forgotten about them. The blister pack crackled again.

"Don't worry, I've left you some." He slipped the pack into my right pocket, his breath tickling neck.

My mind raced. I wouldn't have to feel like this any more. No more endless walking. No more ripping pain in my back. Sure, there would be pain, but afterwards…oblivion. Isn't that what I wanted? I'd planned on dying on this trip anyway. There was nothing left here for me. My baby had died, and Paul had moved on. Only Julie would miss me, if she wasn't already dead.

At my back, the meds were working quickly. Steve's pulse was already slowing, the weight of his body pressing down on me, crushing my lungs.

His head slumped on my shoulder.

"Steve?" I whispered.

He grunted something incoherent. He was losing consciousness. My own brain was hazy—the drugs jumping the fence to invade my body. The woman from the ambulance floated into my mind, her mutilated arm stretching across to touch her child.

Suddenly, something shifted in me. I didn't want to die.

I wanted to live.

But why now, when the world was going to shit? Maybe it was nothing more than my survival instinct kicking in. Maybe Steve had given me purpose. Something, someone else to worry about. I didn't know.

Steve's heartbeat grew weaker. My own heart would stop soon, too. How long did I have? Maybe just minutes. The revelation hit me. If I wanted to live, if I wanted us *both* to live, I had to do something *now*.

If only I had some paddles to defibrillate his heart. A re-boot. But wait, there was something I could try. Would it work? We were dying, anyway. Nothing to lose. Lowering my head, I gripped the railings of the crib and heaved us upright, the pain like a switchblade along my spine. Grimacing under Steve's weight, I dragged us towards the wall, dropping to one knee, thighs burning.

My heart faltered.

"No!" I said. "We're not dying." I gritted my teeth. "Not today."

I thrust my selfie-stick into the electric socket.

WEARING THE STAR CLOAK
Darian Smith

There's a moment, just before waking, when I forget it's gone. I feel the ghost of it on my shoulders, the warmth inside. It boosts my confidence and makes me stronger. I am more myself. I am ready to rule the islands and mould the day to my bidding.

Opening my eyes is a disappointment. My old bones ache with craving. It's been missing from me for almost three decades, but I feel it just the same. I'm simply an old man with his memories and regrets. I had my chance. I was not worthy.

The woven flax that covers my doorway is brushed aside to reveal the antidote to my thoughts. Iolani smiles like the last of the sun glinting off the dark ocean at twilight. They say that our children and grandchildren are our greatest treasure. Iolani is mine.

"Good morning, Grandpa. I brought you breakfast." She lays a tray lined with banana leaves beside my sleeping mat. It is covered in sliced pawpaw, banana and coconut.

"You're a good girl."

Her eyes dance and her smile gets even wider, then her face twitches and the smile disappears.

"What is it?"

She shakes her head. "Nothing, Grandpa. Enjoy your breakfast."

I roll quickly to my feet and tug the flax mat covering the window away.

Sunlight fills the bure. Iolani turns as though to leave, but there's speed in my old bones yet. I grasp her by the shoulders and turn her to face me, peering closer. In the corner of her lip, there is a smudge of blood. "Who did that?"

She shrugs. "Kaha's brothers, of course. He's been the Anela for a long time now so they think they're untouchable."

"And are they right?"

The other corner of her mouth twitches upwards. "The one with the bruised coconuts wasn't."

I laugh. "I hope you kicked him good and hard!"

She tilts her head and looks up from under innocent eyelashes. "I may have. He made me spill the milk I had on your tray."

I find my laugher has gone. "This happened just now?" I frown at the doorway. "On the way here?"

"Yes, but…"

I'm already striding past her, breakfast forgotten. The flax in the doorway is like mist to me. Outside, the sun beats down through the coconut palms, shining brightly coloured on the hibiscus around my home. Four boys are waiting, loitering amongst the tree trunk shadows like eels preying on unwary fish. They're around Iolani's age.

"You don't belong here," I call out. "Get moving."

Two of them shift as if to obey, but the other two hold their ground. "Fuck off, old man. We don't have to do what you say."

"You do if you don't want me to summon the Elders and tell them you've been bullying women."

The ringleader lifts his chin. "Do it. I'll call Kaha'aheo. The Anela beats the Elders."

I stare him in the eye. It is a gaze that quailed enemies in earlier days. Respect fades with power, it seems. "Your brother won't wear the Whetū Korowai forever."

"Oh yeah? Want me to summon him now so you can say that to his face?"

I shrug. "Summon him if you wish. Tell him I will meet him in the choosing circle." No Anela ever returned to the choosing circle willingly. It was too harsh a reminder of what happened to most of them. It'd taken me years before I could face it again.

238

The boy shifts uneasily. "Whatever. Let's get out of here." His brothers move with him, a beast with four heads. They will be back, I'm sure. The fifth brother, the one who wears the star cloak, gives them confidence. He lends them power by association. Power corrupts. I should know.

Iolani waits in the doorway to my bure. The smile is back, although it must hurt her lip to do it. "You're awesome, Grandpa." She throws her arms around me.

The smile is infectious. "Hardly."

"No, it's true. I can just imagine what you were like when you wore the Whetū Korowai. The way you used the magic to defeat the Maloan Islanders. If I ever get the chance to be the Anela, I want to be just like you."

She intends it as a compliment, but when Iolani leaves, her words haunt me. My time in the Whetū Korowai made me a hero to the people and left me with nightmares.

The Maloans had competed for fish in our waters and sometimes their young men would come looking for wives. We would fight them, pushing them back to their own island so we could coexist.

The last time they'd done it, I was new to the star cloak. I believed conquering enemies was a worthy use of the power. I pulled a storm from far out to sea and set it over their island where it raged for five days. When it was over, I led the warriors to finish off our enemy.

The village was like a crab crushed between two rocks. Pieces of broken homes floated in a goo of mud, sticks and blood. Drowned corpses stared at us with bloated faces as the few survivors tried to salvage what they could. When they saw us coming, they cheered, thinking we would be their saviours. Instead, we killed and raped. Our canoes were so laden with pillaged treasure on the way back, I had to use my powers to keep them afloat.

I'd earned the title of conqueror. It wasn't until later, when I looked back, trying to find reasons for my loss, that I realised the horror of what I had done. Of what I'd allowed to be done. My chance to prove myself worthy had come too early in life, before I'd learned what true worth was.

The melancholy stays with me all day and I keep mostly to myself, searching the rock pools for crabs and trapped fish to bring back home. There are more pools now than there used to be. When Kaha'aheo first became the Anela, he amused himself by blasting holes in the rock. The resulting benefit to food gathering was unplanned, but welcome.

The slow, soft brush of waves against the shore marks time until night falls and I leave my basket of collected food at my bure, then make my way to the choosing circle. A few of us gather there every evening to check for the stars' return. I'm barely half way there when I hear the drums.

They have come.

Rough flax, hibiscus and spiky grasses scratch at my legs as I hurry through the scrub. Even now, thirty years beyond being a candidate, the excitement builds in my chest. Iolani is old enough to put herself forward.

My old legs are not as fast as they once were. People have already gathered by the time I arrive. The circle is in fact an oval of hard-packed earth, pressed down by generations of feet. Hollowed half-logs form seats around the edges for those of us tired from the day. The rest stand behind, leaving the circle itself for those who would put themselves forward to wear the Whetū Korowai. At the far, narrow end, three standing stones rise tall and thin above us all. At the top of each is a hole through which one of the coloured stars can be seen. They have aligned once more. It is time for the choosing.

Iolani is among the young people waiting in the circle. The boys who bullied her are there too. She meets my eye and grins, bouncing slightly on the balls of her feet.

The chief stands and the crowd falls silent. "Since the time of the great leader, Haunani, we have seen many young people come forward to prove themselves worthy of his power, the Whetū Korowai. Yet none have kept it. Today, another will be chosen to show their worth."

"No!" It is an anguished cry that pulls at my core. The same cry was ripped from my own throat when the star cloak left me for another. I have heard it many times since then. The stars return to the standing stones every one to three years to choose another Anela. None have proven any more worthy than I did.

Kaha'aheo is fighting it. The crowd parts and I can see him at the edge of the clearing. His arms are wrapped around the trunk of a coconut tree as he tries to resist the inexorable pull back to the standing stones. The Whetū Korowai flutters from his shoulders, streaming like a waterfall of light. It is made of glowing, many-coloured feathers, insubstantial as mist, stronger than stone. As we watch, the feathers grow longer, like fingers, and the cloak bends, wrapping itself around him, pulling his arms away from the tree.

He cries out again, but it is too late. The light of the Whetū Korowai completely envelops him like a glowing cocoon. It floats slowly through the air, past the crowd, toward the circle. As it passes, I hear his sobs from within.

When it reaches the stones, the star cloak unravels and the old Anela is dumped on the dirt. His face is streaked with tears and he reaches toward the magic he has worn for almost two years. It dissolves, and the feathers of light spin up, through the holes in the standing stones and back to the stars.

"Sorry, Kaha." The chief speaks again. "All those who would show themselves worthy to wear Haunani's magic should present themselves now."

Iolani and the others spread out in front of the standing stones, each vying for a position. The stars pulse and the light feathers flood back through the holes in the stone, returning to earth again. They swirl like a swarm of phosphorescent butterflies, swooping around and over the assembled youth.

I hold my breath.

The lights begin to coalesce back into the cloak. Kaha'aheo scrambles to his feet and tries to grab it for himself once more. There is a pulse and he is knocked backward, off his feet.

The feathers ruffle as though in wind. The cloak hovers near Iolani, then swirls around the ringleader of the bullies. My teeth dig into my lower lip. With the power of the Whetū Korowai that boy would be the worst kind of tyrant. A smile begins to form on his lips, then, with a twitch, the cloak flicks away, settling itself around Iolani's shoulders. The light flows into her and around her. Her hair and clothes and the feathers of the star cloak shift in the unfelt wind. There is a pulse of light, and it is done.

The three stars move out of position in the standing stones and continue their passage across the sky.

I clap my hands together. "Iolani! It's you!" My granddaughter is the new Anela. It is bittersweet that I cannot have the Whetū Korowai back, but at least my beloved Iolani can. I pray she can keep it and not have to suffer the way I did. The way Kaha'aheo now suffers.

The boy sobs. He is on his knees, his hands clawing at the dirt. One of his brothers goes to his side and puts a hand on his shoulder. The others seem lost.

I gesture to Iolani. She can afford to be gracious. Perhaps she can offer the boy a token to ease his loss.

She turns to him. "Shut up," she says. She flicks her hand and his body snaps back, spinning into the crowd.

"Iolani!"

Her face is hard. "What? He deserves it. You think he was being nice when he used to explode the rock around me, down at the beach? Not so funny now, is it? Look, I can do it too." A section of the earth next to her explodes outward, showering the crowd with dirt. There are screams.

Though I am unharmed, I feel as if it is my insides that are being pelted with tiny pebbles. My Iolani could not be corrupted so soon. "Iolani, please. You must remember to be worthy. This isn't the way."

She shakes her head. "You're wrong, Grandfather. Strength is worthy. You taught me that. You wiped out the Maloans to stop them harming our people. I will take it further and wipe out those of us who would harm each other."

She turns to the ringleader of the bullies, Kaha'aheo's brother. His eyes are wide. His lip trembles. He stands firm.

"Stand very still," Iolani says. She gestures with her fist and the ground beneath him erupts with the force of a storm. Brown and red geyser upward, then fall like hail and rain. His body lands twisted and broken. He is dead.

Iolani licks her lip where the blood was this morning. It is healed.

People jostle each other as they run. Others are rooted to the spot like a coconut palm—able to do nothing but sway in the wind.

My hands cover my mouth as I murmur my granddaughter's name into my palms. "Iolani. What have you done?"

"What needs doing, Grandpa. And I've just gotten started." The other bullies try to run but an invisible wall boxes them in. Iolani smiles an unpleasant smile. "Not so fun when you're not the one with the power, is it?" She lifts her hand and lightning crackles around her fingers.

"Stop this," I say, my words almost a sob. "Please. It isn't right!" I see the bloated faces of dead Maloans in the broken form of the dead boy. Iolani is going to be just like me. *Worse* than me.

"Yes," she says. "It is."

Her hand raises toward the boys and I move faster than I have in years. I fling myself between my granddaughter and her tormentors. The lightning strikes me in the chest and face. The world explodes in colourful feathers of light, then everything is still and dark.

It is a deeper darkness than night. A quieter stillness than the calm sea at dawn. It is the feeling of death and I make my peace. I have done what I can.

There is a shimmer in the dark, a pinpoint of light like the first tip of colour emerging from a hibiscus bud. It brightens and shifts like a firefly. Another joins it. And another. They circle around me, three stars, swirling, testing, observing. Then they speak, their voices like the distant chiming of delicate bells.

"This one has strength."

"And empathy. It knows loss."

"Sacrifice. And honour."

I can only stare, wordless.

"At last," they say, "the Anela has served its purpose. We have found one willing to stand against the power for the sake of another. He is worthy."

The stars grow brighter, merging into one. Then they merge with me and the world fills with light.

There is a moment, just before waking, when I forget that it is with me. When the memory of my regrets crumbles the strength in my bones and I cry with the need to help my people. I crave a chance for redemption. To calm the hatreds, restore the family bonds, nurture the sea and nourish the land.

I open my eyes to see stars beneath my skin. The Whetū Korowai is no more. Its power is part of me. I am Haunani reborn.

TE HOKINGA MAI (THE RETURN)
by Marolyn Dudfield

MAGNETIC NORTH

I. K. Paterson-Harkness

My entire life I had the feeling that I
had to arrive
here
at this precise point.
It's not on a map, it slides about—
that's something not often known—
but still, it *is* an exact location
at any given moment in time:
Magnetic North.

From the North Pole all roads lead south.
If you stand *there*, right on that spot,
the Earth spins at your feet.
That's not where I am.
I'm on the ever-shifting position in which
Earth's magnetic field points directly
downwards.
I'm at the mercy of the molten core
roiling away beneath me.

I was born different,
sixteen kilos and premature.

My mum stopped heaving me to her hip when I was
five months old.
When I was nine, we did a science project
at school, involving magnets.
They clung to my hands; I couldn't pull them off.
I cried as the family doctor wrenched them from me,
ripping my skin.

They learned I had an inconceivably high iron count.
They said I was a danger
to myself, they said
I was safer, staying with them, for testing.
They found that, like a piece of iron,
when placed within a strong magnetic field
I became magnetised.
But what they didn't expect
was that the effect was permanent.

Inside the hospital walls, the strain was relentless.
Every metallic object hungered for me,
and I for it, so
even in the rain and sleet of winter,
tucked within the scarves and mittens my mum sent me,
I paced the wide yard.
It was strange, but each day I'd unconsciously find myself
pressed against the wooden fence
facing a field of corn with the sun setting to my left.
I yearned for North.

At eighteen, I left that place.
I couldn't take planes; I interfered with their systems.
I've caught bus, train, boat,
I've walked.
I've zigzagged across the Pacific, to Japan, and up through Russia,
stopping only briefly, speaking to no one.

For years, I've journeyed with a force
beyond my control
urging me to continue.

And finally,
here I am.
Magnetic North.
Mum will be beside herself back home.
She begged me not to come;
she hung to my arm, crying, and I
pushed her from me, like everything else.
All my life gone,
for a pure desert of endless ice and sky,
for nothing.

But now that I'm here I doubt that I'll ever
be able to drag myself away.

THE IRON WAHINE
Matt Cowens

Tariana curled her toes in the black sand and surveyed the ocean. A gun-metal grey sky hung heavy over choppy waves, dwindling to blackness at the horizon. Somewhere in the heart of that darkness hearts raced, small hands clung to worn timber and prayers were uttered.

Tariana let out a long, slow karanga to the deep, one node in a nationwide Intercept Recon Outpost Network, watching the sea for survivors. The echoes of her kupu came back as empty pings. There was little hope—refugee ships were cloaked with stealth polymers, their battered hulks invisible to sonar. There was no need to hide from humans now, but the old cloaks could not be shed. The time for refugee quotas and arresting boat people had long since passed. Any life, any survivor was a taonga. All were welcomed, all saved.

Tariana's thrusters fired before she knew she had seen anything. Her metal toes skimmed the waves, dripping iron sand as she barrelled toward the ship on the horizon. The tiny, battered bark had survived the long voyage away from peril. Aotearoa, an island fortress kept free from the worst of the attacks and infestations, was one of the few remaining sanctuaries. Tariana was programmed to make sure no ship failed at the last hurdle. Iron wāhine around the coast answered her call as she plunged beneath the waves. Ships were always pursued by kraken; the wāhine toa were built to fight them.

Beneath the waves, Tariana saw the sea giants swarm. Her body of cogs and motors and hydraulics, driven by AI and aroha, flashed fire from iron fists. She tore a hole through the first of the creatures, rending tentacles and punching through the great beast's eye socket. The swarm turned away from the ship and descended on her. Cold limbs encircled her as maws opened and teeth scraped against her armour. Tariana fought on, drawing the creatures away from the refugee ship as she tumbled deeper. The ship was only minutes from the shore. Her sisters were coming, but the kraken were legion.

Above the waves, the refugees prayed.

ABOUT THE AUTHORS
in order of appearance

Evelyn Doyle (Cover Designer)

Eve is many things: INTJ. Multipotentialite. Graphic Designer. Reader. Writer. Lover of coffee and parataxis. At base, she's a biological system that turns coffee into blog posts, stories, and visual designs...when she's not homeschooling her two boys, or thinking about the philosophical complexities of the Marvel Cinematic Universe. She lives in Hawke's Bay with her husband, two small boys, one canary, and a partridge in a pear tree. Except for the partridge in a pear tree.

www.evelyndoyle.com

Juliet Marillier

Juliet Marillier was born in Dunedin and now lives in Western Australia. She is an award-winning author of historical fantasy novels and short fiction. Among her works are the *Blackthorn & Grim* series and the *Sevenwaters* series. Her lifelong love of folklore, fairy tales and mythology is a major influence on her writing. Juliet's other passion is rescuing and rehabilitating old or sick dogs. She's currently working on a new trilogy, *Warrior Bards*.

www.julietmarillier.com

Eileen Mueller

Eileen Mueller lives on the side of a hill with four dragonets and a shape-shifter. The recipient of two Sir Julius Vogel Awards, she has won various literary contests. Eileen writes for young adults and children, with occasional forays into dark fiction. Free books are available at her website eileenmuellerauthor.com

A.J. Ponder

A.J. Ponder has a head full of monsters, and recklessly spills them out onto the written page. Beware dragons, dreadbeasts, taniwha, and small children—all are equally dangerous, and capable of treading on your heart—or tearing it, still beating, from your chest.
ajponder.wordpress.com & anafflictionofpoetry.blogspot.co.nz

Kevin Berry

Kevin Berry's love of writing began when he handed in a 50,000 word murder mystery for an English assignment to his stunned teacher. More recently, his fiction has received independent writing awards and glowing reviews. He lives in Christchurch, New Zealand, with two sons, and is most definitely a night owl, writing into the early hours.
kevinberrybooks.com

Aaron Compton

Aaron Compton lives in Tūranganui-a-Kiwa (Gisborne) and has had work published by the Tūranganui Poetry Collective (of which he is a founding member) and in the Westerly (the literary journal of the University of Western Australia). He teaches creative writing to primary age children and is proud that one of his students was shortlisted for the 2017 Pikihuia awards for Māori fiction. Aaron is of Pākehā, Rangitāne and Ngāti Kahungunu blood.

Daniel Stride

Daniel Stride has a lifelong love of literature in general and speculative fiction in particular. He writes both short stories and poetry; his first novel, a steampunk-flavoured dark fantasy entitled *Wise Phuul* was published in November 2016, by small UK press, Inspired Quill. Daniel can be found blogging about Tolkien, the fantasy genre, politics, and other random things at A Phuulish Fellow (phuulishfellow.wordpress.com). He lives in Dunedin, New Zealand.

Grant Stone

Grant Stone's stories have appeared in *Island*, *Strange Horizons*, and *Andromeda Spaceways Inflight Magazine*, and have twice won the Sir Julius Vogel Award. grant-stone.com

Mark English

Mark is an astrophysicist and space scientist who worked on the Cassini/Huygens mission to Saturn. Following this he worked in computer consultancy, engineering, and high energy research (with a stint at the JET Fusion Torus). All this science hasn't damped his love of fantasy and science fiction. It has, however, ruined his enjoyment of rainbows, colourful flames on romantic log fires, and rings around the moon. He has previously been published in *Stupefying Stories Showcase*, *Everyday Fiction*, *Escape Pod*, *Perihelion* and also on *Antipodean SF* where he is part of the narration team.

Gregory Dally

Gregory Dally has had poetry and fiction published in various journals, including *Catalyst*, *JAAM*, *Meanjin* and *Takahe*. A number of his short plays have been staged in New Zealand and the United States.

Mike Reeves-McMillan

Mike Reeves-McMillan lives in Auckland, the setting of his *Auckland Allies* contemporary urban fantasy series, and also in his head, where the weather is more reliable and there are a lot more wizards.

He also writes the *Gryphon Clerks* series, steampunkish secondary-world fantasy with heroic civil servants; the sword-and-sorcery heist series *Hand of the Trickster*; and short stories, for venues such as *Compelling Science Fiction* and *Cosmic Roots and Eldritch Shores*.

http://mikerm.blogspot.co.nz

Serena Dawson

Serena Dawson loves painting and sketching the woods and wilds of New Zealand almost as much as exploring them. Also a writer, she is working on a fantasy trilogy and hopes that her first book, *The Oath and the Blade*, will soon be published. She is currently roaming New Zealand in a housetruck with her husband, three girls and one annoying dog. Her interests include archery, bonsai and collecting Suiseki.

See some of her art at: www.facebook.com/Serena.Dawson.art

Kevin G. Maclean

Kevin Maclean lives in Auckland, New Zealand. He gives his profession as "medically-retired computer geek." His short fiction has featured in *Andromeda Spaceways Inflight Magazine*, *Millennium Nights*, *Summoned to Destiny*, and a number of *Pipers' Ash* collections. He is currently working on a trilogy which he describes as "very strange", which, considering he considers H. P. Lovecraft's work "normal", is somewhat worrying. "Eye of the Beholder" appeared in the DAW anthology *Misspelled*, and was an Aurealis Award finalist.

Robinne Weiss

Robinne—an entomologist and educator by training—has never been able to control her writing habit. She has been publishing poetry and short fiction since the 1970s and has been known to answer exam questions in verse. Her books include the middle-grade adventure novels *A Glint of Exoskeleton, The Dragon Slayer's Son* and *The Ipswich Witch*. She has also published the teacher's guide, *Insects in the Classroom*, which draws on her decades of teaching as The Bug Lady, and the kid-friendly companion guide, *Backyard Bugwatcher*.
Robinne writes and blogs from her office at Crazy Corner Farm near Christchurch, New Zealand. Find her online at robinneweiss.com.

Dan Rabarts

Dan Rabarts is an award-winning short fiction author and editor, recipient of New Zealand's Sir Julius Vogel Award for Best New Talent in 2014. His science fiction, dark fantasy and horror short stories have been published in numerous venues around the world, including *Beneath Ceaseless Skies*, *StarShipSofa* and *The Mammoth Book of Dieselpunk*. Together with Lee Murray, he co-edited the anthologies *Baby Teeth—Bite-sized Tales of Terror*, winner of the 2014 SJV for Best Collected Work and the 2014 Australian Shadows Award for Best Edited Work, and *At The Edge*, a collection of Antipodean dark fiction, which won the SJV for Best Edited Work in 2017. His novella *Tipuna Tapu* won the Paul Haines Award for Long Fiction as part of the Australian Shadows Awards in 2017. *Hounds of the Underworld*, Book 1 of the crime/horror series *The Path of Ra*, co-written with Lee Murray and published by Raw Dog Screaming Press (2017), is his first novel. Find out more at dan.rabarts.com.

Sean Monaghan

Sean Monaghan was the 2014 winner of the Jim Baen Memorial Award. His stories have appeared in *Asimov's, Amazing Stories* and *Landfall*, among others. During the day you can usually find him at the Palmerston North City Library. After that, he writes by the light of a single candle, often far too late into the night. Web: seanmonaghan.com.

Grace Bridges

Grace Bridges is a geyser hunter, cat herder, professional editor and translator, and is the current president of SpecFicNZ—having been on the committee since 2012. Indie publishing and freelance editing have been her focus for the past ten years, including 40+ titles in her Splashdown Books brand. She has edited and co-edited a number of short story collections such as *Avenir Eclectia, Aquasynthesis, Aquasynthesis Again,* and *Alter Ego.*
Her novels include space opera, Irish cyberpunk, and the *Earthcore* urban fantasy series set in New Zealand. Several of her works and edited collections have been shortlisted for the Sir Julius Vogel Award. Grace's short stories and non-fiction appear in various anthologies and online magazines.
See www.gracebridges.kiwi for more information.

Matt Cowens

Matt Cowens is a high school teacher, occasional podcast fiction voice artist, doodler and dad. He designed and illustrated the card games Dig, Mob and Cow with his wife Debbie and co-wrote *Mansfield with Monsters.* mattcowens.wordpress.com

Alan Baxter

Alan Baxter is a British-Australian author who writes supernatural thrillers and urban horror, rides a motorcycle and loves his dogs. He also teaches Kung Fu. He lives among dairy paddocks on the beautiful south coast of NSW, Australia, with his wife, son, dogs and cat. He's the multi-award-winning author of several novels and over seventy short stories and novellas. So far. Read extracts from his novels, a novella and short stories at his website—www.warriorscribe.com—or find him on Twitter @AlanBaxter and Facebook, and feel free to tell him what you think. About anything.

Debbie Cowens

Debbie Cowens is a writer and teacher who lives on the Kapiti Coast. She co-authored the Sir Julius Vogel Award winning *Mansfield with Monsters* and her novel *Murder and Matchmaking* is a mash-up of Jane Austen and Sherlock Holmes.

debbiecowens.blogspot.co.nz

Sally McLennan

Sally McLennan's book, *Deputy Dan and the Mysterious Midnight Marauder*, won a Sir Julius Vogel award in 2009. Her short stories have been published in magazines and anthologies in New Zealand, America, England and Australia. These include tales of science fiction, horror, and erotica but Sally's favourite genre is fantasy. Sally has a young adult series of dark fantasy novels in development. Sally lives in an old church in the Wairarapa. On the land around it she breeds Clydesdales and milk goats. Sally enjoys sitting in local cafes, and hugging a cup of tea, while stringing words into a story.

Her website can be found at www.sallymclennan.com.

Piper Mejia

Piper's short fiction appears in a number of anthologies, with *Lockdown*, from the horror flash fiction collection *Baby Teeth: Bite-Sized Tales of Terror*, shortlisted for the Sir Julius Vogel Award for science fiction and fantasy writing. In 2016, she partnered with artist Simone Anderson to tell a tale of domestic violence in the charity publication, *Grim Tales*. Piper currently works as an English teacher in a secondary school where her students provide her plenty of material for her stories.

Paul Mannering

Paul Mannering is an award-winning writer of speculative fiction, comedy, horror and military action novels, short stories, radio plays and the occasional government report. He lives in Wellington, New Zealand with his wife Damaris, and their two cats. Paul harbours a deep suspicion about asparagus and firmly believes we should all make an effort to be more courteous to cheese. Find him online at: www.paulmannering.nz.

Facebook: NZPaulBooks   Twitter: @paul_mannering.

Jane Percival

Jane Percival's first introduction to speculative fiction was a collection of Edgar Allan Poe stories that she found on her parents' bookshelf when she was young. Since then, she has devoured with relish any fantasy, horror, or science fiction story that she could lay her hands on. *The Mysterious Mr Montague* combines her love of the macabre with her childhood memories of Wellington. Jane writes a blog at heni-irihapeti.com.

Mouse Diver-Dudfield

Mouse Diver-Dudfield is an author of sci-fi, horror and mystery novels and lives in the deep dark south of New Zealand. Her passion is to mix horror with history, and meld her sci-fi with a hint of the macabre. She loves writing strong kick-ass heroines in tantalising unique stories, all with a sweet New Zealand connection. Mouse is a nickname given to her as a baby, and it has stuck ever since. mousediver.weebly.com

I. K. Paterson-Harkness

I. K. Paterson-Harkness grew up on the Otago Harbour, but has spent the past decade living on Auckland's K Road. Her output of published works is broad, including short stories, novellas, web series, albums, and a growing collection of poems. Her poetry can be found in *Landfall, JAAM, Takahe* and *Poetry NZ*. Check out her website at www.ikpatersonharkness.com.

Simon Petrie and Edwina Harvey

Simon Petrie is a New Zealander living in Australia. Edwina Harvey is an Australian longing for New Zealand. Simon and Edwina first worked together on *Andromeda Spaceways Inflight Magazine* and have collaborated on other writing and editing projects.

Edwina's most recent book, *An Eclectic Collection of Stuff and Things*, and Simon's latest book, *Wide Brown Land: stories of Titan* are available through Peggy Bright Books, www.peggybrightbooks.com.

"Dancing West to East" is dedicated to Elsie Russell and the inspiration of a lifetime.

Lee Murray

A multi-award-winning writer and editor of science fiction, fantasy, and horror (Sir Julius Vogel, Australasian Shadows), Lee Murray's titles include the military thriller *Into the Mist* and supernatural crime-noir *Hounds of the Underworld* (with Dan Rabarts). She lives in the Land of the Long White Cloud where she conjures up stories from an office overlooking a cow paddock. Find out more at leemurray.info.

Darian Smith

Darian Smith is an Auckland-based fantasy author who likes to mix his magic with a lot of mystery and even a dash of romance. He's the author of the *Agents of Kalanon* series and the Koru Award winning *Currents of Change*. When he's not writing, Darian has been known to get slaughtered on television, work with people who have neuromuscular disabilities, and bake the occasional cake.

You can find more information about Darian and his work at www.darian-smith.com.

Readers: Find more Speculative Fiction stories by Kiwi writers! Browse our database, reviews, and featured books, and stay up to date on new releases.

Writers: Join up and take advantage of member benefits: mentoring, competitions, publishing opportunities, resources, networking and community support, and more!

This means you! Published and aspiring authors, teens and adults, industry professionals such as editors and designers, reviewers and readers.

Find us at...

www.SpecFic.NZ

www.ingramcontent.com/pod-product-compliance
Lightning Source LLC
Chambersburg PA
CBHW031937240626
47153CB00003B/773